William Rathbone Greg

Enigmas of Life

Seventh Edition

William Rathbone Greg

Enigmas of Life
Seventh Edition

ISBN/EAN: 9783337396138

Printed in Europe, USA, Canada, Australia, Japan

Cover: Foto ©Andreas Hilbeck / pixelio.de

More available books at **www.hansebooks.com**

ENIGMAS OF LIFE.

ENIGMAS

OF

LIFE.

BY

W. R. GREG,

AUTHOR OF "THE CREED OF CHRISTENDOM."

"The Soul's dark cottage, battered and decayed,
Lets in new light through chinks that Time has made."
Waller.

SEVENTH EDITION, WITH A POSTSCRIPT.

LONDON:

TRÜBNER & CO., 57 & 59 LUDGATE HILL.

MDCCCLXXIV.

PREFACE.

THE following pages contain rather suggested thoughts that may fructify in other minds than distinct propositions which it is sought argumentatively to prove. In the later years of life the intellectual vision, if often clearer, usually grows less confident and enterprising. Age is content to *think*, where Youth would have been anxious to *demonstrate* and establish; and problems and enigmas which, at thirty, I fancied I might be able to solve, I find, at sixty, I must be satisfied simply to propound.

By the severer class of scientific reasoners, (if I have any such among my readers), it will, I am aware, be noted with disapproval that throughout this little book there runs an undercurrent of belief in two great doctrines, which yet I do not make the slightest attempt to prove. I have every where, it will be said, *assumed* the existence of a Creator and a continued life beyond the grave, though I give no reason for my faith in either; though I obviously do not hold those points of the Christian creed on the ordinary Christian grounds; and though I cannot fail to be conscious that these questions underlie, or inextricably mingle with nearly every one of the subjects I have treated. I have approached, with some pretension to philosophical investigation, a few of the enigmas of human life, yet have deliberately evaded the two deepest and darkest of all, and precisely the two, moreover, whose determination can most satisfactorily solve the rest. I admit the charge, and my defence is simply this.

The religious views in which we have been brought up inevitably colour to the last our tone of thought on all cognate matters, and largely affect the manner and direction of our approach to them, even when every dogma of our early creed has been, if not abandoned, yet deprived of its dogmatic form as well as of its original logical or authoritative basis. Not only are doctrines often persistently retained, though the old foundations of them have been undermined or surrendered ; but beliefs, that have dwelt long in the mind, leave indelible traces of their residence years after they have been discarded and dislodged. It would be more correct to say that they linger with a sort of loving obstinacy in their old abode, long after they have received formal notice to quit. Their chamber is never, to the end of time, quite swept and garnished. The mind is never altogether as if they had not been there. When a "yes" or "no" answer is demanded to a proposition for and against which argument and evidence seem equally balanced, the decision is sure to be different in minds, one of which comes new to the question while the other has held a pre-conceived opinion, even though on grounds which he now recognises as erroneous or insufficient. It was my lot to inherit from Puritan forefathers the strongest impressions as to the great doctrines of Religion at a time when the mind is most plastic and most tenacious of such impressions—

"Wax to receive, and marble to retain."

And though I recognise as fully as any man of science the hollowness of most of the foundations on which those impressions were based, and the entire invalidity of the tenure on which I then held them, yet I by no means feel compelled to throw up the possession merely because the old title deeds were full of flaws. The existence of a wise and beneficent Creator and of a renewed life hereafter are still to me beliefs—especially the first—very nearly reaching the solidity of absolute convictions. The one is almost a Certainty, the other a solemn Hope. And it does not seem to me un-philosophic to allow my contemplation of Life or my speculations on the problems it presents to run in the grooves worn in the mind by its antecedent history, so long as no dogmatism is allowed, and no *disprovable* datum is suffered for a moment to intrude.

The question—when stated with the perfect unreserve which alone befits it—lies in small compass. Of actual *knowledge* we have simply nothing. Those who believe in a Creative Spirit and Ruler of the Universe are forced to admit that they can adduce no proofs or arguments cogent enough to compel conviction from sincere minds constituted in another mould. There are facts, indications, corollaries, which seem to suggest the great inference almost irresistibly to our minds. There are other facts, indications, corollaries, which to other minds seem as irresistibly to negative that inference. Data, admitted by both, appear of very different weight to each. The difficulties in the way of either conclusion are confessedly stupendous. The difficulty of conceiving the eternal pre-existence of a Personal Creator I perceive to be *immense ;*—the difficulty of conceiving the origin and evolution of the actual Universe independently of such Personal Creator I should characterise as *insuperable.* The Positivist— the devotee of pure Science—would simply reverse the adjectives. We can neither of us turn the minor into the major difficulty for the other without altering the constitution of his intelligence. *He* does not say, " There is no God," he merely says, " I see no pheno- mena which irresistibly suggest one ; I see many which negative the suggestion ; and I have greater difficulty in conceiving all that the existence of such a Being would involve than in the contrary assumption.' *I* do not say, " I know there is a God ;" I only say I observe and infer much that forces that conviction in upon me; but I recognise that these observations and inferences would not entitle me to *demand* the same conviction from him. In fine, neither doctrine can be *proved* or *disproved*—the votaries of neither are en- titled to insist upon imposing their conviction upon others, on the plea of its demonstrability. I am entitled, however, to retain mine as, to me, *the* believable one.   Lawyers tell us of a title that is unsaleable, but indefeasible.   Scientific men speak of " Provisional Theories," " good working hypotheses," and the like— the goodness depending upon their value in explaining and elucidating phenomena, not in their capability of being demonstrated.   There is some analogy in the case we are considering.

Again, visible and ascertainable phenomena give no countenance to the theory of a future or spiritual life. It is a matter of intuitive conviction, or of deduction from received or assumed doctrines, not of logical inference from established data.*   I cannot demand assent to it,

---

* I have discussed this question fully in the last chapter of *The Creed of Christendom.*   There is, however, one indication of immortality which was not there dwelt upon, but which ought not to be left out of consideration, though, of course, its value will be very differently estimated by different minds.   I refer to that *spontaneous*, irresistible, and perhaps nearly universal feeling we all experience on watching, just after death, the body of some one we have intimately known ; the conviction, I mean (a sense, a consciousness, an impression *which you have to fight against if you wish to disbelieve or shake it off*), that the form lying there is somehow *not* the EGO you have loved.   It does not produce the effect of that person's personality.   You miss the Ego, though you have the frame.   The visible Presence only makes more vivid the sense of actual Absence.   Every feature, every substance, every phenomenon is there—and is unchanged.   You have seen the eyes as firmly closed, the limbs as motionless, the breath almost as imperceptible, the face as fixed and expressionless, before, in sleep or in trance,—without the same peculiar sensation.   The impression made is indefinable, and is not the result of any conscious process of thought :—that that body, quite unchanged to the eye, is not, and never was, your friend—the Ego you were conversant with ;

with any justice or on any plea of *cogent* argument, from a reasoner who is destitute of my intuitive conviction, or who deems my deductions erroneous, or demurs to the doctrines from which they flow. But, on the other hand, since I can specify undeniable indications which point in that direction, and difficulties which to all appearance that hypothesis only can elucidate, and since he can in no way demonstrate its untenability or its contrariety with known truths, I am entitled to hold it as to me, though not to all, the most credible belief.

These will seem to enthusiastic believers disappointing and timid positions to take up on such momentous questions; but the most advanced positions are not always the most tenable, and the humblest are often the strongest. The safe position for a candid reasoner, and the only true one, is not that which is most menacing to his antagonist, but one from which the holder cannot be dislodged.

---

that his or her individuality was not the garment before you *plus* a galvanic current; that, in fact, the EGO you knew once and seek still *was not that—is not there.* And if not *there,* it must be *elsewhere* or *nowhere;*—and " nowhere" I believe modern science will not suffer us to predicate of either force or substance that once has been.

I have a word or two further to say in reference to each of these main doctrines.

Those who cling most lovingly to faith in a future life, and would avoid the shocks which close thought always causes to it, will do well to guard against every temptation to define or particularise its nature, mode, or conditions, to realise its details or processes, to form a distinct or plausible theory regarding it,—especially a local, physical, or biological one. Let it rest in the vague, if you would have it rest unshaken. For, while it is more than probable that our imagination is utterly incapable of picturing or conceiving, or even conjecturing or approaching, the actual truth about the unseen world, it is certain that our reason will find no difficulty at all in demolishing or discrediting every concrete and systematic conception we might form. The Great Idea—fascinating and maintainable so long as it is suffered to remain nebulous and un-outlined—congeals and carnalises, the moment we endeavour to embody it, into something which is vulnerable at every point, and which we are forced to admit is, on one ground or another, unsustainable.

We all recognise instinctively that a sense of identity, a conscious continuity of the Ego, is an essential element of the doctrine. A life beyond the grave, in other worlds and under other conditions of corporeal or spiritual existence, but devoid of this main feature, would not, it is evident, answer the purposes of the doctrine, nor fulfil those yearnings of the heart and soul which many writers hold to be its most convincing indication. Apart from this consciousness of personal identity, a future life would be simply a new creation,—the beings who came into existence would be other beings, not ourselves awakened and renewed. The curious, but not unattractive, Pythagorean theory of transmigration, reaching, as it did, both to the future and the past, failed altogether in this essential. It is probable that the determination to hold fast by this essential—a determination often half-unconscious and instinctive—fostered, if it did not originate, the astonishing doctrine of the resurrection of the body, which has so strangely and thoughtlessly (like many minor dogmas) found its way into the popular creed. The primitive parents or congealers of that creed, whoever they may have been—innocent of all science and oddly muddled in their metaphysics, but resolute in their conviction that the same persons who died here should be, in very deed, the same who should rise hereafter—systematised their anticipations into the notion that the grave should give up its actual inmates for their ordained transformation and their allotted fate. The current notion of the approaching end of the world no doubt helped to blind them to the vulnerability, and indeed the fatal self-contradictions, of the form in which they had embodied their faith. Of course, if they had taken time to think, or if the Fathers of the Church had been more given to thinking in the rigid meaning of the word, they would have discovered that this special form rendered that faith absurd, indefensible, and virtually impossible. They did not know, or they never considered, that the buried body soon dissolves into its elements, which in the course of generations and centuries pass into other combinations, form part of other living creatures, feed and constitute countless organisations one after another; so that when the graves are summoned "to give up the dead that are in them," and the sea "the dead that are in it," they will be called on to surrender what they no longer possess, and what no supernal power can give back to them. It never occurred to those creed-makers, who thus took upon themselves to carnalise an idea into a fact, that for every atom that once went to make up the body they committed to the earth, there would be scores of claimants before the Great Day of account, and that even Omnipotence could scarcely be expected to make the same component part be in two or ten places at once. The original human frames, therefore, *could not be had* when, as supposed, they would be wanted.

Neither, apparently, did it occur to them that these bodily shells and frames *would not be wanted.* "Flesh and blood cannot inherit the kingdom of God." The perishable carcase could have no part nor lot in the great scene then to be enacted. The perished carcase could not be needed (like the bone "Luz" so queerly invented for the purpose by the later Jews) to supply materials for "the spiritual body," and would not be forthcoming if it were.

Moreover, what could such incongruous elements as nitrogen and phosphates, and sodium and other metallic bases, be doing in immaterial spheres, and before the judgment-seat of God? It was the SOULS of men that were to be the actors in that mighty Drama. And, again, where were those souls during the countless ages that elapse between their exit from the mortal husk and their appearance at the final summons? Speculation has been busy with this problem for long generations; has been always baffled; has never had the sense to perceive, or the candour to admit, that the difficulty was entirely one of its own gratuitous creation. Still, in the orthodox creed, or rather in popular parlance (for real belief was " nowhere " in the matter), the soul—which nobody knew how, even in fancy, to dispose of in the meanwhile — was to be *called* up from somewhere to re-inhabit *pro hac vice* the body, which it was impossible that it should find, and of which it could make no further use in a world that, in philosophical conception, is spiritual, and, according to Scripture, is prohibited to flesh and blood! Endeavour to picture the jumble in the mind of that early Christian who framed the conception (and had influence enough to make after ages repeat it with a submission absolutely servile) of a scene where decayed and dispersed gaseous elements and atoms, collected from ages and places and combinations, were put together once more for one momentary function, and thereafter ——

A more thoughtful age will marvel—as the thoughtful of this age marvel now—that the fancy of the primeval savage, who buries his horse and dog, and spear and arrows, in the same grave with the departed chief, that they may be ready for him in the unseen hunting-grounds whither he is gone, should have been so nearly reproduced in the creed of the most cultivated nation in the most civilised age that human progress has yet reached.

Other illustrations might be given; one or two may be just indicated here. If, as Professor Grote suggests, sympathy with all other beings in the next world will be indiscriminate and perfect, and " undisguisedness " therefore inevitable and absolute, it is difficult to see how separate entity, still more how distinct identity, is to be secured.

" Surely," as the *Spectator* argued, " if sympathy with all is perfect, one of the most effective links of continuity, the limitation of sympathy, will disappear, and the mind understanding all and sympathizing with all equally, all the affections, as we call them, would cease, and all the relations of humanity be meaningless. The ancient and beautiful thought which has cheered so many bereaved ones, that separation is only for a time, would be without object; for though we should meet again, it would be in relations to which the former relations would have no similarity. The love between parent and child, for example, so far as it is not the result of circumstances and physical similarity of constitution—all which circumstances and similarity must cease at death—is the product of superior sympathy, which sympathy would be merged, lost in the universal sympathy of which Professor Grote has spoken. It may be of course that the earthly affections are earthly, and end with earth; but there is no proof of that, and no reason for a suggestion which, besides being a melancholy one, is an additional difficulty in the way of continuity."

Then, again, if there be a hell to which any whom we love are doomed, heaven can only be the place of perfect happiness we picture it, on condition of a narrowing, a worsening, or at all events a change, in our affections and moral nature, so vast as to be fatal to genuine identity.

Lastly, it would seem impossible to frame any scheme of a future life, at once equitable and rational, which should include all human beings and exclude all the rest of the animal creation. Those among us who are most really *intimate* with dogs, horses, elephants, and other *élite* of the fauna of the world, know that there are many animals far more richly endowed with those intellectual and moral qualities which are worth preserving and which imply capacity of cultivation, than many men,—higher, richer, and, above all, more unselfish and devoted, and therefore, we may almost say, more Christian natures. I have seen in the same day, brutes on the summit and men at the foot of the Great St. Bernard, with regard to whom no one would hesitate to assign to the quadruped the superiority in all that we desire should live. Yet, on the other hand, where draw the line, since admittedly the highest animals taper downwards, by wholly inappreciable gradations, to the lowest organisms of simply vegetable life?

Does the following suggestion by an anonymous writer offer a way out of the difficulty?—" I apprehend, that if man's immortality be accepted as proven, a strong presumption may be thence derived in favour of the immortality of those creatures who *attain that moral stage whereat man becomes an immortal being.* What that stage may be we do not presume to guess, but we cannot suppose the tremendous alternative of extinction or immortality to be decided by arrival at any arbitrary or merely *physical* turning-point such as may occur at various epochs either before birth or at the moment of birth. We must believe it to be determined by entrance on some moral or mental stage such as may be represented by the terms Consciousness, Self-Consciousness, Intelligence, Power of Love, or the like; by the development, in short, of the mysterious Somewhat above the purely vegetative or animated life for which such life is the scaffolding. If, then (as we are wont to take for granted), a child of some six or eighteen months old be certainly an immortal being, it follows that the stage of development which involves immortality must be an early one. And if such be the case, that stage is unquestionably attained by animals often, and by some men never.

"I beg that it may be remarked that this argument expressly restricts itself to the case of the *higher* animals, and thus escapes the objection which has always been raised to the hypothesis of the immortality of the humbler creatures, namely, that if we proceed a step below the human race we have no right to stop short of the oyster. I merely contend that where any animal manifestly surpasses an average human infant in those steps of development which can be assumed to involve existence after death, *then* we are logically and religiously justified in expecting that the Creator of both child and brute will show no favouritism for the smooth white skin over the rough hairy coat."

Half the difficulties which lie in the way of believing in a Personal God as the Ruler as well as Creator of the universe are of our own making. They are wholly gratuitous, and arise out of the inconsiderate and unwarranted use of a single word—*Omnipotent*. Thoughtful minds in all ages have experienced the most painful perplexities in the attempt to reconcile certain of the moral and physical phenomena we see around us with. the assumption of a Supreme Being at once All-wise, All-good and Almighty. The mental history of mankind presents few sadder spectacles than is afforded by the acrobatic efforts, the convulsive contortions, the almost incredible feats of subtlety and force, performed by piety and intelligence combined in this self-imposed field of conflict—this torture-chamber of the soul. Thousands have there made shipwreck of their faith,—thousands of their truthfulness and candour,—thousands upon thousands of their peace of mind. When the actual facts of the moral and the natural world came to be fully recognised and understood, it was felt to be inconceivable how or why Infinite Love should have created a scene of teeming life, of which the most salient feature is universal conflict and universal slaughter, — every organic being ceaselessly occupied in trampling down or devouring its neighbour, and dependent for its own existence upon doing this successfully. It was felt to be equally incomprehensible that Infinite Goodness and illimitable Power should have created a world so rife with evil,—into which evil entered so easily, and ruled with so predominant a sway. The origin and meaning of evil, its whence and its why, has always been the crux of the sincerest and profoundest thinkers —the insoluble problem of humanity. It has scattered those who have tried to master it as widely as the fabled tower of Babel. Some it has driven into atheism, some into Manicheism, some into denials of the most obvious facts of life and nature ; some into betrayals of the most fundamental principles of morality; some into elaborate schemes of damnation and redemption, which to unperverted minds seem almost blasphemous in their audacity.

That problem *is* insoluble. Nature never truly set

us such contradictions to reconcile. The conditions of the real problem have been incorrectly stated. What stateable reason, what quotable warrant, have we for assuming that the Creator was, or that the Supreme Being is, " Omnipotent ?" The word originally implied no accurate logical conception of absolute or unlimited power ; but was used to express a relative rather than a positive idea. It was a natural and a fitting epithet to use towards, or of, a Being whose power, as compared with that of man, was simply *immeasurable* and *incalculable,* and might therefore in ordinary parlance be called " Infinite." Those who first used it and those who adopted it never thought of defining the word ; and, never straining their imagination to dream of boundaries or limitations, spoke easily of the boundless and illimitable ; while the incurable vulgar disposition of uncivilised minds to flatter the object of their worship came in aid of the expression, till by degrees the loose language of an age which defined (*précisé*) nothing was invested with the rigid formalism of an age which sought to define everything, and the fine vague description of pcetic piety became the hard and therefore false dogma of the Scholastic creed. That *omnipotence,* in the precise, absolute, metaphysical meaning of the word, should ever have been accepted as an indisputable and essential attribute of the Deity, is one of the most curious instances, among the many which may be traced, of the fatal facility with which in theological fields one age blindly, thoughtlessly, and uninquiringly adopts the notions of its predecessor.

Yet *do* divines even now, when they give themselves the trouble to question their own minds on the subject, really and in very truth attribute absolute omnipotence to the Supreme Being? Do they believe that He can combine inherent contradictions? That He can cause two and two to make five? That He can enable a human creature to be in two places at the same instant of time? If he cannot do these things (and no one will assert that He can), then He *works and lives under limitations and conditions*; and we require no further concession than this to deprive the problem of the existence of evil of half its gloom and difficulty, and though not to solve it, at least to indicate that it is not inherently insoluble. We have only to conceive the Creator, *immeasurably, incalculably* wise, beneficent and mighty—good and powerful to a degree which, in reference to human beings, may fairly be called infinite ; but still " conditioned,"—hampered, it may be, by the attributes, qualities, imperfections of the material on which he had to operate ; bound possibly by laws or properties inherent in the nature of that material ;—and we descend, so to speak, into a breathable intellectual atmosphere at once. We need not attempt to conjecture what those fettering laws or attributes may be; we have only to suppose their existence—a supposition *primâ facie* surely more probable than its opposite,—and it becomes possible at once to believe in and to worship God, without doing violence to our moral sense, or denying or distorting the sorrowful facts that surround our daily life.

TABLE OF CONTENTS.

I.

REALISABLE IDEALS.

THE contrast between the Ideal and the Actual of Humanity lies as a heavy weight upon all tender and reflective minds. Those who believe this contrast to be designed, incurable, and eternal, are driven by their dreary creed to despair, to sensual or semi-sensual egotism, to religion, or that form of religion which is very nearly irreligion. If the countless evils of life are irremediable, or capable only of slight and casual mitigation ; if the swarming multitudes of our race are destined to remain almost as sinful, as ignorant, as degraded, and as wretched as at present ; if the improvements that human effort can effect upon their natures and their lot are to be as trifling as most believe in comparison with the residue of misery and wrong that must remain, as well as with the Possible that may be dreamed ;—then, what is left to us but a selfishness more or less disguised and modified according to our several characters ? The Stoic will train himself to bear what he can, and will leave the scene when he can bear no longer. The cultured Epicurean will strive to harden himself against all warmer, keener, and wider sympathies, and to get what joy and smoothness he can out of life without interfering too greatly with the welfare of those around him. The meaner and coarser Egotist will seek pleasure and shun pain, uncontrolled even by that consideration. The Philosopher will speculate, in ever-growing perplexity and darkness, on the insoluble problem of existence, and on the attributes and plans of the Deity who could have framed so strange a world, till all faith and love dies out of his baffled intellect; while the Religious man —religious either by instinct or by creed—will go on as of old, will transfer his hopes and projects to an ideal scene elsewhere, where he can paint any picture his fancy pleases on the canvas, and seek in a future existence the realisation of those dreams of universal virtue and well-being which it seems forbidden to indulge on earth.

But this creed has always seemed to me as irrational as it is sad and paralysing, and at least as impious as it is unphilosophical. It could never have been received as orthodox, or even as probable or natural, if Priests had not seen fit to congeal and stereotype into articles of faith the crude conceptions of some vigorous minds in early times, puzzling over the problem of life with only a few of its clearly ascertained facts and conditions before them. Practically it is a creed which does not go very deep into our innermost convictions now. Virtually we give it the lie or we tacitly ignore it every hour of our lives. Most of us believe a vast amelioration in the condition of the world to be attainable, both in moral and material things. Many of us systematically strive for this amelioration. The efforts of Government, of Legislation, of Philanthropy, of Science, are all in reality directed to this end. We have all some ideal—though it may be poor, near, and partial—towards which we are pressing, and which we hope more or less perfectly to realise. Perhaps the actual difference between the prevalent speculative views on this subject is that some of us are so much more sanguine than others. Some hope only to make life tolerable ; others trust to make it at length as perfect as in its Creator's original scheme they believe it was designed to. be, or to become. Some believe only that a considerable number of human evils may be materially mitigated ; others, more buoyant, have convinced themselves that, with time, patience, and intelligent exertion, every evil not inherent in or essential to a finite existence may be eliminated, and the yawning gulf between the Actual and the Ideal at last bridged over.

This faith is mine. I hold it with a conviction which I feel for scarcely any other conclusion of the reason. It appears to me the only one compatible with true piety—I mean with a rational conception of the attributes of the Creator ; for I can perceive no beauty and no religion in the notion that God placed us in this world only that we might be for ever working for and hankering after another. It appears to me, also —in spite of the clouds and darkness which are round about us—the only one which reflection and reason will sanction. I am not prepared to give up this life as " a bad job," and to look for reward, compensation, virtue, and happiness solely to another. I distinctly refuse to believe in *inevitable evils*. I recognise in the rectification of existing wrong and the remedy of prevailing wretchedness " the work which is given us to do." For this we are to toil; and not to toil in vain. After this we are to aspire, and not to have our aspirations for ever mocked by the impossibility of their final realisation—

"To seek, to find, to strive, and NOT to yield."

Disease, destitution, endemic misery, certainly—sin and suffering of nearly every sort, probably and mainly —lie at our door, at the door of the aggregate of our race, at that of our ancestors or at our own ; and I hold that what man has caused man may cure. Accidents and death will still remain with the natural but unexaggerated consequences they entail. But how small a residuum should we have to trace to *unavoidable* accidents, if we were only as wise and strong as we might ideally become, and how little of this residuum could fitly be called "evil," we can as yet only guess. Whether Death be indeed an "evil" we need not discuss, for Death is the very condition of our existence here ; yet, if it only took its proper position as one among the many occurrences of life, and only came (as in the ideal state I contemplate it only would come) when it was due, in the fulness of time, we should be amazed to find how rarely it was repined at or unwelcomed, either by the recipients or the spectators of the summons.

The true way to realise to our own minds the curability of all the ills which humanity, individually and collectively, groans under, is to take them one by one, or a few of them as samples, in a colloquial fashion, and ask ourselves if there be any ONE which *must* or *need* have been, which in its inception might not have been avoided, which, in fact, is not distinctly and indisputably traceable to our contravention (through ignorance or wilfulness) of the laws of Nature which lie plain (or discoverable) before us ; the *physical laws* on which health depends, the *moral laws* on which happiness depends, and the *social and economic laws* on which plenty and comfort depend. A very superficial survey will bring us to the conclusion, which the most profound investigation will only serve to deepen into settled conviction, that the world is so constituted that if we were consistently intelligent and morally right we should be socially and physically happy. We have, unquestionably, a terrible inheritance of ancestral errors to redeem, obstacles to remove, mischiefs to undo ; but the recuperative powers of nature are astonishing and nearly inexhaustible, and we only require steadily to go right at once and henceforth, in order ere long to cancel the consequences of having gone wrong for such countless generations.

The evils of our actual social condition may be classed under three heads :—Pain and disease, desti-

tution, and vice or crime.   We believe that all three
may be, if not altogether eliminated, yet reduced to
a minimum that would be easily dealt with and easily
borne; and those will be most inclined to agree with
us who reflect *first*, how curiously the three causes
of our sufferings mutually aid and aggravate each
other; and *secondly*, with what strange, ingenious,
obstinate perversity we have long laboured—individually and collectively, by law and habit, by
action and by abstinence—to foster and propagate
them all.

I. Consider for a moment how vast an amount of
our personal misery, to say nothing of actual sin
and of the wretchedness which our consequent ill-
temper brings on others arises, from *Dyspepsia*.   Perhaps this malady is answerable, directly or indirectly,
for more unhappiness, and does more to lower the
general tone and average of human enjoyment, than
any other.   We all of us know something of it, many
of us know it well ; we can estimate in some measure
how much the cheerfulness and brightness of our daily
life is impaired by its pernicious prevalence, how it
saps good spirits, how it sours good temper.   Well !
how obvious are its causes; in most instances how
possible its cure ?   How many of us toil half our life
to earn it, begin early in its cultivation, dig for it as
for hid treasures ?   We generally lay the foundation
in childhood, or in our first youth, by reckless and
ignorant self-indulgence ;—the fault of parents and
teachers you will say, and what they could have

checked in time had they known and valued the laws of physiology. True, but we ourselves are, or have been, or will be, those very parents and teachers. Then, do we not ourselves commit much the same follies as our children? When we eat, as we habitually do, more than is good for us; when we eat, as most of us do, what we know will disagree with us; when the pleasures of the palate tempt us to do more than satisfy our hunger or recruit our strength; when we drink alcohol, not because we need it, but because we like it; when we take a second glass not because a second was required, but because the first was very good; when smoking becomes a regular habit, instead of an occasional indulgence; in all these cases we are sowing seeds for an inevitable harvest, we are diligently earning our wages and incurring a recorded obligation. If only all wages were as well earned, and all debts as certain to be paid! When we sit lazily in our arm-chair under circumstances which indicate that we ought to be in active exercise; when we sit in close rooms and in a vitiated atmosphere, instead of breathing the clear air of heaven; when we go on toiling and thinking long after our sensations warn us that we have expended the income and are drawing on the capital of our cerebral strength; whenever, in a word, we neglect the plainest physiological laws (which it is difficult not to read whenever our attention is drawn to them), then we are laying the foundation of that functional disorder of the digestive organs which entails so certain and so sad a penalty. I am sceptical about stomachic ailments which a man has done nothing to deserve. I scarcely believe in any which either he or his progenitors have not worked hard to generate. I believe, moreover, that those are few which, however induced originally, may not be cured or kept in bounds, even after mature age is reached, by sedulous care, scientifically directed. We are most of us familiar with the case of Cornaro, who, awakening at forty years of age to the consciousness of a shattered constitution, yet contrived, by sagacious observation and incessant vigilance, to recover the tone of an outraged and enfeebled stomach, and lived in laughing comfort to a green old age.

Again :—few maladies are more distressing, nor we fear more upon the increase, than diseases of the heart.*

* " The tendency of modern investigation into the influence of civilization on longevity seems to show a twofold series of agencies at work. On the one hand, sanitary improvements and the lessened mortality from epidemics undoubtedly tend to diminish the average death-rates ; but, on the other hand, there is practically much less improvement in total death-rates than might be expected if these ameliorating causes were not counterbalanced by the increasing fatality of other classes of disease, such as diseases of the brain and heart. It is important to recognize the precise facts. The excess may, probably, to some extent, be regarded as an unavoidable result of the great mental strain and hurried excitement of these times, in which steam and electricity mark time for us, in an overcrowded community, where competition is carried to the highest point, and where the struggle for existence, not to say for intellectual and other distinction, is carried on with sleepless and exhausting energy. But an evil recognized is sometimes half cured ; and the intellectual classes, looking at figures such as those Dr Quain has displayed at his interesting Lumleian Lectures

Nearly all these, it is now understood, where no hereditary predisposition is responsible, may be traced, either to the high pressure and rapid pace of life generally and in almost all professions, or to violent and excessive muscular exertion in youth, such as physiological knowlege would, if consulted, at once condemn. Where such disorders are inherited, the tendency may usually. be traced to similar neglect of natural laws by parents or ancestors. The same may be said of the three terrible and allied maladies which so extensively corrupt and undermine the health of the English nation, make so many lives miserable, and so many deaths premature; viz. :--consumption, scrofula,

---

at the College of Physicians on Diseases of the Walls of the Heart, may well consider the propriety of attending to the hygiene of their lives, as well as of their houses ; and to remember that, to enjoy and benefit by even pure air, soil, and water, they must avoid disabling heart and brain by the incessant labours which too often make useful lives joyless, and embitter the harvesting of the crop which has been too diligently sown. These warning figures tell that, during the last twenty years, the total of deaths of males at all ages from heart-disease has increased in number from 5,746 in 1851 to 12,428 in 1870. The percentage of deaths from heart-disease for 1,000 of population living was ·755 between the years 1851 and 1855 ; it has risen to 1·085 from 1866 to 1870. This increase, it must be observed too, has taken place wholly in connexion with the working years of active social life. There is no change in the percentage of deaths from this cause in males under 25 years of age. Between 20 and 45 years of age it has risen from ·553 to ·709, and that almost exclusively in males, for there is almost no increase in the percentage of females dying from heart-disease during the 25 years of life from 21 to 45. These figures convey their own lesson, and warn us to take a little more care not to kill ourselves for the sake of living."—*British Medical Journal.*

and gout. The predisposition to these is often, usually perhaps, an inheritance from progenitors who have ignored or set at naught the most obvious conditions of hygiène, even more recklessly than we do ; but no one who knows how latent tendencies are brought out, and the seeds of disease fostered and matured by bad air, unwholesome dwellings, and personal excess, will doubt that " this man has sinned " as well as his parents for this thing to have come upon him. The inherited constitution is no doubt a faulty one, but probably the most experienced physicians will estimate most highly how much may be done to correct and counteract the fault by careful avoidance of all unsanitary conditions, by fresh air, suitable nourishment, and habitual temperance. Three generations of wholesome life might suffice to eliminate the ancestral poison, for the *vis medicatrix naturæ* has wonderful efficacy when allowed free play; and perhaps the time may come when the worst cases shall deem it a plain duty to curse no future generations with the *damnosa hereditas* which has caused such bitter wretchedness to themselves.

It is only now that we are beginning to realise how vast a proportion both of our illnesses and deaths are due to purely and easily preventible causes, and the knowledge has not yet fairly stirred us into action. It is calculated—and the estimate is probably below the truth—that in this country, 100,000 deaths annually can be traced to zymotic diseases and epidemics, generated or propagated distinctly by foul air, defective water, and pernicious food—to filth, noxious gases, and the like—all of which originators and agencies might be extinguished or neutralised by prompt and energetic obedience to well known sanitary laws. It is needless to go into any details on so threadbare a topic. It is certain, and will not be denied, that, for example, to take the metropolis alone, if unwholesome overcrowding were prevented by an adequate supply of dwellings for the poor; and if all those dwellings were well drained and ventilated, and furnished with an ample supply of good water, not only might pestilences and epidemics be almost certainly exterminated, but a number of other evils, now acting and re-acting on each other, would be eliminated or enormously mitigated. First of all, the craving for strong drink, so constantly created and stimulated almost into a passion by breathing fetid air, would be removed, and thus the intemperance arising from *that* cause would be cured, and the destitution, brutality, crime, and sickness thence arising would be subtracted from the sum of human suffering. Next, that further amount of drinking which is incidental to the habit among working men of frequenting public-houses because their own houses offer them no comfortable, warm, cheerful room to sit in, would be minimised :—and few know for how much drunkenness this cause is indirectly, and in its origin, answerable. Then, again, with the universal establishment of wholesome and decent dwellings for the poor, we should escape, not only the 20,000 or 30,000 premature deaths caused by the want of such, and the sapped health and strength of thousands more, but the destitution, misery, and insufficient nourishment of countless families where preventible maladies have swept away the breadwinner, and, in consequence and in addition, at least one-half the pauperism which is eating like a gangrene into the moral and material well-being of the country. For—and this is the encouraging feature of this matter—amendment and reform in one point brings amendment and progress in all others. You cannot improve dwellings without, *pro tanto*, lessening intemperance and vice; you cannot diminish drunkenness without diminishing pauperism and brutality, disease and death; you cannot give people comfortable houses, without sobriety, health, education, virtually if not actually increased wages, and raised moral feeling, inevitably and by a thousand indirect channels, advancing also, and aiding the good work in modes as yet undreamed of. Every valuable influence put in operation is a potent ally of every other. If a man's or a nation's face is once set in the right direction and progress once commenced, unseen influences close in on all sides, half insensibly, to aid the onward march.

Look for a moment very briefly, at the perverse course we have hitherto pursued; how we have fostered all our social maladies as it were with a sort of co-operative zeal; how we have taken every sore which plagues and corrodes our body politic, and not merely " let it alone this year and that year also," but " dug about and dunged it," as if we were determined it should **bear** ample fruit;—and this, not from viciousness, but sometimes from ignorance, sometimes from good feeling gone astray, sometimes from selfishness and careless neglect, usually from sheer stupidity. For generations we have seen that most ominous of all symptoms, that most dangerous if most natural of all tendencies in a productive and advancing country, the concentration of the population into great towns, without—we do not say any attempt to control or counteract it, but—any effort, or any adequate effort, to provide for it, or forestal its consequences. We have scarcely dreamed of the necessity for expanding our social garments as our social body has grown beneath them. The same municipal government—or rather the same municipal makeshifts and neglect—which sufficed for the village or the country town, we have fancied would answer for the vast manufacturing hive. The same drainage system, the same *sort* of water supply, the same hap-hazard mode of multiplying buildings which did for a town of 5,000 inhabitants have been applied to the same town grown to 50,000. Look at London, which needed more care, skill, science, administrative wisdom than any other city, and as the seat of wealth, rank, and the central government, might have been expected to receive more, and consider its contrivances for obtaining gas, water, drainage ; look at its rookeries and its alleys ; its squalid dens ; its mingled luxury and destitution ; its *no* government ; its provision *for* fire, and *against* fire.

Look at pauperism, how we have fed and fostered

it ;—how we shrank from and spoiled and neutralised, the one really scientific piece of legislation which England can boast of, the New Poor Law *as first proposed ;*—how we have kept up and added to those old mediævally-conceived charities which might have been innoxious under altogether different conditions, but which now make mendicancy almost the most profitable trade a miscellaneous town population can pursue. Consider how, when a thorough knowledge and a close and searching investigation into every case of alleged want, offer the only possible means of controlling pauperism and unmasking imposture, we, in our miserable vestry spirit of wasteful parsimony, make all such investigation a mockery and an impossibility by assigning hundreds of families to one relieving officer and an imbecile Board. Consider how public sympathy has been perpetually enlisted on the wrong side by the mingled stupidity and brutality of Boards of Guardians, unjust alike to the ratepayer and the poor, who at the same moment shocked all decent feeling by the cruelty and stinginess of their treatment of the sick and aged, and outraged all common sense by the laxity and feebleness of their dealing with the able-bodied incorrigible pauper, the systematic vagrant, and the drunken casual. Lastly, read and think how the sin and folly of the charitable and religious have combined to convert the East End of London into about the most unmanageable heap of squalor, destitution, drunkenness, imposture, and artificial wretchedness on earth ;—and then some faint idea may be formed of how this monster evil of our country might be got under by sound treatment, from watching how it has been made to flourish under all this lavish and perverse manuring.

Again :—We have fostered our criminal population just as we have fostered our pauper population, till this also has become a flourishing established class, to be numbered, not by tens but by hundreds of thousands. For generations we have laboured with our usual injurious and ever-varying perversity. There is scarcely a single contradictory mistake that we have not committed. It was long before scientific inquiry and reflection let in any light upon the subject; and when light dawned at last, folly and sentimentality refused to follow the guidance of science. For generations our punishments were so savage that juries would not convict. Our constabulary were so scanty and inefficient that crime had practically scarcely any public foe; and when, less than fifty years ago, something like an adequate police began to be set on foot, there was an instant clamour that the liberties of the subject were in danger. Due restraint on known and habitual criminals is still impeded in the name of the same much abused phrase; and burglars and felons are allowed to walk abroad after repeated convictions because the freedom of Englishmen is too sacred to be touched. The most mawkish sentimentality is suffered to prevent the infliction of the only punishments which are really dreaded by the hardened and the ruffianly, as well as those which alone could rescue

and restore the incipient criminal. We will not hang
the murderer, and have only lately and gingerly
begun to flog the garotter and the mutilator; nor
will we give adequately long terms of imprisonment
to the less atrocious and confirmed class of male-
factors. We persist, in spite of all warning and of all
experience, in turning loose our villains on the world,
time after time, as soon as a moderate term of deten-
tion has finished their education and defined their
future course. All who have really studied the
question feel satisfied that professional crime—and
the class that habitually live by violation of the law
—might be well-nigh exterminated by the perpetual
seclusion of the incorrigible, and by the infliction of
the special penalties which are truly deterrent. Yet
still we go on from day to day, making the criminals
as comfortable as we can, pitying them and petting
them when an opportunity occurs, raising an outcry
against any penalties which are painful; and thinking
we have done enough, and arguing as if we had done
all we have a right to do, if we tie the hands of the
most practised robber and ·ruffian for a time. All
wholesomeness of notion in reference to this subject
seemed to have gone out of us, and to be replaced by
sentiment at once shallow and morbid. We have been
feeling towards the criminal neither as Christians, nor
as statesmen, nor as philosophers, nor even as men of
the world. We neither abhor him, nor cure him, nor
disarm him. We do not act either on the reformatory,
or the retributive, or the purely defensive principle,

but on a feeble muddle of all three. So he lives, and thrives, and multiplies ; nourished in the bosom of the silly society on which he preys.

Consider, again, what might fairly be expected to be the present state of the civilized world if the whole influence of the Church had been persistently and sagaciously directed towards the improvement of the moral and material condition of humanity on this earth, instead of towards the promulgation of an astounding scheme for securing it against eternal torments in a future existence ; if, in a word [universal, not selfish] well-being here, instead of what is called salvation hereafter, had been the aim and study of the great organisation called the Church, and of the hundreds of thousands of teachers, both orthodox and unorthodox, who for centuries have ostensibly lived and worked for no other end. It would be rash to say that, on a balance of considerations, the Church and the Clergy of all denominations have in the course of ages done more harm than good to the Christian World ; but probably it would be rasher still to assert the contrary. Certain it is, that in many most material points they have worked counter to the progress of mankind in material and social welfare, and in those departments of moral improvement which spring therefrom. They have inculcated almsgiving on the rich, and (by implication, at least in the matter of early marriages) improvidence on the poor, and have thus been the abettors of incalculable mischief. And they have been able to quote texts in defence of both misteachings. To the rich they have said, "Give to him that asketh of thee;" to the poor, "Take no thought for the morrow, for the morrow shall take thought for the things of itself."* In former days they whetted the angry passions of men by consecrating them and enlisting them in the service of the Church and are answerable for countless cruelties and crimes, perhaps for the very worst that have disgraced history. Something of this tendency, perhaps, still remains, and neither charity nor education can do the good they might, because theology stands in the way.† The entire *theory* of the Church is antagonistic to any concentrated or consistent scheme for raising the earthly condition of the suffering masses; and if practice in this respect has been sounder than theory, the manifest inconsistency of the two has introduced the further evil of a fearful and fundamental insin-

---

* "Another habit of the same category is that of marrying early and in trust. Religion has looked favourably on this habit. 'God himself bade men be fruitful and multiply.' Let young people who fall in love marry, or they may do worse. God will provide food for the mouths he sends into the world.' Our Lord, it is urged, exhorted his disciples to a simple dependence on the heavenly Father who feeds the sparrows, and condemned anxious care about the morrow. To discourage early marriages on prudential grounds has been stigmatised by religious persons as a hard, godless, immoral policy."—Rev. Llewellyn Davies. *Cont. Rev.* Jan. 1871.

† This is the result of much thought and practical experience in a singularly careful, intelligent and pious man. "*In charity as in Education, the supreme evil is religion*—not true religion, not that love which is the fulfilling of the law—but that vile, devil-coined counterfeit which the so-called religious world has stamped with its hall-mark, and agrees to receive as legal tender in place of the true metal."—*Letters of Edward Denison, p.* 229.

cerity. All this has been so well put by other writers that I shall prefer their words to my own.

" With regard to the influence of Christianity it would seem that there is much exaggeration in the views entertained upon that subject, and even a misconception of its true stand-point. The recent arguments upon this subject would, in fact, have been scarcely intelligible to the early fathers and apologists, and if they had understood they would have rejected them. Their conception of Christianity was that it was a preparation for a coming age, and also for another world, not an instrument for the improvement of the present; and this still continues to be the prevalent opinion among those who consider themselves to be especial Christians, members of the body and heirs of the Kingdom of Christ. To be wise, or learned, or rich, or peaceful, or happy, was for the individual believer rather a snare and a peril than an advantage. The kingdom of Christ was not of this world, and its results were not to be looked for here, unless in so far as they were realised by faith. The friendship of this world was enmity with God. If the Christian found himself in harmony with circumstances; if a uniform course of steady and well-directed industry, and an unselfish regard for the rights and feelings of others, had produced their natural consequences of material well-being and social respect, this proof of conformity to the world would at least raise a presumption that he had, in some degree, deserved the enmity of God; at the lowest these temporal blessings might induce him to rest satisfied with his present lot, might dim the eye of faith, and weaken the aspirations or even change the object of hope. These moral virtues, too, were insignificant; they might be splendid sins. Without faith it was impossible to please God, and with faith all other excellences were, at least, implicitly connected; and considering the utter insignificance, on the Christian scheme, of the present life as compared with the eternity that was to follow, no inconvenience or privation or suffering was worthy to be regarded for a moment, if its existence removed an obstacle to the fuller growth of the inward and spiritual life.

" To improve the moral or physical aspect of society was, therefore, no part of the Christian scheme. That it should, in fact, have done so was no subject of congratulation, but rather to be feared and possibly to be regretted ; at any rate it was an absolutely insignificant result. If one soul was lost in consequence, what would the earthly happiness and virtue of millions weigh if balanced against that eternal misery; and if not, what did it matter at the best ? No more than a single smile of an infant in its cradle, procured by some momentary pleasure, as compared with the happiness or misery of its whole future life. There may be a question whether this was the teaching of Jesus, but there can be no question that this is the spirit of orthodox Christianity." *

---

* *The Jesus of History*, p. 13, by Sir R. D. Hanson, Chief Justice of South Australia.

Another writer observes :—

" In our perplexity we naturally direct our attention first to the Church, which we have been taught
to look up to as our guide and instructor in all our
most important concerns. What has been its action
on the progress of the world and the happiness of mankind ? Startling as the avowal must appear, we can
hardly help arriving at the conclusion that the Church
has been rather a hindrance than a helper in the great
business of humanity; and that she is in a great
degree responsible for the fact that so small progress
has been made.

   .   .   .   .   .   .

" Unhappily, the theory on which the Church proceeds is calculated rather to impede than to promote
man's happiness and well-being in this world. It
assumes that this world is a fallen world, and man's
position in it merely a state of preparation for another
and better state of existence ; that man's happiness
here is a matter comparatively of little moment, and
that his main business on earth is to qualify himself for
happiness in that future state. . . . .

" To employ the faculties that God has given us in
endeavouring to discover His laws as displayed in His
works, and to do His will by devoting all our energies
to improve the condition of mankind and to alleviate
the misery so prevalent in the world, and which
mainly arises from ignorance or neglect of those laws;
to endeavour by honest labour to raise ourselves in the
scale of society—this, it is said, although it may be

conducive to man's happiness and well-being here, is
not the way to prepare for a future life. We are to
renounce this world—to lay up no treasures here.
Riches are the root of evil ; the elements of progress
and civilisation are matters of secondary moment. Our
task here is to endeavour, by patience, humility, repen-
tance, faith in the Redeemer, and through the efficacy
of the Sacraments of the Church, to secure eternal
happiness in Heaven. This is the assumption of the
Church. If it be correct, the more zealous the clergy
are, and the more faithful in the discharge of their
duties, the more will they endeavour to withdraw
attention from what concerns the temporal interests of
those committed to their charge, in order to fix it the
more steadily on that which alone, if the Church's
theory be true, is of real worth—the securing of their
happiness in a future life.

"It may perhaps be said that though this is the
theory of the Church, yet, in practice, it does not discourage a reasonable attention to the affairs of this
world, and it is true that there is a great deal of inconsistency between the theory and the practice of the
Church. The clergy do not themselves practise, nor
do they expect their hearers to practise, all that the
theory of the Church requires them to profess. There
is a great deal of conventional insincerity ; but this
very insincerity is one of the serious evils arising out
of the artificial system with which the Church is en-
cumbered. It goes far to explain the discredit into
which the Church has fallen, with the working classes

especially, and the powerlessness of the clergy to make any impression by their teaching." *

Once more :—

" As regards human life in general, it may be said that the industrial theory of it has been treated for the most part as a rival, if not as an enemy, by theological interests. The old traditional teaching of the Church represented it as the business of the Christian to prepare himself for the life to come. The things of this life were snares which he ought, as far as possible, to shun. The love of money was the root of all evil ; it was extremely difficult for a rich man to enter into the kingdom of heaven. The man who accumulated wealth was a fool not to remember that at any moment his soul might be required of him. Mediæval theology, in an uncompromising spirit, asserted the superior credit and reasonableness of a simple ascetic life. It was better that a man should renounce wealth, marriage, comfort, should withdraw himself from the occupations and interests of secular society, and devote himself wholly to the pursuit of salvation. Protestantism recoiled from such a condemnation of the present world, and its trumpet has given an uncertain sound on this question. But its attitude towards industrialism and secular civilization has been generally that of toleration and compromise. Its theology has recommended detachment from the world in the interest of the soul and its salvation. Life is still pictured as a pilgrimage through a

* *The Problem of the World and the Church:* by a Septuagenarian, p. 7.

trying wilderness to Paradise. But for various reasons of necessity and expediency Christians may accommodate themselves innocently and judiciously to the exigencies of this world. Making money is a thing of the earth, earthy; but money is a powerful instrument, and true Christians will not forego the opportunities it gives for promoting the cause of religion." *

It will be admitted at once, that in all the matters above referred to we shall see our blunders, and sooner or later rectify them, and that a vast improvement in the general aspect of social life will be the result. But it may be objected—and the objection indisputably expresses the general sentiment—after all, even when we have come to discern what is wise and right, and to understand thoroughly the unswerving laws which determine political and individual well-being, and estimate adequately the consequences of their neglect or violation, the old, eternal, insuperable difficulty will remain to confront and dishearten us. Our passions will be still in the ascendant, speaking in a louder tone than either interest or duty, and diverting both personal and collective action from that course which alone could realise our visions of attainable good. The ineradicable selfishness of man; the ambition of individuals, of nations, of rulers; the sexual passion (perhaps the most disturbing and unruly of all) will continue to lay waste your ideal future as they have laid waste the melancholy past.

It may be so. But there are three sets of con-

____

* Rev. Llewellyn Davies. *Cont. Rev.* Jan., 1871

siderations which point to a more hopeful issue :—the inevitably vast change which cannot fail to ensue when all the countless influences with hitherto have been working perversely in a wrong direction shall turn their combined forces the other way ; the *reciprocally re-acting* and *cumulative* operation of each step in the right course:—and the illimitable generations and ages which yet lie before humanity ere the goal be reached. Our present condition no doubt is discouraging enough ; we have been sailing for centuries on a wrong tack ; but we are beginning, though only just beginning, to put about the ship. What may we not rationally hope for, when the condition of the masses shall receive that concentrated and urgent attention which has hitherto been directed, permanently if not exclusively, to furthering the interests of more favoured ranks ? What, when charity, 'which for centuries has been doing mischief, shall begin to do good ? What, when the countless pulpits that, so far back as history can reach, have been preaching Catholicism, Anglicanism, Presbyterianism, Calvinism, Wesleyanism, shall set to work to preach Christianity at last ? Do we ever even approach to a due estimate of the degree in which every stronghold of vice or folly overthrown exposes, weakens, and undermines every other ;—of the extent to which every improvement social, moral, or material, makes every other easier ;—of the countless ways in which physical reform re-acts on intellectual and ethical progress ?

What a gradual transformation—transformation almost reaching to transfiguration—will not steal over the aspect of civilised communities when, by a few generations, during which Hygienic science and sense shall have been in the ascendant, the restored health of mankind shall have corrected the *morbid exaggeration* of our appetites;—when the more questionable instincts and passions, less and less exercised and stimulated for centuries, shall have faded into comparative quiescence;—when the disordered constitutions, whether diseased, criminal, or defective, which now spread and propagate so much moral mischief, shall have been eliminated;—when sounder systems of education shall have prevented the too early awakening of natural desires;—when more rational because higher and soberer notions of what is needful and desirable in social life, a lower standard of expenditure, wiser simplicity in living, shall have rendered the legitimate gratification of those desires more easy;—when little in comparison shall be needed for a happy home, and that little shall have become generally attainable by frugality, sobriety, and toil?* It surely is not too

---

* Reflect for a moment on these two examples, applicable to different classes. The (secondary) causes and encouragements of intemperance are bad air and unwholesome diet, sometimes a bad constitution, which create a craving for drink; bad company, which tempts to it; undue facilities, which conduce to it; adulteration of liquors, which exasperates their pernicious influences; squalid homes, which drive men forth for cheerfulness; and the want of other comfortable places of resort, which leaves them no refuge but the publican's parlour. What, again, are the consequences of intemperance? Poverty, squalid homes, brutality, crime, and the transmission of vitiated constitutions. Who can say that all these

Utopian to fancy that our children or our grand-children at least may see a civil state in which wise and effective legislation, backed by adequate administration, shall have made all violation of law—all habitual crime—obviously, inevitably, and instantly a losing game, and therefore an extinct profession; when property shall be respected and not coveted, because possessed or attainable by all; when the distribution of wealth shall receive both from the Statesman and the Economist, that sedulous attention which is now concentrated exclusively on its acquisition; and when,

---

are not preventible? Sound administration might prevent the bad air of unventilated dwellings, the undue multiplication and constant accessibility of gin and beer shops, and the poisoning of wholesome drink. Sound charity might establish, or promote the establishment of workmen's clubs, as rival scenes of cheerfulness and comfort. These, in time, would enormously reduce destitution, and render home more home-like; and brutality, crime, and vitiated constitutions would naturally diminish *pari passu*, till the residuum would become so small in amount that it could be easily dealt with. For let us never forget that it is the magnitude and extent of our social evils that render them so hopeless and unmanageable.

Then, again, look at that sad blot upon our civilisation which we have got to call THE Social Evil, *par excellence*. What are *its* secondary causes? The early awakening of desire by our vicious and careless system of education; our vast population of idle men, whose passions are never sobered by the sanitary blessing of severe toil, and to hundreds of thousands of whom (soldiers and sailors) celibacy is a necessary condition; our want of adequate training and diffused information and legislative and administrative facilities, which prevent those for whom there is no adequate opening to employment and success here from seeking it abroad; our self-indulgence and intemperate habits, which waste the earnings that, well husbanded, might have provided means for an early marriage and a happy home; the wretched notions of luxury which prevail

though relative poverty may still remain, actual and unmerited destitution shall everywhere be as completely eliminated as it has been already in one or two fortunate and limited communities. Few probably have at all realised how near the possibility at least of this consummation may be. An intellectual and moral change—both within moderate and attainable limits—and the adequate and feasible education of all classes, would bring it about in a single genera-

---

through so many strata of society, and frighten away men and women alike from a blended life that would entail frugality and self-denial; the number of women whom our blunders and false notions make redundant, and the yet greater number whom they make destitute and dependent; and, finally, our utterly unsound moral perceptions on this matter. The working of the social evil is simply and obviously to aggravate all these things. But is it quite hopeless to amend our education? Is not the probable tendency of events to diminish the number of mere *fruges consumere nati* by a fairer distribution of wealth; and may we not hope that we are looking, if not actually marching, towards a sounder public opinion that will render idleness and dissipation discreditable? Is it utterly irrational to anticipate the day when the cessation of wars will disband armies, or convert them into a mere police force, to the members of which domestic life will be no impossibility? Are we not already here and there beginning to perceive that large means are not absolutely essential to a comfortable and even refined *ménage?* And the moment simplicity and frugality of living become fashionable, creditable, or even moderately general, at that moment it will become easy, and comparatively early marriages will be feasible without imprudence. When this is achieved, voluntary celibacy will become discreditable, redundant women will be absorbed, and those whose poverty places them now at the mercy of the tempter will become fewer and fewer as the other social improvements which we anticipate begin to operate, and the premature deaths of the bread-winners disappear before sanified cities and vanishing intemperance.

tion. If our working men were as hardy, enduring, and ambitious as the better specimens of the Scotch peasantry, and valued instruction as much, and if they were as frugal, managing, and saving as the French peasantry, the work would be very near completion. If any doubt this, let them carefully ponder the lessons taught experimentally in such narratives as the *Memoirs of William and Robert Chambers*, and Somerville's *Autobiography of a Working Man*, and the facts set forth in *The Proletariat on a False Scent* (*Quarterly Review*, Jan. 1872), and they will doubt no longer.

It may sound romantic, at the end of a decade which has witnessed perhaps the two most fierce and sanguinary wars in the world's history, to hope that this wretched and clumsy mode of settling national quarrels will ere long be obsolete ; but no one can doubt that the commencement of wiser estimates of national interests and needs, the growing devastation and slaughter of modern wars, the increased range and power of implements of destruction which, as they are employable by all combatants, *will grow too tremendous to be employed by any*, and the increasing horror with which a cultivated age cannot avoid regarding such scenes, are all clear, if feeble and inchoate, indications of a tendency towards this blessed consummation.

Europe and England of to-day, and America as well, it is too true, offer many features calculated to try severely our faith that the face of the civilised world is set towards a better day. *Nous avons les defauts de nos qualités.* Our growing tenderness to suffering is accompanied with a corresponding gentleness towards wrong.* Our morality grows laxer as

---

* The following extracts are from one of the most remarkable and suggestive articles I remember to have read, as well as the most beautiful in its turn of thought and power of expression :—

"There is the profoundest danger of the collapse of that highest personal life the glory of which has been shown us, before the confusion of the half lights and half shadows of the new era. Complexity of every kind is the great condition of the new life,—shades of thought too complex to yield up definite opinions,—shades of moral obligation too complex to yield up definite axioms of duty,—shades of insight too various to yield up definite sentences of approval or condemnation for the actions of others. On all subjects not strictly scientific, on all those mental and moral questions which determine conduct and action, the growing sense of complexity and difficulty is rapidly producing a relaxing effect upon the force of individual character. In some sense men are blinded by excess of light. The simple old moral law, 'Thou shalt not kill,' 'Thou shalt not steal,' 'Thou shalt not commit adultery,' 'Thou shalt not covet thy neighbour's goods,' is apt to lose half its meaning before multitudes of distinctions which gradually shade off forbidden acts into the most praiseworthy and delicate sentiments, and leave you wondering where the spirit of the law ends and the letter begins."

.　　　　.　　　　.　　　　.　　　　.

"There is, at all events, an immense growth of this spirit, not amongst those who have most hardship and suffering, but who have least,—amongst those who have chiefly reaped the advantages of the new sciences and arts in easy life, pleasant tastes, languid hopes, and feeble faiths. The fear is, that if civilization succeeds,—and we trust it will succeed,—in raising the mass of men to the same level of comparatively satisfied material and intellectual wants, there will be the same disposition to subside into the limited life of small attainable enjoyments, and to let alone the struggles for perfect freedom and perfect life in God. If it were true that with the beating back of great physical wants,

our hearts grow softer. We are nearly as charitable to the sinner as to the sufferer. We condemn nothing very bitterly. We punish nothing very severely. We scarcely regard anything as wicked which is not cruel. Our social atmosphere is thick and hazy with insincerities and unrealities. We bow down before false gods and we profess ignoble creeds; and, what is almost worse, we neither heartily worship the one nor honestly believe the other. We are not exactly bad, but neither are we strong nor true. The religion we profess has for one of its most significant and salient features the denunciation of wealth as a trust or a pursuit;—Christianity condemns riches and the love of riches as a snare, a danger, and almost a sin; and even Pagan-nurtured sages and statesmen are never weary of pointing out how this disastrous passion vitiates all our estimates of life and its enjoyments, and fosters and exasperates all our social sores. Yet in England and America, perhaps the two most sincerely Christian nations in the world,—one, the

---

the deepest hunger of human nature is to be laid to sleep, and life to be frittered away in small enjoyments, no one could look upon human destiny without a sigh.

"Perhaps it may be thought almost an answer to this fear to point out that with the growth of the self-indulgent spirit there is very apt to grow also a very strong feeling of the worthlessness of life,—a feeling that nothing enjoyed is worth the cost of obtaining it, that life itself is a doubtful good, that the spring and elasticity of youth once over, and the sense of duty smothered in a sea of speculative doubt, it is rather from indolence than from love of life, that men prolong the dreary monotony of unsolved problems and ungranted prayers."—*Spectator*, Oct. 19, 1867.

cradle, the other the offspring, of Puritanism—·the pursuit nearest to a universal one, the passion likest to a national one, is money-getting ;—not the effort after competence or comfort, but the pushing, jostling, trampling struggle for vast possessions or redundant affluence.   Yet already we fancy we can see traces, not so much of positive reaction against these things, as of that sounder *perception* and that sick discontent even in success which precede reaction.   Progress, too, is always fitful, and the errors and backslidings we see around us now may be merely the casual ebb of the advancing wave.   " Time is on our side."   We look to advance by slow accretions.   We calculate on eras almost geological in their duration before the full attainment of an ideal life on earth.   The moral sense will have to be strengthened and purified by long centuries of increasing good before it can do its perfect work.   But what are centuries in the life-time of a Race ?   They are less than as many minutes of individual duration.   " *La Providence a ses aises dans le temps ; elle fait un pas, et des siècles se trou-vent écoulés.*"*   God, who spent ages in fitting the earth for the residence of man, may well spend ages more in fitting rectified man to inhabit a renovated earth.

There are, however, a few recollections and reflec-tions which justify a fancy that possibly our steps forward may ere long be incomparably more rapid than is here supposed.   The *possibilities* of human progress—what Humanity might achieve if its known

---

* Guizot, *Histoire de la Civilisation.*

powers were steadily applied in a determinate and already indicated direction—are simply incalculable. Its *actualities* even—historically recorded or daily witnessed—are startling enough. Our eras of advance have been short and fitful; but they have been wonderful while they lasted, and we can assign no reason why they *need* have ceased. Look back two and twenty centuries. In about two hundred years the Athenians raised themselves from the conditions of a rude and scarcely civilised people to the highest summit which any nation has yet reached—the culminating point of human intelligence.* Conceive that rate of progress continued instead of stopping short, and applied to all departments of man's capacities and wants instead of to a few only, and what might our Race not have been now?

Again, few phenomena are more remarkable, yet few have been less remarked, than the degree in which material civilization,—the progress of mankind in all those contrivances which oil the wheels and promote the comfort of daily life,—has been concentrated into the present century. It is not too much to say that in these respects more has been done, richer and more prolific discoveries have been made, grander achieve-

---

* The summit was attained in the days of Pericles, B.C. 450. Grote considers that the real history of Greece began only in B.C. 776. The Archonship of Kreon, with whom commences the authentic chronology of Athens, dates B.C. 683; but the real progress of Athens is comprised between the time of Solon (594) or that of Pisistratus (560), and that of Pericles (450),—scarcely more than three generations. The grandfather was born in a rude age; the grandson or great grandson flourished in the acme of civilisation.

ments have been realized, in the course of the fifty or seventy years of our own life-time than in all the previous life-time of the race, since states, nations, and politics, such as history makes us acquainted with, have had their being. In some points, no doubt, the opposite of this is true. In speculative philosophy, in poetry, in the arts of sculpture and painting, in the perfection and niceties of language, we can scarcely be said to have made any advance for upwards of two thousand years. Probably no instrument of thought and expression has been or ever will be more perfect than Greek; no poet will surpass Homer or Sophocles; no thinker dive deeper than Plato or Pythagoras; no sculptor produce more glorious marble conceptions than Phidias or Praxiteles. It may well be that David, and Confucius, and Pericles were clothed as richly and comfortably as George III. or Louis XVIII., and far more becomingly. There is every reason to believe that the dwellings of the rich and great among the Romans, Greeks, and Babylonians were as luxurious and well-appointed as our own, as well as incomparably more gorgeous and enduring. It is certain that the palaces belonging to the nobles and monarchs of the Middle Ages,—to say nothing of abbeys, minsters, and temples,—were in nearly all respects equal to those erected in the present day, and in some important points far superior. But in how many other equally significant and valuable particulars has the progress of the world been not only concentrated into these latter days, but astoundingly rapid in its march ?

Consider only the three momentous matters of light, locomotion, and communication, and we shall see that this generation contrasts most surprisingly with the aggregate of the progress effected in all previous generations put together since the earliest dawn of authentic history. The lamps and torches which illuminated Belshazzar's feast were probably just as brilliant, and framed out of nearly the same materials, as those which shone upon the splendid fêtes of Versailles when Marie Antoinette presided over them, or those of the Tuileries during the Imperial magnificence of the First Napoleon. Pine wood, oil, and perhaps wax, lighted the banquet halls of the wealthiest nobles alike in the eighth century before Christ and in the eighteenth century after Christ. There was little difference, except in finish of workmanship and elegance of design—little, if any, advance, we mean, in the illuminating power, or in the source whence that power was drawn—between the lamps used in the days of the Pyramids, the days of the Coliseum, and the days of Kensington Palace. Fifty years ago, that is, we burnt the same articles, and got about the same amount of light from them, as we did four thousand years ago. *Now*, we use gas of which each burner is equal to fifteen or twenty candles; and when we wish for more can have recourse to the electric light or analogous inventions, which are fifty-fold more brilliant. and far-reaching than even the best gas. The streets of cities, which from the days of Pharaoh to those of

Voltaire were dim and gloomy, even where not wholly unlighted, now blaze everywhere (except in London) with something of the brilliancy of moonlight. In a word, all the advance that has been made in these respects has been made since many of us were children. We *remember* light as it was in the days of Solomon, we *see* it as Drummond and Faraday have made it.

The same thing may be said of locomotion. Nimrod and Noah travelled just in the same way, and just at the same rate, as Thomas Assheton Smith and Mr Coke of Norfolk. The chariots of the Olympic Games went just as fast as the chariots that conveyed our nobles to the Derby, " in our hot youth, when George the Third was King." When Abraham wanted to send a message to Lot he despatched a man on horse-back, who galloped twelve miles an hour. When our fathers wanted to send a message to their nephews, they could do no better, and go no quicker. When we were young, if we wished to travel from London to Edinburgh, we thought ourselves lucky if we could average eight miles an hour,—just as Robert Bruce might have done. *Now*, in our old age, we feel ourselves aggrieved if we do not average forty miles. Everything that has been done in this line since the world began,—everything, perhaps, that the capacities of matter and the conditions of the human frame will ever allow to be done,—has been done since we were boys. The same at sea. Probably, when the wind was favourable, Ulysses, who was a bold and skilful navigator, sailed as fast as a Dutch merchantman of the year 1800, nearly as fast at times as an American yacht or clipper of our fathers' day. *Now*, we steam twelve and fifteen miles an hour with wonderful regularity, whether wind and tide be favourable or not;—nor is it likely that we shall ever be able to go much faster. But the progress in the means of communication is the most remarkable of all. In this respect Mr Pitt was no better off than Pericles or Agamemnon. If Ruth had wished to write to Naomi, or David to send a word of love to Jonathan when he was a hundred miles away, they could not possibly have done it under twelve *hours*. Nor could we to our own friends fifty years ago. In 1870 the humblest citizen of Great Britain can send such a message, not a hundred miles, but a thousand, in twelve *minutes*.

Suppose for a moment the advent of another fifty years during which the activity of the human mind should be directed towards Chemistry as applied to Surgery and Medicine and hygienic influences in general, and some of the highest authorities in therapeutics tell us that we can scarcely conjecture the results that might be achieved;—sleep at will, with all the uncalculated gain of time which that implies; the conquest of all pain not needed as a warning; the prevention of infant and gratuitous mortality; the extinction of epidemic diseases, as leprosy and the plague have become extinct in Europe.

But it will be said, all these are material matters, and the vastest advance may be attained in those without any consequent approach to your ideal State. Scarcely :—material victories and achievements make intellectual and moral ones attainable. But suppose again—what no reader of History will deem a wild supposition—suppose the advent of a man, filled and fired with " the enthusiasm of Humanity," and imbued with the true conception of progress—the prophet of a grand yet realisable Ideal. Suppose such seed as he could sow falling on a prepared and fertile soil, and in a favourable season. Such prophets have been raised up in the past, and such happy conjunctions of suitable conditions have occurred. Imagine a Statesman or Leader, of fervid eloquence, convincing logic, with sound conceptions both of ends and means, preaching to an educated people, at a happy epoch,—and why should he not inaugurate a generation of sustained and rightly-guided effort which would revolutionise for good, and for all time, our entire social and moral surroundings? Surely Human Nature is not so changed or sunk that spiritual forces cannot again work greater marvels than mechanical or chemical or economic agencies have done. THOUGHT has not yet grown feebler than electricity and gases in moulding the destinies of man.*

* The following quotation, in an analogous line of thought, will be found suggestive, if not acceptable.—(*Spectator*, Aug. 8, 1868) :—

" We write and chatter, but none of us know what a community in which the majority was sovereign, and each man was as

There are, however, three antagonistic agencies to be considered, the tendency of which appears hostile to all continuous progress or radical and far-reaching amelioration ; and which, if they be really as persistent and incurable as they seem, must be fatal to the realization of our dreams of the ultimate happiness of mankind, or must relegate that realisation to a world

competent to form an opinion as an average county member now is, would be like. That is an advance conceivable without revolution, and no change we have yet encountered could so completely transform Western society, its conditions, its ways, and it may well be, its objects. A happy life might become the ideal instead of a progressive life, and half the existing social motors cease to act. All the new experiments in living tried in America have had that for ultimate end, and have had as chiefs men above the uncultivated class, men usually who have just emerged from the uncivilized stage. Society as it is, is not the ultimate outcome of human thought,—if it be, the best thing men can do is to give up the struggle to improve others, and go in for self-cultivation alone, as the highest Americans seem disposed to do ; but without dreaming of social revolutions, let us think what universal and tolerably equal education really implies. Well, this, for one thing, that work shall be paid for in proportion to its disagreeableness, a very prosaic and undeniable proposition, which of itself and by itself would grind all existing arrangements into powder. Imagine the man who carts muck better paid than the man who sells tapes ! a change actually visible in full work in Illinois and Michigan. There is no need to talk about possible republics and impossible equalities, about the effect of household suffrage or the decay of the feudal idea ; education, if we get it, will of itself be a sufficient solvent ; and getting it, though improbable, is far less impossible than the extinction of feudalism once appeared.

" Or suppose a new creed, or new development of the great existing creed, takes a strong hold of the masses of the West. Observers think they see a strong tendency towards secularism,—a creed that if adopted would pulverize existing society, which, with all its faults, is not based on the theory of securing the greatest comfort in this world ;—but let us imagine that history is true,

of wholly altered conditions. These agencies are,—
first, the alleged perpetual and inevitable struggle
for mere existence,—*secondly,* the multiplication of
the race from its least eligible specimens, or, as it
has been happily termed, the non-survival of the fittest,
—and, *thirdly,* the increasing prevalence of democratic views and institutions—a prevalence which

---

that men will not live without a religious belief, and that the belief
will probably have some connection with the root faith of the last
few centuries, be, in fact, a new form of Christianity. How great,
—let rectors say,—would be the change produced by a general
impression that we ought to live as Christ lived, or as He said we
ought to live, to take His teaching as it stands, and not as the
learned have for a few centuries declared that He meant it to
stand? How would wealth and poverty face each other then?
Or suppose the enthusiasm of humanity to get a strong hold upon
men. It is odd, but it is true, that the only people who seem now-
adays willing to be "faithful unto slaying"—not, be it noticed,
merely "unto being slain,"—are the enthusiasts, the John Browns,
Garibaldis, and Louis Blancs of all sorts upon whom that enthusiasm has descended. How would our social arrangements stand
that new strain? Or suppose the change mainly one of dogma,—
that, for example, Western mankind in general got into its head
the idea, which many English clergymen have got into theirs, that
the prize offered by Christianity *is* eternal life, that the phrases
eternal life and eternal death are literally true, that man either
rejoins Christ or dies like a flower,—would not that act as a pretty
rapid solvent of institutions? We think we could advance some
strong reasons for believing that of all the heresies current among
us, that is, perhaps the most enticing and most dangerous; but
it is but one of a hundred, any one of which may for a moment
prevail, and in prevailing make the next half-century a period of
change before which the last half-century will seem stable and un-
eventful.

"That any change of all those that we have indicated will occur
is perhaps improbable, but not one of them is impossible, and in
each is contained the germ of innovations to which those of our
period of 'concentrated progress' will seem but small and weak."

many deem irresistible and fated. The two former I shall consider in separate chapters; the last, as I propose to deal with it very briefly, I may as well speak of here.

The case is simply this. The ultimate realisation of our ideal depends upon all the influences which determine the condition and improvement of a community —its political and social action, its legislation and administration, the education of the people (using that word in its widest sense, to include the education of life as well as of infancy, the teaching of the pulpit as well as of the school-room), its sanitary laws, its municipal government, its property arrangements—being set and continued in a right direction; that is, being guided by a sincere purpose towards good, and by competent wisdom to determine how that good may most surely be attained. Now, as civilised and social life grows daily more rapid and more complex, and the problems with which it has to deal therefore at once vaster, more difficult, and more urgent, the largest intellects and the widest knowledge are needed to handle them and solve them ; intellects the least liable to be clouded by interest or passion, and the most qualified by training and study to foresee the consequences, and detect the correlations and reciprocal operation on different classes, of each law or executive proceeding. The science of Government is the most intricate and perplexing of all, demanding mental and moral qualities of a higher order than any other. Self-government, as it is not very correctly

termed, is assuredly not the simplest form of rule.
Yet at the very time when the influences which
determine the well-being of the community are growing more numerous and involved, and the problems
of social life more complicated and more vast, the
spread of democratic ideas and institutions is throwing
the control, the management, the ultimate decision
at least of all these influences and problems, the final
guidance of all administrative and legislative action
in short, into the hands of the numerical majority
—of those classes, that is, which, however their
condition as to property and education and morals
may be raised, must always be the *least* educated
portion of the community, the *least* endowed with
political capacity, the *least* possessed of either the
leisure, the characteristics, or the knowledge requisite
for the functions assigned to them or assumed by them.
The masses may no longer be very poor, or very ignorant, or in any way ill-disposed; but under no conditions can they help being *more* ignorant, *more* engrossed with the struggle for individual well-being,
more unqualified to foresee or consider remote and
collateral consequences, *more* unable to deal patiently,
largely, consistently, and profoundly with the questions
which occupy the statesman and affect the life of
nations, than those other classes to whom wealth gives
leisure to grow wise. The few—intellectually at least,
and in all those moral qualifications which directly
or indirectly are connected with intellect — must
always. and as it would seem unavoidably, be fitter

to bear rule, abler to govern righteously and sagaciously than the many.

Yet, unquestionably, the tendency of events in our
days, and in all civilised countries, is to take political
power from the few and confer it on the many ; and
in the view of Tocqueville and his disciples this tendency is absolutely irresistible. If so, what must be
its operation on those who wish to look sanguinely on
the prospects of humanity ? For the few cannot easily
take back power from the many on whom they have
conferred it : and history records no encouraging, instances of the mass voluntarily surrendering a supremacy they have once enjoyed. Nor does our observation
of democratic communities—even the most favoured—
do much to alter ot impair the conclusions at which *à
priori* we have arrived. The United States, France,
and even Switzerland, at present are not consoling
spectacles.

I have little to urge against · the validity of the
above reasoning, or in mitigation of the depressing
conclusions to which it logically points. If democratic
—or I would rather say, ochlocratic—influences and
institutions are to spread and bear sway permanently,
then the day of my cherished vision must indeed be
distant. But I do not believe the tendency to be so
irresistible as is fancied. I am not sure that it may
not contain within it the seeds of a counteracting and
correcting agency. That the concerns and feelings of
the masses are obtaining increased and paramount consideration in our days, is a hopeful sign of the times

at which we must all rejoice. If this had been always so—or had been so in time—probably the occasion for handing over political power to the masses might never have arisen ; nor would the phenomenon have been so formidable when it did arise. If the interests of the lower classes are dealt with, even at this eleventh hour, in a generous, candid, sympathetic spirit, according to the dictates of simple justice, and on principles of wise policy and sound economy, I am even inclined to believe that the *potentiality* of paramount rule in political matters, so rashly conferred upon them, may never be actually realised or exercised. There are two or three very significant and reassuring circumstances which it is desirable to note. Neither in England, nor in America, nor in France, have ochlocratic institutions (those giving political power to the mere masses, the numerical majority) been *obtained* by the masses by their own strength or on their own demand. In every instance they have been conceded by the folly, the weakness, the short-sightedness, and generally by the sinister and clashing interests, of those above them. In America, universal suffrage, conferring electoral rights on Irish and German emigrants before they had acquired any one of the qualifications of good citizens, was the result of unpatriotic and improvident party conflict, for the sake of obtaining a dear-bought victory by the help of " the foreign vote." Bitterly have the Americans paid for their folly, and clearly do they now recognise the error. In precisely the same manner, though in a less extreme and obvious shape, is the household suffrage we have now established here the result of the strife for power between Conservative and Liberal Governments, and perhaps the most pernicious of its consequences. In France, as is every year becoming more recognised by all students of her history, the ochlocracy which is now driving her to seemingly irretrievable downfall is traceable to the fatal weakness of monarch and ministers alike in February, 1848, when a Parliamentary demand for a very moderate extension of a very restricted franchise, was allowed to become first a street riot and then a mob revolution, though ordinary determination and consistency of purpose among the authorities might have prevented it from ever growing beyond the dimensions of a mere police affair, and have crushed it at the outset.

In England, if the latent electoral power of the masses ever becomes noxiously formidable—which no doubt is possible enough, so little wise and patriotic are our general class of politicians—it will be owing to one of two things, or to a combination of both; either to a neglect, or supposed hostility, or disheartening want of sympathy, on the part of the governing classes to the wants and interests of those masses; or, more probably, to the rival factions in the State seeking to use and organise the votes of the working classes on their own behalf respectively, as against their antagonists. As long as property is safe and its rights respected, the legitimate and inevitable influence it must ever wield, directly and through the accessories which belong to it (of which wealth and superior knowledge, refinement,

and intelligence are the principal) is so enormous that
we cannot doubt its winning an easy victory in any
social struggle, and even warding off the near approach
of any such struggle, *provided only the holders of property hang together and recognise in time the danger
of division in their ranks;* and there is surely sagacity
and foresight enough to create close union among all
possessional classes at the first serious menace to the
security and sacredness of property.   This is the first
safeguard we have to trust to.   The second is a plea-
santer one to think of.   It is that the great bulk of
the community—engrossed more or less in daily labour,
interested and occupied mainly in the matters that lie
close about them and concern them most urgently,
caring usually for political questions only or chiefly,
inasmuch as these affect, or are supposed to affect,
their own condition—will be willing enough, partly
from indolence and indifference, partly from a vague impression that their superiors understand these matters,
and that they themselves do not, to leave them in the
hands of the upper classes; provided only these classes
are wise and just enough to take care that no manifest
wrong, no irritating or grinding misery, and no un-
sympathetic or insolent neglect, shall ever rouse the
millions, who would otherwise lie contented and quies-
cent, to seize the reins or to upset the coach.   " Pour
le peuple, ce n'est jamais par envie d'attaquer qu'il se
soulève, mais par impatience de souffrir."   We might,
perhaps, hope that, just in proportion as the working
classes are comfortable, prosperous, and educated,

will they be disinclined to meddle in governmental affairs (which are always laborious and harassing, and seldom remunerative or satisfactory); but this cannot be predicted with any confidence. It is rational however, to anticipate that the better the masses are governed, the less anxious they will be to undertake the heavy burden and the hard task of governing themselves.

II.

MALTHUS NOTWITHSTANDING.

THE hopes of indefinite progress and attainment expressed in the opening chapters are by no means new. They have reappeared at different epochs. They have been cherished by some men in all ages, and by whole nations and continents fitfully and during short periods.

Towards the close of the eighteenth century, more than two generations since, a sudden glow of this sanguine faith in man's future spread over the world. A new era seemed to be opening for humanity. Not only the unthinking multitudes, but men of large experience and devoid neither of great reasoning nor of great observing powers,—not only the young and ardent but the old and the contemplative,—dreamed of perfectibility as well as of progress ; of an approaching time in which both the moral and the physical condition of our species should become thoroughly satisfactory—subject only to the one drawback of mortality, and of mortality reduced to its simplest elements, to the mere fact of death in the ripeness of age and preparation ; of a state of things in which every man having enough of the necessaries, comforts, and even luxuries of life, should have no motive to envy or despoil his neighbour, and in which, therefore, all bad passions would die out from mere lack of nourishment. In a word, "our young men saw visions and our old men dreamed dreams," and they not only cherished but actually believed in their visions and their dreams. Men like Southey and Coleridge and Robert Owen, as in later times and in another country, men like Fourier and St. Simon, had their pictures and their programmes and their panaceas,—and not only men of that stamp, but far soberer and acuter minds. Those who wish to realise to themselves the sort of enthusiasm which anticipation of a state of diffused comfort and universal plenty and well-being excited in the general imagination and of the boundless delight and sweeping confidence with which it was received, and who have not patience to master the whole social and literary history of Europe from 1783 to 1793, should read Godwin's " Political Justice," and ask their grandfathers to describe the glow of generous emotion with which they followed the speculations of that singular book.

An answer, however, shortly appeared to Mr Godwin which shattered all his brilliant pictures of an earthly paradise, and overwhelmed all such philanthropic dreamers with despondency and gloom,—and this cruel shock was administered by a man of singular benevolence and piety, a clergyman of the Church of England. Malthus demonstrated,* or was held to

---

* The first edition of the Essay on the " Principle of Population " was published in 1798.

demonstrate that such a condition of universal comfort and plenty as was shadowed forth *could* never be reached on earth,—inasmuch as there was a constant and irremediable pressure of population on the means of subsistence ; that it was in the nature, in the essence, of human beings to increase in a more rapid ratio than food ; that as long as and whenever population *did* increase faster than its sustenance, the great mass of mankind must be in a state of wretchedness ; and that this incurable tendency could only be counteracted by—what were merely other forms of wretchedness—viz., profligacy, excessive and premature mortality, or abstinence from marriage,—or, as he phrased it, by vice, misery, or moral restraint. In other words, he maintained, and seemed to have proved, that mankind could only secure that sufficiency of food for all, which is the indispensable and main condition of virtue and comfort, on terms which must be held to preclude comfort and imperil virtue—with the majority, with all ordinary men, in fact, to be fatal to both ;— that is, by seeing most of their children die almost as soon as they came into the world, or by themselves and their fellows dying rapidly and prematurely from defect of nutriment; or by wilfully preventing children coming into the world at all; or by resisting and foregoing, habitually and generally, sometimes altogether, always during the most craving period of life, those imperious longings of the senses, and that equally imperious " hunger of the heart," which, combined, constitute the most urgent necessity of our nature, and which the Creator must have made thus urgent foi wise and righteous purposes.

It is obvious on a moment's consideration that the two former of the above three-named terms on which alone, according to the Malthusian theory, plenty can be secured for all, may be left out of consideration, and that practically, the sole condition is the last,— namely, the postponement of marriage as a rule during the years when it is usually most desired, and the abstinence from it in many cases altogether;—in a word, resolute, self-enforced, and prolonged celibacy, precisely at that epoch of life, under those circumstances, and among those classes, in which celibacy is most difficult;—that is (as the rough common feelings of mankind at large would put it), that life in plenty and comfort can only be obtained by the sacrifice of the chief comfort in life, and of those joys without which even a life of material plenty is a very poor and questionable boon. And, be it observed, this is the form the proposition must inevitably assume in the minds not of the vicious, the sensual, the weak or the self-indulgent portion of mankind, but of the *natural*, unsophisticated, right-feeling, sensible,—though, if you will, unregenerate, and unsanctified,—mass of mankind.

No wonder that a proposition, which seemed to condemn the human species to such hopeless, universal, eternal—nay, *ever-increasing* pressure and privation, or to proffer an escape from that lot at a price which few could pay, and few would think worth paying, should have staggered and shocked those to whom it was first propounded. It sounded like the sentence to a doom of utter darkness and despair. It seemed to untrained minds utterly irreconcileable with any intelligent view of the Divine beneficence and wisdom. Yet its author appeared to have framed his conclusion with such caution, and to have clinched it, so to speak, with such close bands of logic and with such a large and indisputable induction of facts, that recalcitration against it was idle, and refutation of it impossible. He maintained it after full discussion and, with some modifications, to the end of his career ; and nearly all political economists of position and repute have accepted his doctrine as a fundamental and established axiom of the science.

Malthus never endeavoured to blink the full scope and severity of his proposition. In an article on Population, which he contributed to the 8th edition of the " Encyclopædia Britannica," and which I believe was the latest of his writings on that subject, he reproduces it in the most uncompromising terms. He lays it down as indisputable and obvious, that population, if unchecked, necessarily increases in a *geometrical* ratio, and that food, the produce of the soil, can only at the outside and under the most favourable circumstances increase in an *arithmetical* ratio. That the inhabitants of a given country or area will, as is seen, actually double their numbers in twenty-five years, and *might* easily double their numbers in a much shorter time ; whereas, even if we concede that in the same twenty-five years the produce of the soil in the same given country or area may be doubled likewise, it is certain that in the *next* twenty-five years, while the population would again double itself or *quadruple* its original numbers, the soil could at the very utmost only again add an equal increment to that of the preceding period, or *treble* its original yield. What is true of a given country, farm, or district, he proceeds to say, must necessarily be true of the whole earth ; and neither emigration, free trade, nor equal distribution of the land can affect the ultimate result. All that these could effect would be a temporary alleviation of the pressure of population and subsistence, and a certain calculable postponement of the day when the ultimate limit of possible numbers and the extreme point of pressure would be reached. "Taking a single farm only into consideration, no man would have the hardihood to assert that its produce could be made permanently to keep pace with a population increasing at such a rate, as it is observed to do, for twenty or thirty years together at particular times and in particular countries." This is obvious and undeniable, and may be conceded at once. But, he goes on to say, "nothing but the confusion and indistinctness arising from the largeness of the subject, and the vague and false notions which prevail respecting the efficacy of emigration, could make persons deny in the case of an extensive territory, *or of the whole earth*, what they could not fail to acknowledge in the case of a single farm, which may be said fairly to represent it." There must always, everywhere, and to the end of time, he maintains—except in the rarest cases, and for the briefest periods—be pressure of population on the means of subsistence. "It is to the laws of nature, therefore, and not to the conduct or institutions of man, that we are to attribute the necessity of a strong and ceaseless check on the natural increase of population."

Malthus' doctrine has been accepted as undeniable by nearly every writer of repute on economical subjects, and by none more unreservedly than by the latest, and in some respects the greatest of them all, J. S. Mill. None of the many authors who have questioned or assailed it, such as Ingram. Alison, Sadler, Doubleday, or Quetelet have been able to shake in any material degree its hold upon the public mind. Various theories have been put forward in competition, but none has obtained any currency, or perhaps deserved any. It has remained the fixed axiomatic belief of the educated world, that pressure of numbers on the means of subsistence is and must remain the normal condition of humanity; that, in consequence, distress or privation, in one shape or another, must be the habitual lot of the great majority of our species; since they can only escape the distress and privation arising from insufficient food by voluntarily embracing the distress and privation involved in long-continued, and perhaps perpetual, celibacy. Reasoning the most careful and cogent seemed to have made this clear, and the observation and experience of every day and every land seemed to illustrate and confirm it.

Some years ago I hoped to be able to show, in opposition to this received doctrine, that, however irrefutable was Malthus' logic, his premises were imperfect, and his conclusions in consequence unsound. It is with some sadness I am now compelled to admit that further investigation and deeper thought have shaken this confidence. I now only venture to suggest as eminently probable what I once fancied I could demonstrate to be certain. I still, however, entertain little doubt of the future discovery and establishment of physiological influences or laws, of which Malthus was not cognisant, and the tendency of which is to counteract and control those which he perceived so clearly ; but I recognise that at present these are not *ascertained ;* and I must therefore confine myself to the task of pointing out a few persuasive indications of the existence of these undiscovered laws, the direction in which they may be looked for, and the vast expanse both of space and time left open wherein they may operate and have their perfect work.

1. Some preliminary misgiving, in the first place, must be aroused by noting that the *actual* fecundity of the human race has never equalled, and scarcely ever even distantly approached, its *possible* fecundity; and that this difference is observable when there is neither vice, misery, nor moral restraint to account for it ;—that in the midst of the most ample supply of food, where there need and can be no anxiety as to the future, where parents are healthy, where the climate is good,—where, in a word, every circumstance is as

favourable as possible to the unchecked multiplication of the species, where everybody marries, and where marriages are as early as is compatible with vigour,— the population does not increase nearly as fast as theoretically it might do. The most rapid known rate of augmentation appears to be that mentioned by Humboldt, in some parts of Mexico, where, judging from the proportion of births and deaths, he calculated that, if there were no interfering circumstances, the population would double itself in 19 years. This was in a tropical climate, where the marriages were unusually early, and the births as numerous as 1 in 17, or occasionally 1 in 15. In the United States and Lower Canada, which come next, it is calculated that when the large immigration is substracted, the period of doubling by natural increase is 25 years. But both these fall far short of the possible rate of theoretical increase; since, adopting data which are actually reached and, indeed, exceeded in some instances, the population of a country can double itself in less than 10 years.

Again, the ordinary size of families in England and Wales, judging by a comparison of the yearly marriages with the yearly births, is now about 4·15 children, and we may fairly assume that with us no artificial means, of abstinence or otherwise, are employed to prevent each marriage yielding its natural number of offspring. But as this mode of ascertaining the number of children to a marriage is only strictly correct when applied to a stationary population, we must add something to the above figures; and there is, I believe, no reason why we may not take Mr. Malthus' calculation, and call the number 4·5. We cannot with any accuracy ascertain the number of children born to a marriage in America, as statistics there are so complicated by immigration, migration, extension, and other causes, but I believe no one would place the average higher than 6. There is, therefore, no reason for believing that the average in the most favourable circumstances exceeds this. But the *possible* number of children to a marriage—the *natural* unchecked number under the best conditions is far beyond this—certainly four-fold. The child-bearing ages of women extend over nearly 30 years—certainly over 25, or from 16 to 40, inclusive, on a moderate estimate. Twenty-five children to each marriage is therefore no impossibility; in favourable conditions we should say no unlikely occurrence. We all of us know individual cases in which it has been realised. In Italy such instances are not very unfrequent—even in England they are not unexampled. In Lower Canada we find they are by no means uncommon;* from 14 to 16 is a usual number. A recent traveller there assured us he had met with one woman who had borne 32 children.

Yet how rarely—even when food is abundant, health

---

* "Social Science Transactions, 1862, p. 894," Mr. Hurlbert's Paper on Canada. In Belgium, perhaps the most fecund as well as the most densely peopled of old civilized states, the average children to a marriage (according to Quetelet) is 4·75 in the least prolific, and 5·21 in the most prolific provinces.

unquestionable, habits good, an entire absence, that is, both of the preventive and the positive check—do we see this potential fecundity even approached! Does not the contrast point to some other, as yet occult, influence, wholly apart from any of those enumerated by Mr. Malthus, which operates as a natural and unconscious limitation on human reproduction?

2. Some doubt as to the completeness of Malthus' premises, and the consequent correctness of his conclusions, appears to be suggested by the fact that every man is able by his own labour to produce food* enough not only to sustain himself and those naturally helpless and dependent upon him, but enough also to exchange for the shelter and clothing which are as necessary as food to the human animal;—and he can do all this and yet leave himself ample leisure for other occupations or amusements. Without endorsing Mr. Godwin's extravagant calculation that half an hour a day devoted by every individual in a community to agricultural labour would suffice to raise an adequate amount of nutriment, there can be no question that a very moderate amount of regular industry, whether applied to the production of one article or of many, would secure to man an abundant supply of all the necessaries, and most of the comforts, of life—at least in all temperate or tropical climates. In the article in

---

* In fact the natural rate of increase of man's food is out of all proportion greater than man's own rate of increase. A couple of human beings multiply three or fourfold in the course of thirty years. One potato sprout multiplies twenty-fold in a single year,—one grain of wheat even two hundred-fold in favouring circumstances.

the Encyclopædia already quoted, Malthus declares that as long as good land was attainable, "the rate at which food could be made to increase would far exceed what was necessary to keep pace with the most rapid increase of population which the laws of nature in relation to human kind permit." It was obvious, therefore, since every man can produce much more than he needs, and since, given the land and the labour, food can be made to increase incomparably faster than population, and would naturally do so, all that is wanted to put man at his ease is a field whereon to bestow his industry. It is not that population has a natural tendency to increase faster than food, or as fast, but simply that the surface of the earth is limited, and portions of that surface not always nor easily accessible.

III. It was pointed out by the late Mr Senior, as another very suggestive fact, that, taking the world as a whole, and history so far as we are acquainted with it, food always *has* increased faster than population, in spite of the alleged *tendency* of population to increase faster than food. Famines, which used to be so frequent in earlier ages and in thickly-peopled countries, are now scarcely ever heard of, while, at the same time, the average condition of the mass of the people has on the whole improved, that is, that they have more of the necessaries of life than formerly. Probably the only cases in our days of scarcity of food amounting to actual famine are to be found where the staple crop of a whole country has been destroyed by locusts, as sometimes in Asia; or by drought, as occasionally in

Hindostan ; or by vegetable disease, as in the potatoe rot of Ireland. In sparsely-peopled Australia famine has often supervened; in densely-peopled Belgium never. " I admit (says Mr. Senior) the abstract *power* of population to increase so as to press upon the means of subsistence. I deny the habitual *tendency*. I believe the tendency to be just the reverse. What is the picture presented by the earliest records of those nations which are now civilized? or, which is the same, what is now the state of savage nations? A state of habitual poverty and occasional famine. . . If a single country can be found in which there is now less poverty than is universal in a savage state, it must be true that under the circumstances in which that country has been placed, the means of subsistence have a tendency to increase faster than the population. Now, this is the case in *every* civilized country. Even Ireland, the country most likely to afford an instance of what Mr. Mill supposes to be the natural course of things, poor and populous as she is, suffers less from want, with her eight millions of people,* than when her only inhabitants were a few septs of hunters and fishers. In our early history, famines and pestilences, the consequence of famine, constantly recur. At present, though our numbers are trebled or quadrupled, they are unheard of. Whole colonies of the first settlers in America perished from absolute want. Their successors struggled long against hardship and privation, but every increase of their numbers seems to have been

* This was written in 1829.

E

accompanied or preceded by increased means of support.

"If it be conceded that there exists in the human race a tendency to rise from barbarism to civilization, and that the means of subsistence are proportionally more abundant in a civilized than in a savage state — and neither of these propositions can be denied—then it must follow that there is a natural tendency in subsistence to increase in a grater ratio than population."— (*Two Lectures delivered at Oxford by N. W. Senior. Lect.* II.)

An interesting correspondence between Mr. Senior and Mr. Malthus followed the publication of these lectures, and was appended to them, leaving the point of the controversy pretty much where it originally stood, viz., that while the theoretic *power* of population to increase faster than food was undoubted, the practical fact was that this power was scarcely ever exercised ;—Mr. Malthus, however, holding to his former doctrine that the reasons of its non-exercise were to be found solely in the severe and general operation of the preventive check.

4. Another class of facts which I shall do no more than allude to, because, though often examined casually, they have, as far as I know, never been thoroughly sifted or brought into a focus, points even more distinctly to the existence of some cause operating, under certain circumstances, to limit human fertility even beyond what is consistent with the multiplication or preservation of the race, or class, or type. I refer to cases in which a family or set of families, or a whole variety,

dies out where no deficiency or difficulty of subsistence can be alleged as the explanation, and where, therefore, some other cause, almost certainly physiological, must be pre-supposed. Such is the case of baronets, whose titles are perpetually lapsing from the failure of male heirs—assuredly not from abstinence from marriage, nor from lack of food. Such, again, is the frequent extinction of peerage families, of whom plentiful sustenance may at least be predicated.* I am aware of Mr Galton's ingenious explanation, based upon the fact of peers so often marrying heiresses, who of course *ex vi termini* come from comparatively unfertile families;—but the explanation itself is a collateral confirmation of the fact I am pointing out,—for whence arise these many unfertile but rich families? If the wealthy who have every facility for prolonging life, and no motive to abstain from marriage, are so often barren and liable to see their families die out or dwindle down to one heiress, does not the circumstance point to the operation of some influence other than Malthus' "pressure on subsistence," almost antagonistic to it, and *especially potent in the most civilised and comfortable forms of life?* I know that other less occult causes of the phenomena in question have been suggested;—but they are not such as can be dis-

---

* A similar, but still more decided, process of gradual extinction of rich and privileged families appears to have been one of the most constant phenomena in the civilised states of the Ancient World,—in Italy and Greece at least. For remarkable examples and ample proof, see *Dureau de la Malle, Economie politique des Romains,* i. p. 417, *et seq.*

cussed here, nor, I believe, could they do anything beyond slightly mitigating the force of my conclusion.— If from classes we turn to races and nations, history affords examples enough of once populous countries now inhabited by comparatively scanty numbers where unwholesomeness and lack of food (or food-producing soil) will do little to account for the decline.* And if, instead of the annals of the past, we read the living history that is before our eyes, we find every-where savage races dying out with the greatest rapidity, —and dying out as much from paucity of births (dim-inished fecundity, that is,) as from increase of deaths,— even where lack of food, or means of procuring it, can scarcely be put forward as *the* reason or an adequate one, (as in the instance of the Maories and the Polynesians); —and where after full allowance has been made for wars,

---

* See *Dureau de la Malle*, liv. ii. ch. 13. Also *Gibbon*, i. ch. 2. *Merivale's Roman Empire*, iv. 433, vii. 602, 604, 608. The process of depopulation in many provinces of the Roman dominions, since the time of the Antonines, has been excessive, and unaccountable on any of Malthus's hypotheses. We may instance especially the north coast of Africa, so populous in the palmy days of Rome, and Asia Minor and Syria,—to say nothing of Turkish countries further east still. According to *Merivale*, Asia Minor and Syria once supported 27,000,000 of people. According to *M'Culloch* they do not now contain more than one-fourth of those numbers. Yet we do not find that they have become either unhealthy or unfertile. Several analogous indications scattered through history point to the depression of spirits or of nervous energy, which seems to accom-pany the decline of Nations and the decay of Races, as exercising a singularly sterilising influence on mankind.

The same wholesale dying out of old families is observable, I believe, in other countries at the present time. M. de Tocqueville told me of one district in France where 200 families had become extinct, as far as the direct line was concerned, in about a century, from a variety of causes.

diseases, and vices, some unexplained residuum is left, which points to a hidden influence, physiological no doubt, but belonging to the nervous and not to the nutritive system. Again, nowhere in the United States, one would suppose, can pressure of population on means of subsistence be alleged as the true acting cause of non-increase of numbers or failing fecundity; yet it is asserted confidently (and there seems every reason to believe with accuracy), that the native-born citizens of some of the New England States cannot—at all events do not—keep up their numbers. *

When astronomers found the calculable influence of the law of gravitation on the motions of the planets disturbed and *pro tanto* counteracted by some unexplained or undiscovered agency, they at once confidently inferred the existence of an unknown body at an unguessed distance but in a specified direction. They believed in Neptune long before they found him. Why should not we do in physiology what they did in physics ? †

5. Lastly. The repellent character of Malthus' conclusion has been usually regarded as in itself a ground for suspecting its truth. Nor do I think this ground, though confessedly open to question, is peremptorily to be put aside as unphilosophical. It is unphilosophical to reject indisputable and proved con-

---

* See especially different monographs by *Dr Storer*, addressed in the first instance, to members of his own profession, and, I believe, confirmed by several of them.

† Consult *Doubleday's true law of Population*, pp. 36., *et. seq.*, also ch. x., xi. And more especially *Darwin's Animals and Plants under Domestication*, ii., 148-171.

clusions because we do not like them, because they
disturb our serenity, shatter our hopes, or run counter
to our prejudices.   It is not unphilosophical to doubt
the accuracy or completeness of any course of reasoning
which has brought us to results at variance with other
results which appear at least equally certain, and
which have been reached by similar processes of
thought.   Nay, more, it would be unwise *not* to
doubt in such cases, not to suspend our judgment, not
to reconsider our inferences and our data.   There are
certain truths which the general sense of mankind has
adopted and clings to as undeniable, partly from instinctive conviction, partly from overpowering proof,
partly from religious teaching,—such as the wisdom,
power, and ultimate, essential, universal goodness of God.
It is right and wise to doubt *provisionally*—not of
course to deny—any doctrine which contradicts or seems
to contradict these truths, and which has been arrived
at by steps of logic.   And it is so for this simple reason,
—that, though we may feel confident of the justness of
our *inferences*, if scientifically drawn by cautious and
well-trained intellects, and sanctioned after due examination by other qualified minds, yet we can scarcely
ever feel similar confidence as to the perfect accuracy
and completeness of our *premises*.   Unless we can be
certain that we know everything bearing upon the
subject, that we are in possession of *every* datum
necessary for framing our conclusions,—a certainty
which is very seldom attainable,—it may well be that
there is something we do *not* know, some facts which
have escaped our observation or research, which, if

taken into account, would have materially modified, or altogether overthrown our conclusions. Logic fails far oftener from defective data than from careless processes. Not only therefore is *doubt* justified by sound philosophy, where improbable doctrines are sought to be thrust upon us by even the most close and cogent steps of ratiocination, but the doctrines may be of such a character, may be so irreconcileable with beliefs that have become axiomatic, may so revolt our most carefully wrought out convictions, that we should be warranted —not indeed in rejecting them if positively proved but —in declaring that there *must* be some deficiency in the premises, some omitted or undiscovered data, which the future progress of knowledge would bring to light, and which, when introduced into the question, would wholly change its present aspect. Now Malthus' theory of population was precisely one of those doctrines, and therefore justly led numbers who could find no flaw in his reasoning, to feel satisfied that there must be some error or hiatus in the bases on which it was grounded ; and who, in consequence, while unable to refute his conclusions, were equally unable to adopt them.

Malthus himself felt this so strongly, that he took much pains to argue that his theory was in no way irreconcileable with the goodness of God, but on the contrary harmonised with what we know of His general dealings with mankind. While admitting that it was incompatible with the happiness, if not the virtue, of the great mass of mankind, that it called upon them to do violence to their strongest instincts·and to some of their best and most natural sentiments, and opened a terrible vista of probable wretchedness for the future of the race, he argued that this world was designed to be a state of probation, not of enjoyment,—that man was called upon to keep all his appetites in check, and was warned and punished by the laws of nature if he did not,—and that only by the exercise of such check could he ever advance in civilization or in moral dignity. The allegations may be quite irrefragable, the plea has no doubt a certain force, but it is impossible not to see and feel that it does not really meet the objection it was intended to neutralise. For, in the first place, though Providence may have designed this world to be a state of probation, he assuredly did not design it to be a state of misery; and a state of misery, or at least of distress, to the majority it must be, as Malthus repeatedly concedes, if his view of the laws of nature be correct and complete. In the next place, though man is bound, both as a condition of progress and under pain of suffering, to *control* his propensities and to *moderate* his appetites and desires, he is not bound to *deny* them. If he is idle and prefers inordinate rest to reasonable work, nature says that he shall starve or live miserably; but nature never says that he shall not sleep or rest at all, or not during the best years of his life, or the dark hours of night. If he eats or drinks immoderately, nature punishes him with dyspepsia and disease, but nature never forbids him to eat when he is hungry, and to drink when he is thirsty, provided he does both with discretion. Indeed she punishes him equally if he abstains as if he exceeds, if he eats too little, or not at all, as if he eats too much. In the same way, if he indulges to excess in the pleasures connected with reproduction, nature punishes him with premature exhaustion, with appropriate maladies, with moral enervation and corruption; but she does not punish the rational and legitimate enjoyments of love. On the contrary she *does* punish enforced and total abstinence, occasionally in the one sex, often, if not habitually, in the other, by nervous disturbance and suffering, and by functional disorder.

Now, if Malthus' doctrine be correct, the great majority of men and women, if they are to escape a condition of perpetual misery and want, must not only keep within moderate bounds the strongest propensity of their nature, but must suppress and deny it altogether, —always for long and craving years, often, and in the case of numbers, for the whole of life. Observe, too, that the desire in question is the especial one of all our animal wants which is redeemed from animalism by being blended with our strongest and least selfish affections, which is ennobled by its associations in a way in which the appetites of eating and drinking and sleeping can never be ennobled,—in a degree to which the pleasures of the eye and ear can be ennobled only by assiduous and lofty culture. Yet this longing— which lies at the root of life, which enters largely into the elements of chivalry, which nature has inextricably intertwisted with the holy joys of maternity—is singled out as the one, and the only one, which must be smothered, if we would live in plenty or in peace. Do the laws of nature say this? If so, they speak in a language which is wholly exceptional, and which here, and here only, has to be interpreted in a "non-natural" sense. Is there any other instance in which Nature says in the most distinct and imperious language, "Thou shalt do this?"—and also in language equally imperious, if not equally distinct, "If thou dost, thou shalt be punished as in other cases those only are punished who *transgress* my laws?" I know of no analogous instance.*

The various considerations suggested above appear to point irresistibly to the conclusion—though to

---

* Two antagonistic considerations should be noticed here. It has been suggested that the paramount and despotic strength which the instinct in question has now assumed is not *natural*, but excessive; the excess being due to ages of unrestrained indulgence added to other bad influences in the present. Probably this is so; to a large extent I have no doubt it is, and this is one reason why I venture to entertain better hopes for the future. But it must be admitted without doubt, I fancy, that at all events the instinct in man is perennial, not periodic; and that on Malthus' theory the utmost anticipateable moderation in its exercise would virtually be just as certain to result in over-population and discomforting pressure on subsistence, as its present pampered and abnormal development.

Mr Darwin's views and researches, again, remind us that the universal law of all vegetable and animal life is the struggle for subsistence, and that the conclusion we deprecate and deem improbable is merely the natural inference that man is no exception to the permanent and general rule. Certainly this is undeniable; but surely the marvellous *primacy* of man, cerebrally, and therefore mentally, renders it at least reasonable to seek to vindicate for him an exceptional destiny, notwithstanding a common origin.

justify it, or even fully to develope it, would require a separate treatise, and not a mere incidental chapter like the present—that Malthus' logic, though so keen and cogent, was at fault, because based on imperfect and insufficient premises ; that in addition to the positive and preventive checks to over-population notified by him, *there exist physiological checks which escaped his search, and which will prove adequate for the work they have to do* ; that if we were wise and virtuous, the positive check would entirely disappear (with the exception of death, in the fulness of time), and the prudential check be only called upon to operate to that degree which is needed to elevate and purify and regulate the animal instinct, and which is quite reconcileable with and conducive to virtue, happiness, and health ;—in fine, that Providence will be vindicated from our premature misgivings when we discover that there exist natural laws, *whose operation is to modify and diminish human fecundity in proportion as mankind advances in real civilization,* in moral and intellectual development ; and that these laws will (unless we thwart them) have ample time and space wherein to produce their effect, long before that ultimate crisis shall arrive which the Malthusian theory taught us so to dread. I briefly touch upon this point first.

If any one island of limited extent and already moderately peopled, Great Britain, for example, were to be effectually isolated from the rest of the world, either by natural causes or by human laws, it is obvious that, in a comparatively short time,—the reproductive faculty remaining "excessive," as it is now, and as it probably would continue to be—population would press upon the means of subsistence, and either increased mortality, or increased privation and distress from the necessity of an augmented severity in the preventive check, must be the result. But no country is thus completely isolated, and no near approach to such isolation can arise, except from human folly, indolence, or ignorance. Such isolation and absolute impossibility of expansion as would render the Malthusian theory self-evident and indisputably true, would be traceable, not, as he alleges, to the laws of nature but to man's interference with those laws.

Again, since a man can produce from the soil a great deal more than is needed for his own subsistence, and since in consequence, food will and may increase faster than population,—*granted only an unlimited supply of available land*,—it is obvious that there can be no *necessary* pressure on the means of subsistence, until all the available surface of the globe is taken up and fully cultivated. Any pressure that occurs before that extreme point is reached, it is clear, can only be caused by impediments to expansion; and all these impediments are to civilized man artificial, not natural—of human, not of Providential origin. It is obvious that a single family or a single tribe, surrounded by an unlimited territory of uninhabited and productive soil, might go on multiplying indefinitely and without restraint, on the sole condition *of spread-*

ing as they multiplied; and that, so long as they fulfilled this condition, they would never have an idea of what pressure of population on subsistence meant, till they had reached the bounds and exhausted the resources of the habitable earth.

Now what are the practicable impediments to this gradual extension of man over the earth, analysed and traced back to their source ? Why do men not thus spread as they multiply ? • Why have they not always done so ? That they have a natural tendency to do so we know. It is the dictate of nature and of common sense to take in a fresh field from the outlying waste, or to extend their forays over a larger hunting-ground, as children grow up and marry, and as more mouths have to be fed. It has been the practice of mankind to act thus in all times and in some form, so far as history can reach back. There are two ways in which men may spread : they may either actually disperse and settle on other lands, or they may remain at home and exchange the products of their industry for the products of those other lands. The one is emigration, the other is manufacture and commerce. The process by which the earth has been peopled has been usually a mixture of the two, and for the purpose of our argument it is immaterial which is followed, or in what manner the two are blended. People who multiply and live in plenty bring new land into cultivation, and virtually spread themselves, whether they cultivate that new land with their own hands, or through the instrumentality of others whom they employ and pay.

The impediments to the spread of man over the
globe are either natural or artificial, physical or moral.
The physical 'ones, properly regarded, will be seen to
be, and to have usually been, nearly inoperative. They
are climate, sea, and distance. As far as distance is
concerned, this is practically an impediment chiefly in
the case of too dense populations situated in the
interior of Continents and Countries, and hemmed in
and kept at a distance from available spare land by
surrounding numbers. Locomotion, no doubt, is
difficult and costly to the poor ; but in civilised States
neither the difficulty nor the cost are insuperable.
In the beginning, of course, a community spreads from
the outside and *gradually*, and as it spreads, and as civilization increases with numbers and dispersion, roads are
made, and means of communication are opened up in all
directions. Even mountains and rivers are mere difficulties to be overcome, not obstacles to prevent. Sea,
as we know, operated to check expansion only in the
earliest times, in a very slight degree, and in rare and
isolated spots, such as some of the remoter Polynesian
islands. To civilized man it is a prepared highway, a
channel of communication, not a barrier to migration.
Climate, where, as in all natural cases, the expansion
of the community is gradual, merely *directs* the course
of population, and does not check it. Man accommo-
dates himself to climate and provides against its rigours
as long as it yields him a fair recompense for his labour.
When it ceases to do this, if he lives according to
nature, he turns elsewhere, and virtually the limits of

the habitable world, or at least of available land, have been reached in that direction.

The real impediments to expansion—the reasons why man has not spread freely as he multiplied—have all been of a different order, and have proceeded from himself alone. The first has been his *indolence.* He was too lazy or unenterprising to go far afield for his food ; he preferred to remain on the land where he was born ; he chose to be satisfied with scanty food at home rather than seek plenty a few miles away; he was willing even in barbarous times to fight with his brethren for subsistence, or to abstain from marriage, or to let his children die from insufficient nutriment, often indeed to kill them, rather than rouse himself to the exertion of seeking abundance in a new home. This indisposition to spread operates everywhere and always in some measure and in some form. With some it is ignorance of what new fields offer them, and how easily they can be reached—as with the Dorsetshire peasants. With others it is mere "concentrativeness"—a tendency to the *maladie du pays*—as with the French and some Celtic nations. But in all cases, so long as the land is there, and the means of reaching it exists, the impediment is human ; and man has no right to speak of "pressure of population on subsistence," and to reproach Providence in his heart.

The second impediment is meeting with hostile nations who compress each other and forbid mutual expansion. They may not be to blame ; for as long as boundless, unoccupied lands exist, each tribe may bo entitled to say to every other, " Go and expand elsewhere, and leave us alone." But this impediment, like the other, is to be surmounted by sense and energy, and comes not from God but, from man.

A third set of obstacles is often interposed by human laws. Restrictions on migration and restrictions on commercial interchange are such obstacles. The old law of settlement which forbade the Buckinghamshire labourer starving on seven shillings a week to migrate to Lancashire where he might earn twelve shillings, or which discouraged his doing so, and the old corn laws, and other analogous fiscal enactments, which debarred Englishmen from the free use of the rich lands of the Mississippi, are specimens in point. No one can call obstacles of this sort natural.

It remains plain, therefore, that even granting the premises of Malthus to be complete, and his reasoning irrefragable, there can be no NECESSARY insufficiency of food, or pressure of population on subsistence, or indispensable demand for the preventive check, till the whole earth is peopled up to the limits of its productive powers, or till all available land is brought into cultivation : and that any pressure of population on subsistence, and consequent misery which may arise previous to that distant time, is traceable solely to human agency or human short-comings. Since, if men were wise and well-trained enough to know their interests, and to follow them ; to see their duty, and to do it—if they knew what boundless fertile lands lie around them, and within reach ; if they were energetic enough to make the necessary efforts to reach them, and to assist their less capable brethren to do so, and to do this in time; if all laws directly or indirectly interfering with free expansion and free intercourse were repealed, and their lingering consequences neutralized; if, in a word, there were only among us thorough freedom, thorough sense, and a reasonable amount of goodness, mankind might multiply unchecked, if only they would disperse unchecked.* And that pressure of population on the means of subsistence, with all the misery it involves, which Malthus held to be not only *ultimately,* but *perpetually* inevitable, is—at least in its severer form—mainly gratuitous and nearly always premature, and under wise regulations ought never to be encountered till that future day, of whose distance from our era the following concise summary of a number of carefully collected facts will give some idea.

Not to interrupt the argument, I give the details of these data and calculations in the appendix:— They demonstrate that even the most densely populated countries in Europe are probably not peopled up to the full numbers they might comfortably maintain; that many of them fall vastly short of the maximum actually reached by others not more favoured by nature; and that as a whole there

---

* J. S. Mill dwells urgently on the necessity of workmen limiting their numbers, if they wish their wages to increase and their condition to improve. I wish to show that the object will be as effectually gained by *dispersion* as by *limitation.* It is not multiplication, but multiplication *on a restricted field,* on a given area, that lowers wages and brings privation.

is every reason to believe that the European continent could support three or four times its present numbers. They show that a similar conclusion may be adopted with almost equal certainty in reference to a great part of Asia, and perhaps the whole of Africa ; that probably in Africa, and certainly in the two Americas, there are vast tracts of fertile land, with fair, if not splendid climates, which are scarcely inhabited at all, and others which contain a mere sprinkling of human beings ; and that in Australasia the case is even stronger. In fine, while Belgium and Lombardy, which are the best peopled districts in Europe, con- tain about 400 souls to the square mile, Paraguay contains only 4, Brazil only 3, and the Argentine Republic only 1. From the aggregate of these facts we are warranted in concluding that an indefinite number of generations and long periods of time must elapse before the world can be fully peopled,—that before that consummation shall be reached we have cycles of years to traverse, ample to afford space for all the influences which civilization may develope to operate to their uttermost extent.

But this is not all. Not only are few countries in the world adequately peopled, but none even of the most peopled countries are adequately cultivated. England has the best tilled soil in the world, though by no means the best climate ; yet in England the average produce of the soil is not half—perhaps not a third—what it might be, and what in many districts it actually is. But the average yield of France, usually regarded as a very productive country, is only half that of England ; nay, the average yield of the splendid grain-growing provinces in America, which ought greatly to exceed that of England, falls short of it by one half. Without bringing a single additional acre under the plough, the production of the world, by decent cultivation, might be easily trebled or quadrupled. In addition to this hopeful prospect, we see ample ground for expanding still further our conception of the amount of human life that might be maintained in comfort on the earth's surface, in the wasted or neglected riches of the sea, in the utilisation of lands now devoted to the production of needless or noxious superfluities, in the more skilful extraction from the materials of our food of the real nutriment they contain, and in the transfer of much land from pasture to cereals, and in other economies too numerous to mention.

The above considerations prove that *the world* is in no danger of being over peopled just at present, whatever *local* congestion may exist ; that centuries must elapse before population really presses, or, at least, need to press severely, on the means of subsistence ; and that civilization will have time enough to do its work, to perfect its resources, and to bring all lands and all mankind under its modifying influences. Now, my conviction is, that there are certain influences, more or less occult, attendant on civilisation, and which may be made to attend it yet more surely, universally, and promptly than hitherto—which operate insensibly to check fecundity and reduce the rate of increase, so that possibly the danger *ultimately* to be apprehended may be the very reverse of that which Malthus dreaded ; that, in fact, when we have reached that point of universal plenty and universal cultivation to which human progress ought to bring us, the race will multiply too slowly rather than too fast.   One such influence may be specified with considerable confidence,—namely, THE TENDENCY OF CEREBRAL DEVELOPMENT TO LESSEN FECUNDITY.*

To dwell on the various evidences which might be adduced to establish the existence of this tendency would obviously be out of place in a work designed for

---

* It was at one time fancied that a second physiological law might be made good, as operating in the same direction. Mr Doubleday and others, arguing from the facts that scanty nutriment often stimulated reproduction, as rich soils and abundant food in many cases checked it, drew the conclusion that merely ample and sufficient nourishment (such as the progress of civilisation might be expected to bring to all men) would progressively lower the average fecundity of the race. But I believe further investigation has not favoured this theory, at least certainly not in the broad extent·and positive form in which it was first stated by Mr Doubleday. But loose as are both his arguments and statements, I think it is scarcely possible not to recognise some residuum of suggestive truth, at least in several of them ; and Mr Spencer's antagonistic theory appears to be laid down in too unmitigated a form. My own strong opinion is, that other physiological causes of anti-fecund tendency are yet to be discovered ; and that races, nations, and families would not so often die out, were it not so. It is impossible to read the Eighteenth Chapter of Mr Darwin's great work on Domestication without recognising how far we yet are from having got to the bottom of this question, and without receiving a strong conviction of the existence of a variety of *hidden* causes affecting the fertility of animals, especially when in what we

general perusal, and the subject could only be adequately discussed in a physiological treatise. I shall, therefore, not attempt any proof or elucidation here. Meantime it is a great satisfaction to me to find, since these pages were written (now some years ago), that one of our most eminent and profound thinkers, Mr Herbert Spencer, has arrived at almost an identical conclusion, though starting from a different standpoint, pursuing a far more systematic and strictly scientific train of reasoning, and working on a vast induction of facts drawn from all forms of organic life. He not only concludes, as I do, that fecundity diminishes with that intellectual and moral development

---

may term, for them, a state of civilisation. The *modus operandi* of some of these influences may be conjectured : others appear at present quite inexplicable; but all confirming Mr Darwin's conclusion as " to the remarkable and specific power which changed conditions of life possess of acting repressively on the reproductive system." The non-breeding of tamed Indian elephants—though living in their native country and climate, well treated, allowed considerable freedom, amply supplied with food, and in perfect health—seems to me a singularly suggestive phenomenon. It looks almost analogous to the cases of tribes and races, which have died or are dying out in the midst of plenty, under the mysterious influence of some mental condition like depression of spirits, despondency, restraint, the *gêne* of a settled life, &c., &c. It appears to be in those animals which, for nervous development and intelligence most resemble man, and *which share the subtle and complex influences of that artificial life which we call civilisation,* that we find the most curious and anomalous modifications of fecundity. May it not be abnormal cerebral culture in the tamed elephant which so strangely interferes with the procreative tendency or power ?—as in the case of barren marriages which are observably so frequent among persons of preponderatingly *cephalic* temperaments.

of the race which constitutes, causes, and results from what we call civilisation, but he appears irrefragably to demonstrate (what I could do little more than surmise) that such diminished fecundity and reduction in the rate of increase *must* physiologically ensue from mental action and advance.* The chief difference between our views seems to be that he conceives this corrective process must arise specifically if not directly from the stimulus given to the brain and nervous system by the perpetual struggle for subsistence ; while I should be inclined to hope that a sound career of progress, once inaugurated, would continue, and bring with it that cerebral development which is the corrective of undue fertility, even though free expansion into wider areas should have made the pressure of that struggle almost unfelt.†

Mr Spencer's ultimate conclusion is as follows :—

" It is manifest that in the end pressure of population and its accompanying evils will disappear ;. and will leave a state of things requiring from each individual no more than a normal and pleasur-

---

* *Principles of Biology*, ii., chap. 13, which is a master-piece of rigid reasoning, and fine but carefully controlled imagination.

† The continuous pressure which he anticipates, however, he does not regard as a necessary cause of suffering :—"The higher nervous development and greater expenditure in nervous action, here described as indirectly brought about by increase of numbers, and as thereafter becoming a check upon the increase of numbers, must not be taken to imply an intenser strain—a mentally laborious life. The greater emotional and intellectual power and activity above contemplated must be understood as becoming, by small increments, organic, spontaneous, and pleasurable. As, even when relieved from the pressure of necessity, large-brained Europeans voluntarily enter on enterprises and activities which the savage could not keep

able activity. Cessation in the decrease of fertility implies cessation in the development of the nervous system ; and this implies a nervous system that has become equal to all that is demanded of it —has not to do more than is natural to it. But that exercise of faculties which does not exceed what is natural, constitutes gratification. In the end, therefore, the obtainment of subsistence and the discharge of all the parental and social duties will require just that kind and amount of action needful to health and happiness.

"The necessary antagonism of Individuation and Genesis then, not only fulfils with precision the *à priori* law of maintenance of race, from the Monad up to Man, but ensures the final attainment of the highest form of this maintenance—the form in which the amount of life shall be the greatest possible, and the births and deaths the fewest possible. *The excess of fertility has rendered the process of civilisation inevitable; and the process of civilisation must inevitably diminish fertility, and at last destroy its excess.* From the beginning, pressure of population has been the proximate cause of progress. It produced the original diffusion of the race. It compelled men to abandon predatory habits and take to agriculture. It led to the clearing of the earth's surface. It forced men into the social state ; made social organisation inevitable; and has developed the social sentiments. It has stimulated to progressive improvements in production, and to increased skill and intelligence. It is daily thrusting us into closer contact and more mutually dependent relationships. And after having caused, as it ultimately must, the due peopling of the globe, and the raising of all its habitable parts into the highest state of culture—after having brought all processes for the satisfaction of

up even to satisfy urgent wants; so their still larger-brained descendants will, in a still higher degree find their gratifications in careers entailing still greater mental expenditures. This enhanced demand for materials to establish and carry on the psychical functions, will be a constitutional demand. We must conceive the type gradually so modified, that the more developed nervous system irresistibly draws off, for its normal and enforced activities, a larger proportion of the common stock of nutriment, and while thus increasing the intensity, completeness, and length of the individual life, necessarily diminishing the reserve applicable to the setting up of new lives—no longer required to be so numerous."—*Principles of Biology,* vol. ii., p. 520.

human wants to perfection—after having, at the same time, developed the intellect into complete competency for its work, and the feelings into complete fitness for social life—the pressure of population as it gradually finishes its work, must gradually bring itself to an end."[*]

In fine, that pressure of population on the means of subsistence, which was originally fancied to doom the human race to perpetual struggle, discomfort, and misery, and to frown away all dreams for its steady progress and ultimate perfectibility, is the very instrumentality through which that final issue is wrought out ; and through which, if man were only reasonably intelligent, it might be wrought out with no more suffering or *géne* in the process than is requisite to supply the needful stimulus to the natural inertia of the undeveloped brain. The *necessity for exertion* is all that Malthus' law *indispensably* implies and involves—and this exertion is of itself or soon becomes a pleasure. The righteousness, wisdom, and beneficence of the arrangement are thus vindicated the moment we catch a glimpse of " its perfect work."

Another formidable obstacle to the realisation of our ideal has now to be considered—the tendency in civilised societies to multiply the race from its inferior specimens.

---

[*] Principles of Biology, Part vi., § 376.

III.

CIVILISATION ANTAGONISTIC

TO

THE LAW OF "NATURAL SELECTION."

EVERY one now is familiar with the Darwinian theory
of the origin of species, at least in its main principles
and outlines : and nearly all men qualified to form an
opinion are convinced of its substantial truth.   That
theory explains how races of animals vary as ages roll
on, so as to adapt themselves to the changing external
conditions which those ages bring about.   At every
given moment, in every given spot on the earth's surface, a 'struggle for existence' is going on among all
the forms of organic life, animal and vegetable, then
and there alive ; a struggle in which, as there is not
room for all, the weaker and less adapted succumb,
while the stronger and better adapted survive and
multiply.   As surrounding circumstances, climatic or
geological, vary and are modified, corresponding variations (such as are always incidentally appearing among
the offspring of all creatures) in the inhabitants of
each district crop up,. increase, spread, and become
permanent.   The creatures that are most in harmony
with surrounding circumstances have a manifest daily
and hourly advantage over those which are less in
harmony : live when they die ; flourish when they
fade ; endure through what kills others ; can find

food, catch prey, escape enemies, when their feebler,
slower, blinder brethren, are starved and slain.* Thus
the most perfect specimens of each race and tribe, the
strongest, the swiftest, the healthiest, the most
sagacious, the most courageous—those fullest of vitality
—live longest, feed best, overcome their competitors in

---

* 'The grand feature in the multiplication of organic life is that
of close general resemblance, combined with more or less individual
variation. The child resembles its parents or ancestors more or less
closely in all its peculiarities, deformities, or beauties; it resembles
them in general more than it does any other individuals; yet
children of the same parents are not all alike, and it often happens
that they differ very considerably from their parents and from each
other. This is equally true of man, of all animals, and of all
plants. Moreover, it is found that individuals do not differ from
their parents in certain particulars only, while in all others they are
exact duplicates of them. They differ from them and from each
other in every particular: in form, in size, in colour, in the structure
of internal as well as of external organs; in those subtle peculiarities which produce differences of constitution, as well as in those
still more subtle ones which lead to modifications of mind and
character. In other words, in every possible way, in every organ
and in every function, individuals of the same stock vary.
'Now, health, strength, and long life are the results of a harmony
between the individual and the universe, that surrounds it. Let
us suppose that at any given moment this harmony is perfect. A
certain animal is exactly fitted to secure its prey, to escape from
its enemies, to resist the inclemencies of the seasons, and to rear a
numerous and healthy offspring. But a change now takes place.
A series of cold winters, for instance, come on, making food scarce,
and bringing an immigration of some other animals to compete
with the former inhabitants of the district. The new immigrant
is swift of foot, and surpasses its rivals in the pursuit of game; the
winter nights are colder, and require a thicker fur as a protection, and more nourishing food to keep up the heat of the system.
Our supposed perfect animal is no longer in harmony with its
universe; it is in danger of dying of cold or of starvation. But
the animal varies in its offspring. Some of these are swifter than

the choice of mates ; and, in virtue of these advantages, become—as it is desirable they should be—the progenitors of the future race. The poorer specimens, the sick, the foolish, the faulty, the weak, are slain or drop out of existence ; are distanced in the chase, are beaten in the fight, can find no females to match with

---

others—they still manage to catch food enough; some are hardier and more thickly furred—they manage in the cold nights to keep warm enough ; the slow, the weak, and the thinly clad soon die off. Again and again, in each succeeding generation, the same thing takes place. By this natural process, which is so inevitable that it cannot be conceived not to act, those best adapted to live, live; those least adapted, die. It is sometimes said that we have no direct evidence of the action of this selecting power in nature. But it seems to me we have better evidence than even direct observation would be, because it is more universal, viz. the evidence of necessity. It must be so ; for, as all wild animals increase in a geometrical ratio, while their actual numbers remain on the average stationary, it follows that as many die annually as are born. If, therefore, we deny natural selection, it can only be by asserting that in such a case as I have supposed the strong, the healthy, the swift, the well clad, the well organised animals in every respect, have no advantage over,—do not on the average live longer than, the weak, the unhealthy, the slow, the ill clad, and the imperfectly organised individuals ; and this no sane man has yet been found hardy enough to assert. But this is not all ; for the offspring on the average resemble their parents, and the selected portion of each succeeding generation will therefore be stronger, swifter, and more thickly furred than the last ; and if this process goes on for thousands of generations, our animal will have again become thoroughly in harmony with the new conditions in which he is placed. But he will now be a different creature. He will be not only swifter and stronger, and more furry ; he will also probably have changed in colour, in form, perhaps have acquired a longer tail, or differently shaped ears ; for it is an ascertained fact, that when one part of an animal is modified, some other parts almost always change as it were in sympathy with it.'—*Wallace* '*On Natural Selection,* ch. ix.

them; and the species is propagated and continued mainly, increasingly, if not exclusively, from its finest and most selected individuals—in a word, its *élite*. Thus is established what Mr Herbert Spencer calls the law of " the Survival of the fittest."

This explains not only those extraordinary changes in the form and habits of the same animals which, when aided and aggravated by man's requirements and careful management, strike us so forcibly in domesticated races, but also those purely natural though far slower modifications which geological researches have brought to our knowledge. Mr Wallace, in the admirable paper just quoted — which is a perfect model of succinct statement and lucid reasoning—has pointed out how this principle of natural selection has been modified, and in a manner veiled and disguised, though by no means either neutralised or suspended, in the case of MAN; so that neither history nor geology enable us to trace any changes in his external structure analogous to those which we find in such abundance and to such a remarkable extent in the case of the lower animals. He adapts himself, just as they do, to the altered conditions of external nature, but he does it by mental not by bodily modifications. As with them, so with him, the best adapted to surrounded circumstances, the most in harmony with the imperious necessities of life, surmount, survive, and multiply; but in his case the adaption is made and the harmony secured by intellectual and moral efforts and qualities, which leave no stamp on the corporeal frame. As with them, inferior varieties and individuals succumb and die out in the eternal and universal 'struggle for existence;' only, in the case of man, the inferiority which determines their fate is not so much inferiority of muscle, of stomach, or of skin, as of brain.

In man, as we now behold him, this is different. He is social and sympathetic. In the rudest tribes the sick are assisted at least with food; less robust health and vigour than the average does not entail death. Neither does the want of perfect limbs or other organs produce the same effect as among the lower animals. Some division of labour takes place; the swiftest hunt, the less active fish or gather fruits; food is to some extent exchanged or divided. The action of natural selection is therefore checked, the weaker, the dwarfish, those of less active limbs or less piercing eyesight, do not suffer the extreme penalty which falls on animals so defective.

In proportion as these physical characteristics become of less importance, mental and moral qualities will have increasing influence on the well-being of the race   Capacity for acting in concert, for protection and for the acquisition of food and shelter; sympathy, which leads all in turn to assist each other; the sense of right, which checks depredations upon our fellows; the decrease of the combative and destructive propensities; self-restraint in present appetites; and that intelligent foresight which prepares for the future, are all qualities that from their earliest appearance must have been for the benefit of each community, and would, therefore, have become the subjects of " natural selection." For it is evident that such qualities would be for the well-being of man ; would guard him against external enemies, against internal dissensions, and against the effects of inclement seasons and impending famine, more surely than could any merely physical modification. Tribes in which such mental and moral qualities were predominant, would therefore have an advantage in the struggle for existence over other tribes in which they were less developed, would live and maintain their numbers, while the others would decrease and finally succumb.

Again, when any slow changes of physical geography, or of

climate, make it necessary for an animal to alter its food, its clothing, or its weapons, it can only do so by a corresponding change in
its own bodily structure and internal organisation. If a larger or
more powerful beast is to be captured and devoured, as when a
carnivorous animal which has hitherto preyed on sheep is obliged
from their decreasing numbers to attack buffaloes, it is only the
strongest who can hold,—those with most powerful claws, and
formidable canine teeth that can struggle with and overcome such
an animal. Natural selection immediately comes into play, and by its
action these organs gradually become adapted to their new requirements. But man, under similar circumstances, does not require
longer nails or teeth, greater bodily strength or swiftness. He
makes sharper spears, or a better bow, or he constructs a cunning
pitfall, or combines in a hunting party to circumvent his new prey.
The capacities which enable him to do this are what he requires to
be strengthened, and these will, therefore, be gradually modified
by "natural selection," while the form and structure of his body
will remain unchanged. So when a glacial epoch comes on, some
animals must acquire warmer fur, or a covering of fat, or else die
of cold. Those best clothed by nature are, therefore, preserved by
natural selection. Man, under the same circumstances, will make
himself warmer clothing, and build better houses ; and the necessity of doing this will react upon his mental organisation and social
condition—will advance them while his natural body remains
naked as before.

When the accustomed food of some animal becomes scarce or
totally fails, it can only exist by becoming adapted to a new kind
of food, a food perhaps less nourishing and less digestible.
"Natural selection" will now act upon the stomach and intestines,
and all their individual variations will be taken advantage of to
modify the race into harmony with its new food. In many cases,
however, it is probable that this cannot be done. The internal
organs may not vary quick enough, and then the animal will
decrease in numbers and finally become extinct. But man guards
himself from such accidents by superintending and guiding the
operations of nature. He plants the seed of his most agreeable
food, and thus procures a supply independent of the accidents of
varying seasons or natural extinction. He domesticates animals
which serve him either to capture food or for food itself, and thus
changes of any great extent in his teeth or digestive organs are
rendered unnecessary. Man, too, has everywhere the use of fire,

and by its means can render palatable a variety of animal and vegetable substances, which he could hardly otherwise make use of, and thus obtains for himself a supply of food far more varied and abundant than that which any animal can command.

Thus man, by the mere capacity of clothing himself, and making weapons and tools, has taken away from nature that power of changing the external form and structure which she exercises over all other animals. As the competing races by which they were surrounded, the climate, the vegetation, or the animals which serve them for food, are slowly changing, they must undergo a corresponding change in their structure, habits, and constitution, to keep them in harmony with the new conditions—to enable them to live and maintain their numbers. But man does this by means of his intellect alone; which enables him with an unchanged body still to keep in harmony with the changing universe.

From the time, therefore, when the social and sympathetic feelings came into active operation, and the intellectual and moral faculties became fairly developed, man would cease to be influenced by "natural selection" in his physical form and structure; as an animal he would remain almost stationary; the changes of the surrounding universe would cease to have upon him that powerful modifying effect which they exercise over other parts of the organic world. But from the moment that his body became stationary, his mind would become subject to those very influences from which his body had escaped; every slight variation in his mental and moral nature which should enable him better to guard against adverse circumstances, and combine for mutual comfort and protection, would be preserved and accumulated; the better and higher specimens of our race would therefore increase and spread, the lower and more brutal would give way and successively die out, and that rapid advancement of mental organisation would occur, which has raised the very lowest races of man so far above the brutes (although differing so little from some of them in physical structure), and, in conjunction with scarcely perceptible modifications of form, has developed the wonderful intellect of the Germanic races.

But this is by no means the whole of the case. As we follow out the reflections suggested by this argument, an entirely new series of consequences and

operations opens before us. We perceive that the
working of the law of "natural selection," and of
" the preservation of favoured races and individuals in
the struggle for existence," has become in the course of
man's progress not only thus modified, as Mr Wallace
points out, and directed to one part of his organisation
(the brain) alone, but positively suspended, and in many
instances almost *reversed.* It even dawns upon us that
our existing civilisation, which is the result of the operation of this law in past ages, may be actually retarded
and endangered by its tendency to neutralise that law
in one or two most material and significant particulars.
The great, wise, righteous, and beneficent principle
which in all other animals, and in man himself, up to
a certain stage of his progress, tends to the improvement and perfection of the race, would appear to be
forcibly interfered with and nearly set aside ; nay, to
be set aside pretty much in direct proportion to the
complication, completeness, and *culmination* of our
civilisation. I do not assert that if our civilisation
were purely and philosophically ideal—perfect in
character as well as splendid and lofty in degree—this
result would follow, or would continue ; but it certainly does follow now, and it delays and positively
menaces the attainment of that ideal condition. My
thesis is this : that the indisputable effect of the state
of social progress and culture we have reached, of our
high civilisation in its present stage and actual
form, is to *counteract and suspend* the operation of
that righteous and salutary law of " natural selection"

in virtue of which the best specimens of the race —the strongest, the finest, the worthiest—are those which survive, multiply, become paramount, and take precedence ; succeed and triumph in the struggle for existence, become the especial progenitors of future generations, continue the species, and propagate an ever improving and perfecting type of humanity.

The principle of the 'Survival of the Fittest' does not appear to fail in the case of *races* of men. Here the abler, the stronger, the more advanced, the finer in short, are still the favoured ones; succeed in the competition, exterminate, govern, supersede, fight, eat, or work the inferior tribes out of existence. The process is quite as certain, and nearly as rapid, whether we are just or unjust ; whether we use carefulness or cruelty. Everywhere the savage tribes of mankind die out at the contact of the civilised ones. Sometimes they are extinguished by conquest and the sword ; sometimes by the excessive toil which avaricious victors impose upon the feeble vanquished ; often by the diseases which the more artificial man brings with him and which flourish with fearful vigour in a virgin soil ; occasionally they fade away before the superior vitality and prolific energy of the invading race in lands where there is not room for both :—they are crushed, in fact, by the severity of competition ; in some cases they sink under the new and unsuitable habits which civilisation tries to introduce among them; not unfrequently it would seem from some mysterious blight which the mere presence of a superior form of humanity casts over them. But, in every part of the world and in every instance, the result has been the same; the process of extinction is either completed or actively at work. The Indians of the Antilles, the Red man of North America, the South Sea Islanders, the Australians, even the New Zealanders (the finest and most pliable and teachable of savages), are all alike dying out with strange rapidity—in consequence of the harshness, or in spite of the forbearance and protection, of the stronger and more capable European. The negro alone survives—and seems likely to survive. He only has been able to hold his own after a fashion, and to live and flourish side by side with masterful and mightier races, though in a questionable relation and with questionable results. But the exception is a confirmation of the general law. The negro is not only strong, docile, and prolific, but in some respects he is better adapted to surrounding conditions than his European neighbour, conqueror, or master; in certain climates he, and not the white man, is 'the favoured race;' and for many generations, perhaps for ages, in the burning regions about the equator, a black skin may take precedence of a large brain, and be a more indispensable condition of existence; or possibly the brain may grow larger without the skin growing any whiter. The principle of 'natural selection' therefore —of the superior and fitter races of mankind trampling out and replacing the poorer races, in virtue of their superior fitness—would seem to hold good universally.

So probably it does also, and always has done, in the case of *nations*; and the apparent exceptions to the rule may be due only to our erroneous estimate of the true elements of superiority. In the dawn of history the more cultivated and energetic races conquered the weaker and less advanced, reduced them to slavery, or taught them civilisation. It is true that in the case of the Greeks and Romans the coarser organisation and less developed brain of the latter overpowered and overshadowed probably the finest physical and intellectual nature that has yet appeared upon the earth; but the Greeks, when they thus succumbed, had fallen away from the perfection of their palmier days; they had grown enervated and corrupt; and the tougher fibre, the robuster will and the unequalled political genius of their Roman conquerors constituted an undeniable superiority. They triumphed by the law of the strongest—though their strength might not lie precisely in the noblest portion of man's nature. Intellectually the inferiors of the Greeks whom they subdued, they were morally and *volitionally* more vigorous. The same may be said of those rude Northern warriors who at a later period flowed over and mastered the degenerate Roman world. They had no culture, but they had vast capacities; and they brought with them a renovating irruption of that hard energy and redundant vitality which luxury and success had nearly extinguished among those they conquered. They were then 'the most favoured race,' the fittest for the exigencies of the hour, the best adapted to the conditions of the life around them ; they prevailed, therefore, by reason of a very indisputable, though not the most refined sort of, superiority. With the nations of modern history, the same rule has governed the main current of the world, though perhaps with more instances of at least apparent exception. Each nation that has dominated in turn, or occupied the first post in the world's annals, has done so by right of some one quality, achievement, or possession—then especially needed—which made it for the time the stronger, if not intrinsically the nobler among many rivals. Intellect, and intellect applied alike to art, to commerce, and to science, at one period made the Italians the most prominent people in Europe. There was an undeniable grandeur in the Spanish nation in its culminating years towards the close of the fifteenth century which gave it a right to rule, and at once explained and justified both its discoveries and its conquests. No one can say that France did not fairly win her vast influence and her epochs of predominance by her wonderful military spirit and the peculiarity of her singularly clear, keen, restless, but not rich intelligence. England owes her world-wide dominion and (what is far more significant and a greater subject for felicitation) the wide diffusion of her race over the globe, to a daring and persistent energy with which no other variety of mankind is so largely dowered. Even the Ottoman and Arabian races had special qualities or elements of superiority which warranted their temporary sway. And if in modern conflicts might has sometimes triumphed over right, and the finer and kinder people fallen before the assaults of the stronger and harsher, and the events of history run counter to all our truer and juster sympathies ; it is probably because in the counsels of the Most High, energy is seen to be more needed than culture to carry on the advancement of humanity, and a commanding will, at least in this stage of our progress, to be a more essential endowment than an amiable temper or a good heart. At all events it is those who in some sense are the STRONGEST and the fittest who most prevail, multiply and spread, and become in the largest measure the progenitors of future nations.

But when we come to the case of individuals in a people, or classes in a community—the phase of the question which has far the most practical and immediate interest for ourselves—the principle would appear to fail, and the law is no longer supreme. Civilisation, with its social, moral, and material complications, has introduced a disturbing and conflicting element. It is not now, as Mr Wallace depicts, that intellectual has been substituted for physical superiority, but that artificial and conventional have taken the place of natural advantages as the ruling and deciding force. It is no longer the strongest, the healthiest, the most perfectly organised ; it is not men of the finest *physique*, the largest brain, the most developed intelligence, the best *morale*, that are 'favoured' and successful 'in the struggle for existence'—that survive, that rise to the surface, that 'natural selection' makes the parents of future generations, the continuators of a picked and perfected race. It is still 'the most favoured,' no doubt, in some sense, who bear away the palm, but the indispensable favour is too often that of fortune, not of nature. The various influences of our social system combine to traverse the righteous and salutary law which God ordained for the preservation of a worthy and improving humanity; and the 'varieties' of man that endure and multiply their likenesses, and mould the features of the coming times, are not the soundest constitutions that can be found among us, nor the most subtle and resourceful minds, nor the most amiable or self-denying tempers, nor the most sagacious judgments, nor even the most imperious and persistent wills, but often the precise reverse—often those emasculated by luxury and those damaged by want, those rendered reckless by squalid poverty, and those whose physical and mental energies have been sapped, and whose characters have been grievously impaired, by long indulgence and forestalled desires.

The two great instruments and achievements of civilisation, are respect for life and respect for property. In proportion as both are secure, as life is prolonged and as wealth is accumulated, and as the poor and weak are cared for, so nations rise—or consider that they have risen. Among wild animals the sick and maimed are slain; among savages they succumb and die or are suppressed; among us they are cared for, kept alive, enabled to marry and multiply. In uncivilised tribes, the ineffective and incapable, the weak in body or in mind, are unable to provide themselves food ; they fall behind in the chase or in the march; they fall out, therefore, in the race of life. With us, sustenance and shelter are provided for them, and they survive. We pride ourselves—and justly—on the increased length of life which has been effected by our science and our humanity. But we forget that this higher average of *life* may be compatible with, and may in a measure result from, a lower average of *health*. We have kept alive those who, in a more natural and less advanced state, would have died—and who, looking at the physical perfection of the race alone, had better have been left to die. Among savages, the vigorous and sound alone survive ; among us, the diseased and enfeebled survive as well ;—but is either the physique or the intelligence of cultivated man the gainer by the change ? In a wild state, by the law of natural selection, only or chiefly, the sounder and stronger specimens were allowed to continue their species ; with us, thousands with tainted constitutions, frames weakened by malady or waste, brains bearing subtle and hereditary mischief in their recesses, are suffered to transmit their terrible inheritance of evil to other generations, and to spread it through a whole community.

Security of property, security for its transmission as well as for its enjoyment, is one of our chief boasts. Thousands upon thousands who never could themselves have acquired property by industry, or conquered it by courage, or kept it by strength or ingenuity, and who are utterly incompetent to use it well, are yet enabled by law to inherit and retain it. They are born to wealth, they revel in wealth, though destitute of all the qualities by which wealth is won, or its possession made a blessing to the community. In a natural state of society they would have been pushed out of existence, stripped of their inherited and ill-used possessions, jostled aside in the struggle and the race, and left by the wayside to die. In civilised communities they are protected, fostered, flattered, married, and empowered to hand down their vapid incapacities to numerous offspring, whom perhaps they can leave wealthy too. In old and highly advanced nations, the classes who wield power and affluence and social supremacy as a consequence of the security of property, do not as a rule consist—nay, may consist in a very small measure—of individuals who have won, or could have won, those influences for themselves—of natural "kings of men;" the *élite* lots in life do not fall to the *élite* of the race or the community.* Those possessions and that position, which in more simply

---

* Mr Darwin points out here as a *per contra*, the validity of which is great and indisputable, the good effect of this transmission of property in securing the existence of a leisured class adapted for literature, government, and thought. "The presence of a body of well-instructed men, who have not to labour for their daily bread, is important to a degree that can hardly be overestimated; as all high intellectual work is carried on by them, and on such work material progress of all kinds mainly depends,—not to mention other and higher advantages."—*Descent of Man*, i., p. 169.

But do the majority of this rich and leisured class occupy themselves with "high intellectual work"?

organised tribes would be an indication and a proof either of strength, of intelligence, or of some happy adaptation to surrounding exigencies, now in our complicated world indicate nothing—at least in five cases out of six—but merit or energy or luck in some ancestor, perhaps inconceivably remote, who has bequeathed his rank and property to his successors, but without the qualities which won them and warranted them. Yet this property and rank still enable their possibly unworthy and incapable inheritors to take precedence over others in many of the walks of life, to carry off the most desirable brides from less favoured though far nobler rivals, and (what is our present point) to make those brides the mothers of a degenerating, instead of an ever improving race.

But even this by no means presents the whole strength of the case. Not only does civilisation, as it exists among us, enable rank and wealth, however diseased, enfeebled, or unintelligent, to become the continuators of the species in preference to larger brains, stronger frames and sounder constitutions; but that very rank and wealth, thus inherited without effort and in absolute security, often tend to produce enervated and unintelligent offspring. To be born in the purple is not the right introduction to healthy energy; to be surrounded from the cradle with all temptations and facilities to self-indulgence, is not the best safeguard against those indulgences which weaken the intellect and exhaust the frame. No doubt *noblesse oblige*, and riches can buy the highest education— always excepting that education by surrounding circumstances which is really the only one that tells very effectually on the youthful plant. No doubt, too, there are splendid and numerous exceptions—instances in which rank is used to mould its heir to its duties, and in which wealth is used to purchase and achieve all that makes life noble and beneficent. But we have only to look around us, and a little below the surface, and then ask ourselves whether, as a rule, the owners of rank and wealth——still more the owners of wealth without rank—are those from whose paternity we should have most right to anticipate a healthy, a noble, an energetic, or a truly intellectual offspring—a race fitted to control and guide themselves as well as others, to subdue the earth as well as to replenish it, to govern, to civilise, to illustrate, to carry forward, the future destinies of man ?

And if it is not from the highest and most opulent that we can expect this desiderated posterity, assuredly it is not from the lowest. and most indigent. The *physique* and the *morale* of both the extreme classes are imperfect and impaired. The *physique* of the rich is injured by indulgence and excess—that of the poor by privation and want. The *morale* of the former has never been duly called forth by the necessity for exertion and self-denial; that of the latter has never been adequately cultivated by training and instruction. The intellects of each have been exposed to opposite disadvantages. The organisations of neither class are the best in the community; the constitutions of neither are the soundest or most untainted. Yet these two classes are precisely those which are, or are likely to be, preponderatingly, the fathers of the coming generation. Both marry as early as they please and have as many children as they please,—the rich because it is in their power, the poor because they have no motive for abstinence:—and scanty food and hard circumstances do not oppose but rather encourage procreation.   Malthus' "prudential check" rarely operates upon the lowest classes; the poorer they are, usually, the faster do they multiply; certainly the more reckless they are in reference to multiplication. It is the middle classes, those who form the energetic, reliable, improving element of the population, those who wish to rise and do not choose to sink, those in a word who constitute the true strength and wealth and dignity of nations, —it is these who abstain from marriage or postpone it.* Thus the imprudent, the desperate,—those whose standard is low, those who have no hope, no ambition, no self-denial,—on the one side, and the pampered favourites of fortune on the other, take precedence in the race of fatherhood, to the disadvantage or the exclusion of the prudent, the resolute, the striving and the self-restrained. The very men whom a philosophic statesman, or a guide of some superior nature would select as most qualified and deserving to continue

---

* Galton's *Hereditary Genius*, p. 352.—"Certain influences retard the average age of marriage while others hasten it. . . . . The wisest policy is that which results in retarding the average age of marriage among the weak, and hastening it among the vigorous classes; whereas, most unhappily for us, the influence of numerous social influences has been strongly and banefully exerted in our community at least, precisely the opposite direction."

the race, are precisely those who do so in the scantiest measure.* Those who have no need for exertion, and those who have no opportunities for culture, those whose frames are damaged by indulgence, and those whose frames are weakened by privation, breed *ad libitum:* while those whose minds and bodies have been hardened, strengthened and purified by temperance and toil, are elbowed quietly aside in the unequal press. Surely the "selection" is no longer "natural." The careless, squalid, unaspiring Irishman, fed on potatoes, living in a pig-stye, doting on a superstition, multiplies like rabbits or ephemera :—the frugal, fore-

---

*Those who may be disposed to make light of the injurious operation, on the well-being of a community or the improvement of the race, of this positive or comparative abstention from the functions of paternity on the part of the true *élite* of a people,—would do well to study Mr Galton's picture of the effect of two analogous facts on the progress of Europe during the middle ages. In his rich and suggestive book on *Hereditary Genius* (p. 357-359) he points how effectually, though unintentionally, " the Church brutalised and demoralised the breed of our forefathers," by, in the *first* place, condemning to celibacy all those gentler, kindlier, more cultured and thoughtful natures who sought refuge in the cloister in those troubled times,—leaving only the ruder and coarser organisations to marry and multiply ; and, in the *second* place, by burning all the more powerful, free and daring thinkers of those days, and thus as far as possible crushing out the class.—" Having first captured all the gentler natures and condemned them to celibacy, she made another sweep of her huge nets,—this time fishing in troubled waters—to catch those who were the most fearless, truth-loving, and intelligent in their modes of thought, *and therefore the most suitable parents of a high civilisation,*—and put a strong check, if not a direct stop, to their progeny. Those she reserved, as it were, to breed the generations of the future, were the rough and ferocious, or the servile, the indifferent, and the stupid."

seeing, self-respecting, ambitious Scot, stern in his morality, spiritual in his faith, sagacious and disciplined in his intelligence, passes his best years in struggle and in celibacy, marries late, and leaves few behind him. Given a land originally peopled by a thousand Saxons and a thousand Celts,—and in a dozen generations, five-sixths of the population would be Celts, but five sixths of the property, the power, and the intellect, would belong to the one-sixth of Saxons that remained. In the eternal " struggle for existence," it would be the inferior and *less* favoured race that had prevailed,—and prevailed by virtue not of its qualities but of its faults, by reason not of its stronger vitality but of its weaker reticence and its narrower brain.

Of course it will be urged that the principle of natural selection fails thus utterly because our civilisation is imperfect and misdirected; because our laws are insufficient ; because our social arrangements are unwise; because our moral sense is languid or unenlightened. No doubt, if our legislators and rulers were quite sagacious and quite stern, and our people in all ranks quite wise and good, the beneficent tendencies of nature would continue to operate uncounteracted. No constitutions would be impaired by insufficient nutriment and none by unhealthy excess. No classes would be so undeveloped either in mind or muscle as to be unfitted for procreating sound and vigorous offspring. The sick, the tainted, and the maimed, would be too sensible and too unselfish to dream of marrying and handing down to their children the curse of diseased or feeble frames;—or if they did not thus control themselves, the state would exercise a salutary but unrelenting paternal despotism, and supply the deficiency by vigilant and timely prohibition. A republic is *conceivable* in which paupers should be forbidden to propagate; in which all candidates for the proud and solemn privilege of continuing an untainted and perfecting race should be subjected to a pass or a competitive examination, and those only be suffered to transmit their names and families to future generations who had a pure, vigorous and well-developed constitution to transmit; —so that paternity should be the right and function exclusively of the *élite* of the nation, and humanity be thus enabled to march on securely and without drawback to its ultimate possibilities of progress. Every damaged or inferior temperament might be eliminated, and every special and superior one be selected and enthroned, till the human race, both in its manhood and its womanhood, became one glorious fellowship of saints, sages, and athletes; till we were all Blondins, all Shakespeares, Pericles', Socrates', Columbuses, and Fénelons. But no nation—in modern times at least—has ever yet approached or aimed at this ideal; no such wisdom or virtue has ever been found except in isolated individual instances; no government and no statesman has ever yet dared thus to supplement the inadequacy of personal patriotism by laws so sapiently despotic. The faces of the leading peoples

of the existing world are not even set in this direction
—at present notably the reverse.   The more marked
tendencies of the age are three ; and all three run
counter to the operation of the wholesome law of
' natural selection.'   We are learning to insist more
and more on the freedom of the individual will, the
right of every one to judge and act for himself.   We
are growing daily more foolishly and criminally lenient
to every natural propensity, less and less inclined to
resent, or control, or punish its indulgence.   We absolutely refuse to let the poor, the incapable, the lazy,
or the diseased die ; we enable or allow them, if we
do not actually encourage them, to propagate their
incapacity,   poverty,   and   constitutional   disorders.
And, lastly, democracy is every year advancing in
power, and claiming the supreme right to govern and
to guide ; and democracy means the management and
control of social arrangements by the least educated
classes,—by those least trained to foresee or measure
consequences,—least   acquainted   with   the   fearfully
rigid laws of hereditary transmission,—least habi-
tuated to repress desires, or to forego immediate
enjoyment for future and remote good.

Obviously, no artificial prohibitions or restraints,
no laws imposed from above and from without, can
restore the principle of ' natural selection' to its due
supremacy among the human race.   No people in our
days would endure the necessary interference and control ; and perhaps a result so acquired might not be
worth the cost of acquisition.   We can only trust to

H

the slow influences of enlightenment and moral susceptibility, percolating downwards and in time permeating all ranks. We can only watch and be careful that any other influences we do set in motion shall be such as, where they work at all, may work in the right direction. At present the prospect is not reassuring. We are progressing fast in many points, no doubt, but the progress is not wholly nor always of the right sort, nor without a large *per contra*. Legislation and philanthropy are improving the condition of the masses, but they are more and more losing the guidance and governance of the masses. Wealth accumulates above, and wages rise below ; but the cost of living augments with both operations, till those classes—the stamina of the nation—which are neither too rich nor too poor to fear a fall, find marriage a hazardous adventure, and dread the burden of large families. Medical science is mitigating suffering, and achieving some success in its warfare against disease; but at the same time it enables the diseased to live. It controls and sometimes half cures the maladies that spring from profligacy and excess, but in so doing it encourages both, by stepping in between the cause and its consequence, and saving them from their natural and deterring penalties. It reduces the aggregate mortality by sanitary improvements and precautions ; but those whom it saves from dying prematurely it preserves to propagate dismal and imperfect lives. In our complicated modern communities a race is being run between moral and mental enlightenment and the deterioration of the physical and moral constitution through the defeasance of the law of natural selection ; and on the issues of that race the destinies of humanity depend.

Mr Francis Galton (who had followed the same line of thought as myself, though both, till after the publication of our respective speculations, were unacquainted with the other's writings), estimates almost more gravely than I have done the mischief and the menace of this tendency of civilised nations to multiply from their lower specimens. He condemns " the Peerage as a disastrous institution, owing to its destructive effects on our valuable races. The most highly-gifted men are ennobled ; their elder sons are tempted [for the sake of means to keep up their titles] to marry heiresses [who are habitually sterile] ; and their younger sons do not marry at all, not having fortune enough to support both a family and an aristocratic position. So the side-shoots of the genealogical tree are hacked off, the leading shoot is blighted, and the breed is lost for ever." . . . . . Further on he says :—" It is a maxim of Malthus that the period of marriage ought to be delayed in order that the earth may not be overcrowded by a population for whom there is no place at all at the great table of Nature. If this doctrine influenced all classes alike, I should have nothing to say about it here, one way or the other, as it would hardly affect ·the discussions in this book ;—but when it is put forward as a rule of conduct for the prudent part of mankind to follow, whilst the imprudent are necessarily left free to disregard it, I have no hesitation in saying that it is a most pernicious rule of conduct in its bearing on the race. Its effect would be to cause the race of the prudent to fall after a few centuries into an almost incredible numerical inferiority to that of the imprudent, and therefore to bring utter ruin upon the breed of any country where the doctrine prevailed. *I protest against the abler races being encouraged to withdraw in this way from the struggle for existence.* It may seem monstrous that the weak should be crowded out by the strong, but it is still more monstrous that the races best fitted to play their part on the stage of life should be crowded out by the incompetent, the ailing, and the feeble."

Mr Galton gives us a sort of formula by which we may form some faint conception of the magnitude of the evil thus wrought—or likely to be wrought—by the operation of this doctrine. He points out that— of two classes in a community starting with equal numbers, but one class marrying habitually at twenty-two years of age, and the other at thirty-three years —the first class will in less than a century be twice as numerous, and in two centuries six times as numerous, as the second. We have only to follow out this thought, and picture to ourselves, if imagination is equal to the task, the contrast between two communities at the end of either period, one a nation where the early-marrying class had been the educated, the temperate, the energetic, and the self-restrained; and the other a nation where this class had consisted of the reckless, the indolent, the vicious, and the diseased. The latter would probably have degenerated nearly to the race of Papuans; the former might have surpassed even the Athenians in their palmiest days.[*]

Mr Darwin,[†] who has done me the honour to quote a monograph which I wrote four or five years ago on this subject, equally regards the operation in question

---

[*] Mr Galton (p. 361) has a passage which suggests a wide and fertile field of investigation,—namely, how far the decay of old civilisations (one of the perplexing phenomena of history) may be traceable to the circumstance we have been considering.—" In an old civilisation the agencies are more complex. Among the active, ambitious classes, none but the inheritors of fortune are likely to marry young. Those whose future fortune is not insured can scarcely succeed well and rise high in society, if they hamper themselves with a wife and children in their early manhood. . . . Thence result the evils I have already described, in speaking of the marriages of eldest sons with heiresses, and of the suppression of the marriages of the younger sons. Again, there is a constant tendency of the best men in a country to settle in the great cities, where marriages are less prolific, and children less likely to live. Owing to these several causes, *there is a steady check in an old civilisation on the fertility of the abler classes:—the improvident and unambitious are those who chiefly keep up the breed. So the race gradually degenerates, becoming with each successive generation less fitted for a high civilisation,* although it retains the external appearances of one: *until the time comes when the whole political and social fabric caves in,* and a greater or less relapse towards barbarism takes place." I have long been convinced that the startling contrast between the France of to-day and the France of one or two centuries ago, is in a vast measure due to the dying (or killing) out of the old Frankish and Norman elements, and the growing predominance of the Celtic one. Probably the equally startling difference between the America of Washington and the America of Andrew Johnson, may be greatly traced to the immigration of old days consisting of Cavaliers and Pilgrim Fathers, and the recent immigration being made up of Irish cottiers and German boors, and loose or criminal fugitives from everywhere.

[†] " Descent of Man," i. p. 168.

as a most serious one; and though he mentions a number of compensating influences, he evidently does not consider them as at all adequate or effectual. " With savages, the weak in body or mind are soon eliminated; and those that survive commonly exhibit a vigorous state of health. *We civilised men, on the other hand, do our utmost to check the process of elimination;* we build asylums for the imbecile, the maimed, and the sick; we institute poor-laws; and our medical men exert their greatest skill to save the life of every one to the last moment. There is reason to believe that vaccination has preserved thousands, who, from a weak constitution, would formerly have succumbed to small-pox. Thus the weak members of civilised societies propagate their kind. No one who has attended to the breeding of domestic animals will doubt that this must be highly injurious to the race. It is surprising how soon a want of care, or care wrongly directed, leads to the degeneration of a domestic race : but, *excepting in the case of man himself, hardly any one is so ignorant as to allow his worst animals to breed.*"

It cannot be denied, then, that the tendency, in communities of advanced and complicated civilisation, to multiply from their lower rather than their higher specimens, constitutes one of the most formidable dangers with which that civilisation is threatened; and, if not counterworked in time, must bring about eventually the physical, and along with that the moral and intellectual deterioration of the race. But in civilisation itself—in the spreading intelligence, in the matured wisdom, in the ripened self-control, in the social virtues, which civilisation nurtures and in which it ought to culminate—may be found, ought to be found, and, we hope, will be found, the counter-acting influences required. A few of these may be briefly intimated. The longer lives, the sounder health, the smaller mortality in infancy, among the better classes (using the word better to include all the elements of true superiority), will do something to antagonise the greater fertility of the inferior. As political wisdom improves—forced upon us by increasing social perils, by severe experience, and by exhaustive error, I consider that pauperism—and with it the propagation of paupers—will be nearly extinguished by the control and organisation of charity, and the ultimate abolition of compulsory poor-rates. Even now we are beginning, at least, to *look* in that direction; and, as I pointed out in the first chapter, pauperism is the result of our fostering, if not actually our own creation. I notice that there are countries in which it exists in a very mitigated form, even if at all. I do not think it over san-guine to anticipate the time when wealth, under wider views of economic science, may be far more equitably and beneficently distributed than now. We may conceive even, and should aspire after, such a rational and sober simplicity of living, that marriage would become prudent and easy to thousands of the middle and upper classes, to whom it now seems an absolute impossibility. The higher orders of society would become less extravagantly provident as the lower orders learned to be reasonably so. It does not seem to me quite unreasonable to hope that the means, or at least the prospect, of being able to maintain children shall be regarded practically as an essential pre-requisite to producing them,—probably under the control of an enlightened social opinion,—possibly, as is not unknown in certain continental States,* under legal pressure. I cannot see why—when the working-classes are educated in some proportion to those now above them, and possess property of their own,—whether in acres, or consols, or shares, as they assuredly may do, and soon will †—they should not become so provident and so well-conditioned, that they will be no unfit fathers for coming generations. For we must never forget that it is not poverty, but squalor—not a hard life, but insufficient nutriment—not strenuous bodily exertion, but excessive and *exhausting* toil—that disqualify men from transmitting a sound physical and mental constitution to their off-spring. A sanified city population and a well-fed agricultural population may be not only a wholesome but a necessary element to share the functions of paternity with the more elaborately prudent and cerebrally over-developed classes higher in the social scale. Lastly, I look forward to a not very distant

---

* Laing's "Notes of a Traveller." "Travels in Sweden and Norway."

† See *Quarterly Review*, January 1872, " Proletariat on a False Scent."

day when, as the moral tone of society advances, and men rise to some larger and more vivid perceptions of their mutual obligations, the propagation of vitiated constitutions, as well as of positive disease, will be universally condemned as culpable, and possibly prohibited as criminal. Some classes and communities have already, from time to time, reached this slight rising-ground in social virtue, in reference to the three fearful maladies of insanity, leprosy, and cretinism. Surely a further progress in knowledge and reflection, and a somewhat wider range of sympathy, may extend the list to scrofula, syphilis, and consumption. I can discern no reason—beyond our own halting wisdom and deficient sense of right, the strange ignorance of some classes, and the stranger senselessness of others, our utterly wonderful and persistent errors in political and social philosophy in nearly every line—why a very few generations should not have nearly eliminated from the community those who ought not to breed at all, and have taught prudence to those who ought to breed only in moderate and just proportions.

In comparing the conclusions arrived at in this chapter with those of the preceding one, a certain *primâ facie* inconsistency is observable, which must not be evaded or ignored. If that gradual decrease in fecundity which, in the ripeness of time, will render the population of the earth naturally and without effort stationary, is to result, as we anticipate, mainly from the increased culture and development of brain which civilisation brings about, it seems obvious to infer that such decrease will take place earliest and most decidedly in the classes and races most marked by cerebral superiority, that is, by mental power and moral pre-eminence. If the cultivation of the higher elements of humanity has, as we allege, the distinctive tendency, in the long run, and on a general survey, to retard the rate of increase of the species, then this retarding operation should be strong and manifest in proportion to the spread of that cultivation, and in those quarters where its progress and predominance are most undeniable. If so, the tendency of man in the more civilised stages of society to multiply rather from his lower than his higher forms, which in this chapter we have been deploring and would seek to check, would appear to be not only one of the greatest dangers and drawbacks of civilisation, but precisely its most inevitable issue;—and the very advance of improvement and cerebral culture, to which we look ultimately for the solution of the problem and the perfection of the race, would seem to negative that prospect, by withdrawing, *pro tanto* and *pari passu*, from the privileges of paternity the best qualified portion of the community, and virtually throwing the function of continuing the race mainly upon the classes least capable of transmitting healthy organisations and fine intellects to their offspring. If the superior sections and specimens of humanity are to lose relatively their procreative power in virtue of and in proportion to that superiority, how is culture or progress to be propagated so as to benefit the species as a whole, and how are those gradually amended organisations from which we hope so much to be secured ?   If, indeed, it were ignorance, stupidity, and destitution, instead of mental and moral development, that were the *sterilising* influences, then the improvement of the race would go on swimmingly, and in an ever-accelerating ratio.   But since the conditions are exactly reversed, how should not an exactly opposite direction be pursued ?   How should the race *not* deteriorate, when those who morally and hygienically are fittest to perpetuate it are (relatively), by a law of physiology, those least likely to do so ?   Does it not appear as if nature herself were pursuing a pernicious course, precisely analogous to that which M. Galton attributes to the Church in the middle ages, and as if the very influence which we pointed out in the last chapter as rendering the perfection of the race feasible, must have a distinctively antagonistic operation ?

The reply to the foregoing objection is simply this : —In the preceding chapter we were considering specifically the influence of natural laws, more or less occult, but all self-operating and *involuntary*, which reduced fecundity as cerebral development advanced and spread.   In the present chapter we have been dealing exclusively with *voluntary* human influences, with the operation of social tendencies and regulations in causing an abnormal and not natural withdrawal (relatively) from the function of perpetuating the race, on the part of the classes fittest for that duty.   The former influence will work out its beneficent issues gradually and in the fulness of time; the latter is operating artificially and mischievously under our eyes. True culture, as it spreads—the influence of a really enlightened civilisation, in our age and country, ought to have a double operation; in the creation, on one side, of a class of healthy and educated, and laborious but no longer stinted poor, whose redundant fertility will be controlled at once by greater providence and more developed brains, and, on the other side, in the growth of wiser and more right-minded superior classes, estimating more truly the vital essentials of a happy and worthy existence, less fearing a social fall and less ambitious of a social rise, less straitened and less deterred from marriage than at present, and therefore both positively and relatively more prolific. The problem of progress may thus be successfully wrought out, in perfect conformity with the physiological laws we had assumed, by the mitigated fecundity of the multitude in proportion to their culture and social elevation, and the simultaneously augmented fecundity of the ranks above them, as they learn the true philosophy of life.

I think it may serve the elucidation of a subject, the importance of which can scarcely be exaggerated, if I subjoin here a criticism by one of our subtlest and finest thinkers, which appeared in *The Spectator* when my argument was first propounded, as well as my rejoinder.

. . . " No doubt the laws of property, do secure to a vast number the means of living and of giving life to others who would not seem well qualified for ' the struggle of existence,' and who might have succumbed if they had had to win the means of living for themselves by shouldering their own way in life. Still, not only does this tell as strongly for the energetic who inherit, as for the *dilettanti* who inherit, not only does it leave it quite as certain as ever that those who have no moral capacity to rise will scarcely fail to fall, will be quick to lose their inheritance to those who would have had power to gain it,—not only is this so, but in fact this transmission of a great bulk of property to persons not well fitted to make or save it, is a necessary condition of detecting and developing capacities, of the first value to our race, which would be utterly drowned and lost in the mere conflict for material sustenance. No test could be coarser or more ineffectual of the sort of intellectual and moral energy which gives value to life, than the test of ability to win money without the help of accumulated capital. Such a test would put out of court at one blow, as unfit for ' the struggle for existence,' three-fourths of the religious teachers, the thinkers, the discoverers, the poets, the artists, the philanthropists, the reformers. If we are to assume that all who inherit are drones, unless they show the power to win what they inherit, we should have to assume that there is no true sort of energy at all, except it admits of diversion into a channel wherein pounds, shillings, and pence could be rapidly accumulated. And it is obvious enough that such a test would be quite false.

" Still, what we have said as yet, is but preliminary to the true answer to the essayist we refer to. The real answer to him is this,—that directly you reach man in the ascending stages of animal life, you reach a point where the competitive principle of ' natural selection' is more or less superseded by a higher principle, of which the key-note is not ' Let the strong trample out the weak,' but ' Let the strong sacrifice themselves for the weak.' This is really the law of supernatural selection, as distinguished from the law which governs the selection of races in the lower animal world. It is from reverence for this law that men value so highly the healing art which helps us to restore the weak instead of to trample them out,—the arts of political organisation which teach us to feed and clothe those who are, without their own fault, hungry and naked, instead of to leave them to destruction,—the charity which bestows a new language on the dumb, teaches the blind to see with their fingers, brightens the hopeless fate even of the idiotic and the insane, nay, reforms even criminals if it be possible, instead of exterminating them. The history of all Christian and many other Churches is at bottom little but the history of the growth of human reverence for that law of supernatural selection which supersedes the law ruling in the merely animal world. If we are to complain that the Darwinian theorem does not apply to man, we are complaining that we are in the truest sense men at all. The law of self-sacrifice, the law of the Cross, the law the religious root of which lies in the teaching that One, ' being in the form of God,' made himself of no reputation, and took upon himself the form of a servant, to raise creatures infinitely below Himself up to His own level, to give them of His life, and breathe into them His spirit, is in its very essence and conception a reversal of the law of ' natural selection,' at least so far as man dreams of making himself in purpose and in spirit the executioner of that law. Christ tells us *not* to help to extinguish poor and maimed and blighted forms of life, lest they spoil the breed, but to have faith that every act of wise self-sacrifice, *i.e.*, every transfer of blessings from the strong, happy, or wealthy, who can spare them, to the weak, miserable, or poor who might otherwise dwindle and perish, is a vindication of that higher law of supernatural selection, by virtue of which the ' weak things of the world confound the mighty, and the things which are not bring to naught the things which are.'

" But then how far is this reversal of the Darwinian law of 'conflict for existence,' in the life of man, a true abrogation of the ' Providential' principle, as our essayist calls it, which secures a gradual amelioration of the organisms of the animal world ? Can we properly say that the principle of competition, so far as it secures the recognition of every new faculty, and the appropriate reward of strength, and industry, and ingenuity, and invention, is not wanted, and not in the highest degree beneficent, in the human world as well as the world below it ? If not, where are we to draw the line ? Where does the Darwinian principle end, and the Christian begin ? Where does it cease to be mischievous, to give aid to lower forms of life which we should be glad in the abstract to see disappear ? Where does it become beneficent to lend artificial succour to those who may transmit the seeds of misery and even crime to distant generations ? Of course these are questions by no means easy to answer. Each one must try and answer them for himself. But it is easy to perceive that, judging even by the coldest light of reason, the *race* would lose infinitely more of greatness, of energy, of variety of activity, of mental and moral stimulus of every kind, by the extinction of the principle of self-sacrifice, by the rigid application of the animal law of natural selection to human affairs and purposes, than it could possibly gain in purity of breed. In fact, there would be no room at all left for the highest dispositions which we hope to see transmitted to our children, if the 'catch-who-can' principle of natural selection is to govern the conscience and inform the motives of men. In endeavouring to purify the breed, we should at once extinguish every character of the highest calibre, and make the breed no longer worth a future destiny at all. In pushing on the competitive principle, pure and simple, beyond its legitimate point, and making it supreme over the life of a being capable of self-sacrifice, we should only degrade man to the level next beneath him, and cut off at a blow the last upward step of his progress. Indeed, whatever risk there is of artificially preserving and perpetuating low types of humanity by our charitable institutions and the higher principles of our civilisation, there is infinitely more risk of failing to preserve and perpetuate that very highest of all types of life which cares more to draw up those beneath it than even to climb itself,—or rather which climbs itself by virtue, chiefly, of the endeavour to draw up those beneath it. Grant, if you will, that the true physician may sometimes save from extinction a life which propagates the seeds of crime and suffering. Grant, if you will, that the giver who saves the wretched from destruction may sometimes have lent a helping hand to physical and moral mediocrities whose posterity will start from a very low level of natural advantage. Still you cannot arrest the hand of either, without arresting an infinitely grander stimulus to all the higher human energies,—intellectual no less than moral,—than can for a moment be compared with the loss which may result from the perpetuation of some low types of organisation. The higher virtues, or rather the characteristic impulses and dispositions in which they are rooted, are amongst the most transmissible of hereditary moral qualities. The children of the purely selfish start from a selfish basis of character. The children of the self-denying start from a freer and nobler capacity for impulse. Enthrone the principle of natural selection, and even if you succeed in diminishing the number of transmitted mischiefs, you diminish infinitely more the number of transmitted goods.

The plan of God seems to be to ennoble the higher part of His universe at least, *not* so much by eliminating imperfection, as by multiplying graces and virtues. He balances the new evils peculiar to human life by infinitely greater weights in the scale of the good which is also peculiar to human life. 'Natural selection' has its place and its function, doubtless, even amongst us. But over it, and high above it, is growing up a principle of supernatural selection, by our free participation in which we can alone become brethren of Christ and children of God."

My rejoinder was as follows :—

Some of the criticisms in the first part of your paper I accept and acquiesce in. My argument, I know, was stated broadly and, perhaps, too extremely —in somewhat harsh outline, and, as it were, without *atmosphere.* But I believe this is the best plan, in the first instance, at least; it arrests attention and makes the meaning clear, and enables readers to judge whether the main essence of the thesis is correct or not. Modifications and limitations come afterwards, and from other quarters ; and some of these you have helped to supply. But I do not think—and I infer that you scarcely think yourself—that you have materially invalidated my chief position — which is that civilization and humanity—our tenderness to life and our respect for property—have, amid their many beneficent and elevating influences, the mischievous operation of preserving, placing in situations of advantage, and enabling to perpetuate themselves classes, individuals, and types of organization at once imperfect, degraded, feeble, and diseased, in their moral and intellectual as well as physical characteristics.

Now, this I hold to be a grave evil ; you, on the contrary, with your inveterate disposition to look at every subject through the misty medium of morals, maintain it to be a great good. You argue that the exercise and discipline which these damaged and diseased organizations afford to healthier and higher ones, in relieving their sufferings, bearing with their infirmities, improving their condition, — " strength sacrificing itself to weakness," in short,—on the whole and in the end cultivate and create a nobler average type of humanity than would have existed were these faulty and bad specimens trampled out or suffered to die out, as they would do in a state of nature. Well, it is an arguable position, no doubt, and has an air of disinterestedness and religious elevation which will throw fascination round it for many minds, and carry conviction to some. But let us state it broadly and without the halo which your language throws round it, and follow it out into a few of its applications. Strip it naked, and see how it looks then. To judge of the symmetry or non-symmetry of a form or figure, you must relieve it of all disguising drapery or tinted clouds which may conceal any defects and suggest any beauties. To estimate the correctness of a logical position, you must see if it will bear being announced in a *positive*, if not extreme shape, and in perfectly plain and unattractive, if not cynically harsh terms. Men fight best, at least they ascertain most speedily and certainly which is strongest,

I

when they fight in the closest conflict, and neither give nor take quarter.

I fully admit that what we want for the human race is not simply nor chiefly the strongest and healthiest physical type, but the highest and noblest physical, intellectual and moral type *combined*, that can by all material and psychological influences be produced. I fully recognize, also, that the existence of misery to be relieved, of sufferings to be sympathized with, of weakness to be borne with, of poverty to be assisted, of diseases to be treated, of degradation to be raised, is a most efficient, nay, perhaps an absolutely necessary instrument for the education and development of the best portions of our nature, and for bringing man up to the highest perfection that he is capable of attaining. But then I hold that it is by *curing* disease, by *eradicating* wretchedness, by *precluding* poverty, by *preventing* suffering, that the needed moral discipline is to be sought and gained; not by perpetuating these evils, or permitting them to propagate themselves. I would seek the perfectation of the race by the extermination, so far as possible, of these things. You, or at least your argument, would maintain these things, or welcome their maintenance, for the education of the race. I would establish hospitals to extinguish maladies; you would establish them to instruct physicians, to train nurses, to exercise the charity of subscribers. I would discourage and eradicate (not " stamp out") the hopeless pauper, the congenitally morbid, the incurably idiotic or defective—all degraded types, in short; you would treat them tenderly, as "dispensations" sent for our good, as whetstones for our virtue to sharpen itself upon, and allow them to multiply other "dispensations" like themselves. As the ascetic fakir rejoices when he can devise a new torment to exercise the spirit and mortify the flesh, so your self-sacrificing theory would hail with joy the advent and multiplication of a one-armed or one-eyed family in the human race, in order that the more perfect human beings with two arms and two eyes might attain moral eminence by "sacrificing themselves" for their deficient or mutilated brethren. Are not these legitimate, even if extreme, inferences from your position ?

I grant without reserve what you urge, viz., that moral qualities are at least as transmissible by inheritance as physical ones, and, therefore, that we shall best further the aggregate and ultimate perfection of the race by cultivating those moral qualities through generous effort and self-denial. There will always be enough suffering and evil in the world for this purpose without permitting inferior and diseased organizations to propagate, and to propagate *par préférence*. But what I pointed out as so mischievous and mistaken in the tendency of our actual civilization is that those classes and individuals whose moral excellencies have been most cultivated by exertion and self-control, on whom the loftier influences that you so value have wrought their perfect work, and who, therefore, are precisely the men and women whom both you and I would wish to see the progenitors of the future race, are precisely those *who are not so*, or not so in preponderating or even proportionate measure, and (what is more to the purpose) *are precisely those whom your doctrine of self-sacrifice withholds from being so.* They stand aside, and abstain from marriage, or marry late, effacing themselves, "sacrificing" themselves, denying themselves, in order (practically, if not designedly) that the luxurious rich and the reckless poor, the degraded organizations that have no notion of self-sacrifice or self-control, may breed other degraded organizations like themselves. Or, in conclusion, and once again to state the argument so nakedly and broadly that it cannot be misconceived,—when the existence and propagation of those degraded types, whose perpetuation I deprecate and you defend, has created a race of generous and noble natures, philanthropic ascetics, and gentle *sœurs de charité*, disciplined to the last perfection of Christian devotion to others, it is not *they* who transmit their tried virtues to future generations, and so gradually build up a Humanity such as God designed ;—they remain barren saints and barren vestals ; and, in the vast disciplining and ennobling hospital that you would make of earth, it is the patients, not the physicians or the nurses,—the degraded, not the purified,—the whetstones, not the razors, that are to propagate their species and their maladies. The virtues and the virtuous are to be sacrificed or postponed to the evils which God sent to practise and to train them.

IV.

LIMITS AND DIRECTION

OF

HUMAN DEVELOPMENT.

The great Enigma of Human Destiny, which has saddened so many bright hearts and baffled so many noble understandings, is apparently not intended to be wholly or satisfactorily solved on earth. Man has worked at it in all ages, in every land, and under every condition,—and constantly in vain. The existence of the Individual and of the Race,—their laws, significance, origin, and goal—constitute the problem which has alternately attracted and beaten back every order of intellect and every variety of character. From the earliest times of which we have any record we find that men had begun to question of these things; the most ancient literature we possess contains speculations upon them as ingenious, as profound, and as unsatisfactory as any that can be found in the ablest philosophical productions of to-day,—for alas! on these topics the veriest child can propound inquiries which the wisest Sage cannot answer—the simplest mind perceives the darkness which the acutest and most powerful cannot pierce or dissipate—and the young and buoyant spirit which comes fresh to the endeavour finds itself at once hemmed in by the barriers and limitations which the intellect that has worked longest in this field is unable to remove or overstep. Carlyle and Goëthe, Bacon and Rousseau, attained no nearer to the golden secret than

Job or Solomon, Anaxagoras or Plato. Generation after generation still sends forth new speculators, ardent, sanguine, and undiscouraged by the failure of their predecessors,—to toil at the same Sisyphæan task, to be met by the same impassable bounds, to catch the same vanishing and partial glimpses, to be conscious of the same incompetency, to confess to the same utter and disheartening defeat. One after another they retire from their voyage of discovery weary and baffled; —some in the exasperation of mortified ambition— some having learned the rich lesson of humility; a few in faith and hope—many in bewilderment and despair;—but none in knowledge—scarcely any (and those only the weakest) even in the delusion of fancied attainment.

Why does Genius ever wear a crown of thorns, self-woven, and inherent in the very conditions of its being? Why does a cloud of lofty sadness ever brood over the profoundest minds?* Why does a bitterness, as of

---

* Because the few with signal virtue crowned,
   The heights and pinnacles of Human mind,
Sadder and wearier than the rest are found,—
   Wish not thy soul less wise or less refined.
True, that the dear delights that every day
   Cheer and distract the pilgrim are not theirs;
True, that, though free from Passion's lawless sway,
   A loftier being brings severer cares;
Yet have they special pleasures—even mirth—
   By those undreamed of who have only trod
Life's valley smooth; and if the rolling earth
   To their nice ear have many a painful tone,
   They know man does not live by joy alone,
But by the presence of the power of God.

LORD HOUGHTON.

Gethsemane, mingle with or pervade the productions of even the serenest Intelligences, if all human emotion be not dead within them ? Why have Statesmen, Philosophers, Warriors, and Poets—men of action and men of thought — men who have sought to influence and men who have sought to comprehend Humanity, in its wild fever and its strange anomalies —why have so many of them, in the intervals of repose and at the close of life, been conscious of an indescribable melancholy and a sombre shadow, which yet had in it nothing selfish and nothing morbid ? Why—but because these are the minds which have seen further, and penetrated deeper, and comprehended more, and deceived themselves less than others; because, precisely in proportion as their experience was profound, as their insight was piercing, as their investigations were sincere, as their contemplations were patient and continuous, did they recognise the mighty vastness of the problem, its awful significance, and the inadequacy of the human faculties to deal with it; because just in proportion as they had higher perceptions of what *might be* or might have been, the contrast of what *is* and of what appeared as if it inevitably *must be*, became more irreconcilable and more appalling; because they felt painfully conscious that *they could not see their way*, and could arrive only at conclusions both in speculation and in actual life, from which it was impossible to escape, yet in which it was impossible to rest. Grand capacities, which seemed adequate to the mightiest achievements; inwoven weaknesses which dishonoured those capacities and rendered those achievements hopeless and unattainable; germs and specimens of virtues approaching the divine and promising a glorious future, yet dashed with imperfections and impurities which seem to hint of a low origin and a still lower destiny; vast steps forward to a lofty goal—recreant backslidings towards the bottomless abyss; ages of progress and enlightenment, followed by ages of darkness and retrogression; unmistakable indications of a mighty purpose and an ulterior career—undeniable facts which make those indications seem a silly mockery; much to excite the fondest hopes—much to warrant the uttermost despair; beautiful affections, noble aspirations, pure tastes, fine intellects, measureless delights, all the elements of paradise,—

"But the trail of the Serpent still over them all."

And as, from their watch-tower of contemplation, the wise and good have brooded over these baffling contradictions, what marvel that one by one they should have dropped off into the grave,—sorrowing, and wondering if peradventure behind the great black Veil of Death they might find the key to the mysteries which saddened their noble spirits upon earth.

Still we go on ruminating over the stupendous enigma from age to age, and occasionally obtaining or seeming to obtain new facts and truths bearing upon it,—which, however, are for the most part contributions rather to a clearer statement of its conditions than to an elucidation of its difficulties. The true solution is perhaps no nearer to us than before, but false ones are disproved and discarded; positive Science, which is always advancing, lends its aid not so much to disperse the darkness as to expose the *ignes fatui* which we mistook for light; and we are brought into a more hopeful state of progress and sent further on our way, in proportion as wider knowledge and exacter observation unroofs one after another of the errors in which we had sought a shelter and fancied we could find repose. Perhaps, after all, our discomfitures hitherto are attributable less to the inadequacy of our speculative faculties than to the poverty of our positive knowledge; the problem may appear insoluble simply because we have not yet accumulated the materials necessary for approaching it; and the higher branches of Physiology may yet point the path to the Great Secret.

Man is a composite Being, and possesses a complex organisation. We must use ordinary language, even though inaccurate and unphilosophic, so long as it conveys to others the same meaning as to ourselves : to affect a precision, which in reality exists neither in thought nor in the instrument of thought, would be at once to deceive and to hamper ourselves. We must accept the common parlance of educated men as a rough approximation to the truth, and at least as the nearest approximation we can, on the whole, make to our conception of the truth. We say then,

—as we are most of us in the habit of thinking——that
Man is made up of three elements——body, mind, and
spirit ;——the BODY, which is the material organ of our
inner being, the seat of the senses through which we
communicate with the outer world, the means by which
we move and act ;——the MIND, which reasons, under-
stands, judges and wills, of which the body is the imperfect servant, often the ruthless tyrant, always the
sympathising companion, possibly, as some think, the
medium by which alone it operates ;——and the SOUL
or SPIRIT, that element and ingredient of our nature
which we believe, or fancy, to be something distinct
from the understanding, which is the seat of our moral
nature, our emotions and affections, which is the
embodiment of our consciousness, which we feel to be
more peculiarly *ourselves*, which we think to be undying,——in virtue of which we live in the future and
aspire to the Eternal,——by which we come into relation with the unseen and spiritual world.   It is possible, as materialists say, that this division may be
mere delusion, that we ought to speak rather of the
Nervous and Muscular systems,——that Mind, Thought,
may be merely a state or operation of the physical
brain,——and that the Soul has no existence whatever,
but that what we call such is only a finer function or
development of the. reason.   But, be this as it may,
we are compelled to accept this threefold division and
employ expressions which assume it to be a reality,
because only thus can we state, *or bring our language
into harmony with*, the known facts of our Nature,

without having recourse to periphrases, qualifications, technical terms, logical and metaphysical definitions which—while perhaps they ensured no higher degree of correctness but merely substituted one inaccuracy for another—would effectually confuse and mystify our meaning.

Man, then we say, has received from the hands of his Maker a composite nature, fitted for the part he is to play, and the work he has to do. In the consentaneous cultivation, in the equal and harmonious development of all the elements of this nature, must lie its earthly perfection and his earthly destiny. By "harmonious development" we mean the fullest elaboration and *perfectation* of each element, which is compatible with the fullest culture, the completest exercise, the healthiest and most vigorous condition of every other ; that justly balanced progress towards the extreme of capability, in which no part profits, or is fostered, to the injury of the rest.

Experience, however, soon teaches us that no one of the three elements of our composite Being *can reach this fullest development except at the expense of the others ;* that each is capable of an abnormal scope and strength by impoverishing the other components and impairing the harmony of the whole :—*but only thus.* The highest flight, the furthest range of each portion of our Nature is purchasable only at the cost of full and fair justice to the rest. The perfection of humanity is one thing : the perfection of the Spiritual, Intellectual, or Animal Man, *severally,* is a different thing,

—and they would seem mutually to exclude each other. ⌐

There can be no doubt that a healthy condition of the body greatly contributes to the healthy action of the mind, to a clear perception and a sane judgment. It may be questioned indeed whether a man with a disordered liver or a dyspeptic habit *can* see things in a precisely true light, or take a just view and an unexaggerated estimate of their proportions. At any rate, it is certain that any weakness or derangement in the corporeal functions has a tendency to introduce corresponding disorder into the mental operations—a tendency which only the utmost vigilance of observation and the utmost energy of will can counteract. A sound constitution is the best handmaid to a sound intellect, and only a frame naturally strong can carry men uninjured through the fatigues of severe and unremitting mental labour. The brain becomes injured by over pressure and the other organs and functions suffer secondarily or by sympathy. So far then, we fully recognise that a perfectly sound and normal state of the mental element demands and belongs to a sound and normal state of the corporeal element of our nature—and *vice versâ*. So true is this, that there are some cases in which torpor of the mind produces maladies of the body; and maladies of the body for which mental activity and moral stimulus are the promptest and most appropriate remedies. Ennui or apathy is as real a source of illness as malaria or alcohol.   And we have all of us heard of instances in which a sudden shock to the feelings or a startling idea conveyed to the mind has restored action to paralytic limbs, life to the languishing, and transient strength to atrophy itself.

But, on the other hand, though the physical frame must be kept in a sound and well disciplined condition in order to be a faithful servant and an adequate and effective organ of the Mind, it is equally true that the highest development of the bodily, and the highest development of the mental, powers must be sought for by a very different course of training, and cannot (except in abnormal and exceptional cases) be attained in the same individual or under the same circumstances. The perfection of the human ANIMAL, and the perfection of the human BEING are probably quite incompatible.   Where do we find the most astonishing strength, the most wonderful feats of activity, the hardiest nerves, the keenest and most unerring senses, in a word, the culminating point of the corporeal faculties and functions?   In the brutal gladiators of Greece or Rome; in the mind-less Matadors of Spain, in the filthy savages of North America, in the empty acrobats and circus-riders of our theatres, in the nearly idiotic prize-fighters of our pugilistic rings.   In the low narrow forehead, the small brain, the scowling brow, the animal expression of the ancient Gladiator and Athlete, contrasted with his quick eye, his spare form, his well-developed muscles, as pliant as whale-bone and as hard as steel, his firm, well-knit, elastic frame, may be seen a further illustration;—an illustration which will be at once confirmed when we converse with the dull and unintelligent of the pugilists or posture-masters of our country, or take the trouble to observe among the circle of our own acquaintances what sort of intellects take most kindly to bodily exercises and are most eminent for feats of agility and strength.

Again. Take a man whose whole life, whose every day is spent in severe physical labour—the wood cutter for example—every muscle of whose brawny frame is trained and hardened to the *ne plus ultra* of capacity, whose every organ is performing its allotted function to perfection, whose every nerve and fibre is glowing with health, to whom pain, weakness, and malady are altogether strangers. Call upon that man for even moderate mental effort, and you find that a child might overmatch him. I will suppose him a man of education—there are many such in the Colonies and the backwoods—but set him down to a problem or a book, and he is certain to fall asleep; task his mind in conversation, and he cannot follow you, or if he does for a while, he feels as wearied as if he had walked fifty miles or felled trees for twelve hours; test his intellectual faculties in any way you please, and you will find them quite sound perhaps, but incapacitated because unexercised. *His* development has gone in a different direction.

Or let the practised student or the trained literary man examine himself as to the times and conditions in which he finds himself capable of the highest flight, or the most severe and sustained toil. Is it when the *animal* part of him is in the healthiest and most natural condition,—when the body is nourished with ample and succulent food,—when the limbs are wearied with salutary exercise,—when he has passed hours inhaling the fresh mountain breezes and bringing his muscles into fit development by the oar, the foil, or a gallop with the Melton fox-hounds? On the contrary, at such times, although conscious that he is then in the most natural and soundest condition *on the whole*, he feels less capable than usual of concentrated thought, less disposed for patient and prolonged research, more ready to enjoy, less ready to contemplate or to soar. Nourishing food clouds his mind; ample exercise brings inevitable somnolence; the Soul is, as it were, clogged by the rude health of the body; the animal nature begins to encroach upon the spiritual, or, to speak more correctly, to insist upon its dues.

The conclusion to which all these observations point is simply that which the physiologist would arrive at *à priori*. The brain, he is well aware, is the organ by means of which the intellect does its work—the organ of Thought; just as the lungs are the organ of respiration, the heart that of circulation, and the nerves and muscles those of action and volition. It is a law of physiology that every bodily organ strengthens and enlarges in proportion as it is exercised, and shrinks and becomes enfeebled if it be comparatively unattended to and unemployed. It is in the power

of the individual to throw, as it were, the whole
vigour of the constitution into any one part, and by
giving to this part exclusive or excessive attention, to
develop it at the expense and to the neglect of the
others. Thus the brain of the thinker, and the lungs
of the glass-blower, attain a partial and abnormal
development by engrossing the exercise and nourishment which ought to have been more equally distributed
to all the functions;—the right arm of the fencer, and
the left arm of the rider become peculiarly strong; and
while the legs of the pedestrian acquire an exaggerated
size and vigour in which the upper extremities do not
share, those of the Indian of the Pampas, on the other
hand, who is always on horseback, are feeble, emaciated
and comparatively useless instruments. He is insignificant and impotent on foot. A special training and
management is required according to the result you wish
to produce; for the pugilist you develop the muscles of
the arm—for the runner those of the legs and loins; the
organization you cultivate in the racer is quite different
and incompatible with that needed in the carthorse;—
and in like manner the discipline by which is sought
the completest and most thorough elaboration of the
physical or that of the intellectual Man, is entirely
divergent. The *fullest* development of either cannot
be united with the *harmonious and equal* development of both. To produce the highest mental
result we cultivate the body only in as far as is
necessary to keep it in that degree of *health* suited
to the favourable and unimpeded operation of the

brain, caring nothing for its condition of strength or agility. To produce the highest corporeal result, we attend to the mind only enough to keep it in that state of gentle stimulus and moderate activity which experience has found conducive to the development of the physical capacities. Like skilful generals, we concentrate our whole force upon that central division of our army with which we intend to operate, taking care merely that in doing so we do not impoverish the other wings to an extent which would disable them from rendering the efficient support which is indispensable.

What is true of the Body is true of the Mind likewise. Its highest condition is an *abnormal* condition. Its loftiest and grandest developments are attainable only at the expense of the corporeal frame and of the natural affections. Its greatest achievements are dearly paid for. Its most towering pinnacle is also the most perilous position it can reach. The mightiest and most glorious human Intellect is *ipso facto* imperfect as a man—more imperfect than many of his fellow-beings. The ordinary mental operations and exertions, those in which the intellect is merely exercised, not strained, may be carried on not only without injury, but even with benefit to the body. But severe and prolonged mental labour, that devotion of the whole faculties to the pursuit before them, that concentration of the powers on one object or on one point, without which anything great or eminent can rarely be attained, this, we know, tells terribly upon physical health and strength. Every year, to the disgrace of our Educators and our Doctors, shows us young men who break down in the struggle for University honours, or sink into permanent valetudinarianism as soon as the unnatural strain is withdrawn. Every physician can point to students whose splendid cerebral development has been paid for by emaciated limbs, enfeebled digestion and disordered lungs. Every biography of the intellectual Great records the dangers they have encountered, often those to which they have succumbed, in overstepping the ordinary bounds of human capacity ; and, while beckoning onward to the glories of their almost preternatural achievements, registers by way of warning the fearful penalty of disease, suffering, and bodily infirmity which Nature exacts as the price for this partial and in-harmonious grandeur. It cannot be otherwise. The brain cannot take more than its share without injury to other organs. It cannot *do* more than its share without depriving other organs of that exercise and nourishment which are essential to their health and vigour. The imaginative efforts and the frequent and prolonged state of cerebral excitation requisite for the production of the finest poetry, involve inevitable reaction, lassitude, and weakness. The profound reflection, the laborious and resolute abstraction, by which alone the penetralia of the inner world can be explored and the hardest problems of philosophy are to be solved, sap the vital energy to a degree that only experience can convince us of, impair the sleep, weaken the digestion, and exhaust the frame.   Perhaps severer than all is the *continuity* of application needed for great achievements either in literature or science.   Sir Isaac Newton was wont to say that he owed his success and whatever apparent superiority over other men he might have shown, to his faculty of thinking continuously on the same subject for twenty or thirty hours together.   But this continuous exercise of one organ is precisely the most fatiguing and weakening of all things.   We may keep in bodily exercise for twelve hours without injury or lassitude, provided we vary frequently enough the muscles which are brought into play.   But who can walk, or fence, or hammer or blow glass for twelve hours without injury or peril ? Again, many can use their brains for twelve hours, and use them energetically too, without being the worse for it, if the subjects of their attention are changed from time to time.   But this dissipation of the mind over many topics is precisely the habit which is antagonistic to all those great achievements of which concentration and continuity of thought are the indispensable conditions.

Once more.   *Sleep*, sufficient in quantity and sound in quality, is essential to the health, strength, and normal perfection of man.   Yet not only is severe mental application unfavourable to sleep and apt to deprive it of that character of complete unconsciousness necessary for thorough refreshment and repose, but life is short, the work of the intellectual aspirant is multifarious and vast, and the residue of time left after the due demands of the body for sleep have been satisfied, is seldom sufficient for all that has to be learned and done. Hence we find that nearly all the loftiest and grandest minds—those, we mean, who have pushed forward their intellectual nature to its culminating point—have cut short their hours of slumber, have defrauded the body of its needful rest, and have impaired its strength and effectiveness accordingly. Severe study, too, injures the sight; sedentary habits are incompatible with muscular activity, a strong stomach, or serene nerves; yet without severe study and sedentary habits, it is difficult to see, how, in our time at least, the summits of intellect are to be scaled or the arcana of the Universe laid bare.

It appears, then, that the ultimate development of which the intellect is capable and its highest possible attainments, can only be reached by an exclusive cultivation and attention which entails upon its physical companion impoverishment, weakness, and disease. But this is not all. It seems even that bodily pain and disease are not only compatible with, but may indirectly contribute to the loftiest efforts of the intellect. They sometimes positively enhance its powers. The effect of some disorders and of certain sorts of pain upon the nerves is to produce a cerebral excitation; and the stimulus thus communicated to the material organ of thought renders it for the time capable of unusual effort.* Men under the stirring influence of severe pain are capable of a degree of imaginative and ratiocinative brilliancy which astonishes themselves and all who have known them only in ordinary moods of comfort. Extinct faculties come back to them. Torpid faculties become vigorous and sparkling. Forgotten knowledge is recovered. Marvellous gleams of insight are vouchsafed to them. The wonderful eloquence of Robert Hall was doubtless greatly owing to the stimulating influence of a terrible spinal malady. Dr Conolly mentions a gentleman whose mental faculties never reached their full power except under the irritation of a blister. Abnormal and unsound conditions of the bodily organs sometimes give us glimpses of mental powers and possibilities far exceeding anything of which ordinary health is capable. The phenomena of some nervous disorders are positive revelations, and most startling ones, of what the human intellect, disengaged from matter or under favouring material conditions, might achieve and learn. The partial powers alleged to appear in catalepsy are most singular. Insanity, which is clearly a disorder of the brain, is not without

---

* Those who wish to follow up this train of thought may find much suggestive matter in Abercrombie's " Intellectual Powers," third edition, pp. 140, 141, 142, 285, 291, 297, 310, 363, 274.

Dr Wigan—" Duality of Mind," pp. 78, 265, 361, 378, 283 284.

Dr Conolly—" Indications of Insanity," pp. 214, 221.

its strange analogous suggestions. The approach of
death—that is to say, the culmination of disease—
has occasionally given wonderful depth, clearness, and
insight, to the mental powers. In fact, when we
become acquainted with all the remarkable cases of
these and cognate phenomena on record, it seems
scarcely exaggeration to say that the *supreme* point
of vigour, brilliancy, and penetration of the human
faculties *can* only be reached under unsound conditions of the body.

There can, we apprehend, be no doubt that in proportion as a man is deficient in the natural affections,
in proportion as those sympathies which bind him to
individual fellow beings are either originally cold and
languid, or have become so by the accidents of life, or
have been wilfully bounded or suppressed,—in that
proportion does he recede from the ideal of a perfect
human being. We all instinctively feel that a man
of pure intellect, however grand and powerful that
intellect may be,—a man in whom the rational too
completely predominates over the emotional,—is incomplete and unsatisfactory. He is *inharmoniously
developed.* We shrink . from these incarnations of
Mind as something portentous and unnatural, and
leave them alone in their desolate and solitary grandeur.
Yet it can scarcely be questioned not only that the
most intense cultivation of the understanding has

a tendency to starve and chill the gentler and tenderer affections, but that this suppression of them is necessary to permit the attainment of the very loftiest summits of thought. The conquest of the remoter and profounder realms of Reason demands not only the concentrated devotion of the whole intellect, but a calmness and serenity of Soul which is unattainable by those who still breathe the atmosphere of the domestic hearth, and are liable to be swayed and perturbed by the emotions inseparable from the love of the earthly, the perishable, and the imperfect. Ancient Philosophers, Poets, Mystics, Artists, religious Enthusiasts, have all felt the same need, all acknowledged the same inevitable price, all preached the same cold doctrine, with more or less of insight and consistency. The absence of disturbing emotions, the undivided direction and engrossment of the intellect, is the one indispensable condition.* "Not in vain did the old Rosicrucians—those spiritual aspirants who

---

* " ' And once more,' I cried, 'ye stars, ye waters,
    On my heart your mighty charm renew;
Still, still, let me as I gaze upon you,
    Feel my Soul becoming vast like you.'

From the intense, clear, star-sown vault of Heaven,
    Over the lit Sea's unquiet way,
Through the rustling night air came the answer—
    ' Wouldst thou be as these are?—*live* as they.

'Unaffrighted by the silence round them,
    Undistracted by the sights they see,
These demand not that the things without them
    Yield them love, amusement, sympathy.

aimed at an earthly immortality and superhuman powers, and fancied that some had won them,—teach that the extinction of all earthly passions, fear, love, hate, pity, ambition, must precede the attainment of the 'Arch Secret,' and the initiation into the sublime existence which they sought. Not without reason did they feign that all their occult knowledge and their wondrous faculties were unavailing for the aid or protection of those to whom they were bound by the sweet ties of human affection or earthly interest, inasmuch as the least shade of natural sympathy at once struck these abnormal powers with impotence and blindness. Those powers are granted, they taught, to him only who could become a passionless, impressionless, serene Intelligence."

The truth is, PEACE is necessary to all the higher intellectual operations. Great *feats* may be done while the Soul is tempest-tossed : great heights achieved— no !—Poets may strike out splendid passages, sparkling with passionate beauty and a sort of gorgeous and turbid inspiration, and Orators may astonish us with brilliant flights of power and pathos, redolent of the

---

'But with joy the Stars perform their shining,
  And the Sea its long moon-silvered roll,—
For *alone* they live, nor pine with noting
  All the fever of some differing soul.

'Bounded by themselves, and unobservant
  In what state God's other works may be,—
In their own task all their powers pouring,
  These attain the mighty life you see.'

M. ARNOLD.

excitement which gave them birth; and all this may be done while the heart is torn by internal conflict or by wild emotion, or yearning with unanswered love, or sick and faint with passionate desire; nay, it may be done while the conscience is heavy with the load of recent sin, or distracted in a danger wherein it sees no light and is conscious of no strength; it may be done while the spirit is burdened with a hopeless or melted with a tender grief, and while the mind is clouded and bewildered by strife and pain, and the mistiness of the moral vision. But THOUGHT, insight, sound clear vision of the Truth, wisdom at once piercing and comprehensive, the noblest and divinest achievements of the REASON, demand serenity of Soul as their imperative condition. Passion clouds the mental Eye; emotion disturbs the organ of discovery; as the astronomer can only rely upon his nicest and loftiest observations when the air is still and the telescope is isolated from all the tremulous movements of terrestrial surroundings, so the Thinker can only see justly and penetrate far, when all that could agitate his Spirit is buried deep, or put quite away, or laid eternally to rest. The conscience must slumber either in conscious innocence or in recognised forgiveness; the aspirations and desires must be calm, simple, and chastised; the keener sympathies must be still; the heart must repose upon a love at once serene, satisfied, and certain—

—— " Such love as Spirits feel
In worlds whose course is equable and pure;
No fears to beat away, no strife to heal,
The past unsighed for, and the future sure."

Or the needed Peace must be sought in a sadder and a surer mode. There is the peace of surrendered, as well as of fulfilled hopes,—the peace, not of satisfied, but of extinguished, longings—the peace, not of the happy love and the secure fireside, but of unmurmuring and accepted loneliness,—the peace not of the heart which lives in joyful serenity afar from trouble and from strife, but of the heart whose conflicts are over and whose hopes are buried—the peace of the passionless as well as the peace of the happy,—not the peace which brooded over Eden, but that which crowned Gethsemane. Perhaps *this* peace—if there be no sourness or morbid melancholy mingled with it—is even more favourable than its brighter prototype to depth of mental vision and power of intellectual effort ; because—though with less of elastic energy—its source lies deeper, its nature is more thorough, it is less liable to disturbance from without. With it

> " The future cannot contradict the past,
> Mortality's last exercise and proof
> Is undergone."

The solitude of Soul, which is its worst sting, is also its surest seal. The deepest discernment and the highest wisdom ever proceed either from the throne of the crowned, or the grave of the buried, Love.

If there is something sad in the idea that the brightest torch of the mind should be kindled at the funeral pile of earthly happiness; that in the slaughter or suicide of the affections should be found the entrance to the inner courts of wisdom ; that men should be compelled " to learn in suffering what they teach in song ; " yet it is much that griefs arising from crushed or wounded human tenderness should be able to find a refuge and a substitute in the loftier and serener realm of thought,—though to taste this balm effectually, a man must not only be *able* to trample out his tenderness, but must *feel it right* to do so,—perhaps must have this task made naturally easy to him.*

But to men of gentler and more genial natures—men in whose nature Love is as undestructible as Thought, who cannot slay their affections, and would not if they could,—the great drag and penalty upon intellectual progress is the sense that it is and must be made at the hazard and to the mortification of the warmer sympathies,—often to the loss of

> " The thousand still sweet joys of such
> As hand in hand face earthly life."

The most painful portion of the martyrdom which awaits

---

* " Wilhelm von Humboldt seemed to have acquired this peace by closing his mind to all disturbing calls or feelings from without —to have kept his spirit as if it were in an iron safe."—*Thoughts of a Statesman.* " Goethe, probably the most powerful and comprehensive genius among the moderns, appears to have been by temperament cold and unsympathising—not absolutely heartless, but only feeling superficially,—and to have cultivated this coldness as an invaluable mental aid."—*Conversations with Eckerman.* " It is a great folly to hope that other men will harmonize with us :— I have never hoped this. I have always regarded each man as an independent individual, whom I endeavoured to study, and to understand with all his peculiarities; but from whom I desired no further sympathy."

the emancipation and the growth of mind is that it so often compels us to leave those we have loved and lived with behind; those who once marched side by side with us, with parallel steps and equal vigour, grow languid, fall behind, tread in our footsteps only feebly, timidly and at a distance, and at length stand still and gaze after us with grief, exasperation or despair; those who used to be our sought and cherished comrades in our moments of deepest feeling and of highest elevation, are now reserved for the hours when we unbend ourselves and sink down to the simplicities and genialities of fond human affections; and the friend of the inner becomes but the companion of the outer life. All this is exquisitely sad : and thousands among the searchers after truth " sicken at the unshared light " they reach at last.

It would seem, then, that those fond and expansive affections which are so essential to the perfect ideal of humanity, and without which we feel it to be defective, are hostile to the grandest development of the intellectual faculties,—and on the other hand that the supremacy of these faculties does not favour those softer sentiments and sympathies which are among the better portions of our nature. A confirmatory indication may be found in the comparative and often singular inadequacy of the mental powers of the men of whom warm-heartedness is the predominant characteristic. Why are Philanthropists generally so weak—or at all events so wanting in commanding talents, and even in

common sense ?   Why are their schemes so constantly
futile, abortive, and even mischievous ?   Why is their
career so strewed with failures, wrecks and ruins,—
beyond the example of men of harder hearts and less
generous emotions ?   There are, no doubt, a few
brilliant exceptions ; and cases might be pointed out
in which real, permanent and signal good has resulted
from the exertions of these worthy men; but the
good has generally flowed, not from the adoption of
their plans, but from their zeal having compelled the
attention of colder and abler men to the work to be
accomplished.   Their views are so often injudicious,
and their schemes so noxious, that a great portion of
existing evils may be traced, either in their origin or
their present aggravated form, to benevolent interfer-
ences for their removal; and it may be said, with
little exaggeration, that in this world a large part of
the business of the wise is to counteract the efforts of
the good.

Much of this apparent anomaly we believe to be
simply explicable by the fact that in these cases one
part of their nature has been inordinately developed
at the expense of the others—as it must be in all
inordinate developments.   But besides this, there is
another cause.   The extent and severity of human
miseries are so enormous, and the depth to which the
roots of them have struck is so measureless, that few
men of keen or ready sympathies can study or contemplate them with a calm mind,—without either
falling into despair, or losing that power of patient

investigation and passionless reflection, from which alone any sound projects for their cure can spring.   Human tenderness is a sad disturber of human intelligence.* In truth those only can safely and serviceably encounter social evils who can both watch and in some measure imitate God's mode of dealing with them. Patience; slow and flank approaches; a dealing with roots, not branches—with the seat not the symptom of the epidemic horror; the *preparing*, rather than the *ordaining*, of a change or cure:—these characterise the treatment of the world's wounds and maladies by Him who is "patient because Eternal,"— together with a majestic indifference to, or rather a sublime endurance of, sorrow, suffering, and sin,

---

* Her heart is sick with thinking
      Of the misery of her kind;
  Her mind is almost sinking,
      That once so buoyant mind.
  She cries, " these things confound me,
      They settle on my brain,
  The very air around me
      Is universal pain.
  The earth is damp with weeping,
      Rarely the sun shines clear
  On any but those sleeping
      Upon the quiet bier.
  I envy not hard hearts, but yet
  I would I could *sometimes* forget;
  I would, though but for moments, look
  With comfort into Nature's book,
  Nor read that everlasting frown
  Whose terror bows me wholly down."

                                    R. M. MILNES.

during the intervening time, however long, till the seed has borne fruit, and the cause has worked onward to its issue.   Few, we believe, will ever effect real, radical, permanent social amelioration, who endeavour to cure evils by direct enactment; whose feelings are too keen and sensitive to wait the time of the Most High, and to contemplate with unflinching faith and patience the sufferings continued through or by reason of the remedial process, sometimes even aggravated by it.* Hence the coldest tempers are generally, in matters of philanthropy, the soundest thinkers and the safest guides and administrators.   A tender hearted statesman is almost more to be dreaded than a despot or an adventurer.   To be worthy and efficient coadjutors of God, on the great arena of the world, we must be able to borrow some of the sublime impassive calm with which, age after age, He has looked down upon the slow progress and the lingering miseries of His children.

Again.   The loftiest culture of the intellect is not favourable either to undoubting conviction of any truth or to unhesitating devotion to any cause.   It has been truly said of the most profound and comprehensive order of minds : *Ils font penser : il ne font pas croire.*"—" The greater the knowledge the greater the doubt," said Goëthe.   And the faithfullest thinkers

---

* " Such are the men whose best hope for the world
   Is ever that the world is near its end ;
   Impatient of the stars that keep their course,
   And make no pathway for the coming Judge."
SPANISH GYPSY.

L

have felt more painfully than others that the deeper
they go often the less easy it is to reach soundings;
—in a word the more thorough their study of the
grandest subjects of human interest, the further do
they get, not to, but from, *certainty :* the more fully
they can see all sides and enter into all considerations,
the less able do they feel to pronounce dogmatically or
to act decidedly.   " The tree of knowledge is not that
of life : "—profound thought, if thoroughly honest and
courageous, is deplorably apt to sap the foundation
and impair the strength of our moral as well as
of our intellectual convictions.*   It weakens the power
of self-sacrifice inevitably, by weakening that positive
undoubting confidence in the correctness of our conclusions and the soundness of our cause from which all
the great marvels of self-sacrifice have sprung.   The
age of Martyrdom is not the age of Thought.†   The
men who can die for a faith are not the same who

---

* It is worthy of remark that Opium, which with some men is
a wonderful clarifier and intensifier of the intellectual powers, is
singularly weakening to the moral nature, appears to cloud the
conscience and benumb the will.

† " Look at the History of any great movement for good in
the world, and ask who took the first critical step in advance?
Whom it was that the wavering and undecided crowd chose to
rally round as their leader and their champion?   And will not the
answer always be, as it was in the Apostolic age—not the man of
wide and comprehensive thought, nor of deep and fervent love,
but the characters of simple unhesitating zeal, which act instead
of reflecting, which venture instead of calculating, which cannot
or will not see the difficulties with which the first struggle of an
untried reformation are of necessity accompanied."—*Stanley on
the Apostolic Age.*

can investigate it closely, or judge it fairly.   The discovery of *truth* belongs to an age of inquiry: the promulgation and triumph of a *creed* belongs to an age of unasking and unreasoning belief.   We laugh at the scholastic nonsense of Irenæus and are disgusted at the unseemly violence of Tertullian :— but these men were ready to die for their opinions, and *we are not.*   The fact is, it is only minds which see but a little way that see clearly and fancy they see all ; it is only those who see but one side that can feel confident there is no other ; it is those only whom study has never taught how wide is the question which seems to them so narrow—how questionable the facts which seem to them so certain—how feeble the arguments which seem to them so impregnable— that can be positive in their beliefs ; it is those only whom inquiry has never compelled to abandon any of their past opinions who can feel sure enough to encounter martyrdom for present ones.   Philosophers can neither burn nor be burned for a creed :—for after all may they not be mistaken now as they have often been before?—It may well be doubted whether some degree of *fanaticism*—i.e. wrong appreciation of the essential value of things—is not necessary to prompt the higher efforts of self-sacrifice ;* whether any calm - judging, far-seeing, profoundly sagacious man, would think *any opinion certain enough or any cause valuable or spotless enough,* to be worth dying for— except, indeed, the right of free action and free

---

* *Natural History of Enthusiasm.*—Isaac Taylor.

thought. If all men had been deep thinkers—had seen every thing correctly, valued every thing at its precise worth, measured the relative importance of each object, estimated accurately *the degree of certainty attainable regarding each opinion or each faith,*— could we ever have had those martyrs who have conquered for us our present freedom ?—and who won it, so to speak, *incidentally* and by a sort of fluke ; for they died, not for the right of every man to maintain whatever he thought true, but for *their* right to hold and to proclaim their own special form of error.   Where is the Believer who does not now admit that many of these men went to the scaffold for an error—*were martyrs by mistake ?* Where is the Philosopher who does not suspect that *all* may have thus nobly blundered ?

In speaking of the Intellectual faculties it is probable that I have anticipated much that might as fittingly have been treated under the head of Spiritual faculties; for the line of demarcation which separates the two is often faint, obscure and not easily definable.   And here I must repeat the remark made at the opening of this chapter, as to the inevitable looseness and inaccuracy of our language when treading this debateable ground.   Whether the spiritual faculties be in any true and specific sense distinguishable from the intellectual ; or whether, as is probably the case, the real distinction does not lie between the *imaginative* and the *ratiocinative* powers of mind, I will not

discuss.   In using the phrase 'Spiritual faculties,' we
mean those powers or portions of our mind by which
we contemplate the unseen, the immaterial, the Divine,
which take cognizance of that wide range of sentiments
and subjects coming under the vague denomination of
'*religious*,'—those faculties, in a word, by virtue of
which we commune or endeavour to commune with
our God, and believe in or are conscious of a Soul.
Now, these faculties are not the most vigorous, piercing or exalted in the strongest frames or the most
powerful intellects—but rather the reverse; and their
highest development is reached generally in the less
sound and well-balanced cerebral organisations, and
under conditions both of body and mind which either
are morbid or inevitably tend to become so.   Of course
we meet with many healthy and strong men who are
pious, and many able men who are unfeignedly devout,
and many eminently religious men whose sanity and
vigour both of mind and body are above the ordinary
standard : we even find exceptional cases where the
eminently spiritual are eminently intellectual also ; but
as a general rule the observation of mankind will, we
think, sanction the above broad position.

The imaginative faculties are those by which we
take cognisance of and aspire to things supernal, future,
and unseen—'things spiritual' in a word.   "Spiritual
things (says St. Paul) are spiritually discerned."   But
the logical or reasoning faculties are those by which we
obtain positive and certain knowledge, and correct the
errors and check the vagaries of the imagination.   The

two are not exactly antagonistic but reciprocally vigilant. We soar by the one; we make firm the ground beneath our feet by the other. By the one we conceive, form hypotheses, catch glimpses; by the other we judge, compare, and sift. The one is the sail: the other is the rudder and the ballast. It is natural that the culmination of the two should be mutually excluding and incompatible; and that which is the most exercised will infallibly become the strongest. Moreover, the spiritual or religious imagination is concerned with matters of which the simple reason can judge only partially and doubtingly, as having defective premises and a limited jurisdiction; the provinces of the two faculties are in a great measure distinct. The Soul has, or assumes to have, its own senses and perceptions; it sees, feels, is conscious of things which the pure intellect can neither discern nor pass judgment upon—which lie out of its range. It sometimes conveys to us information which the reason can pronounce false, because inconsistent with known truths; but for the most part when the Spirit says "I know, I see;"—all that the Intellect can say is, "It may be so: I cannot tell."

We have seen that it is the law of our being that the exclusive or paramount exercise of any one part of our composite nature should be followed by correspondingly disproportionate development and predominance of that part. Hence we need feel no surprise at observing that many of the most magnificent and comprehensive intellects the world has known, even when gifted with fine imaginations, have not been peculiarly or obviously 'spiritually-minded' —rather the contrary. The very acuteness and vigour of their reason taught them to distrust what may be called the Senses of the Soul, and to avoid cultivating what they believed a misleading and a dangerous faculty. The converse of this proposition is equally true. Few of those in whom the religious element has been disproportionally developed have been men of the soundest or most powerful minds. Often they have been gifted with brilliant eloquence and poetic genius of an elevated order: often have they, in virtue of these gifts, and aided by that earnestness of purpose and tenacity of aim which strong religious convictions bestow in surpassing measure, been able to sway the minds of men and to guide the destinies of the world, far more powerfully than philosophers or sages;—but they have exercised this influence in virtue of their moral and not their intellectual qualities. Wisdom has a poor chance against the zeal of an unhesitating conviction. The weakest of the wise men who smiled or mourned over the crusading folly of the Middle Ages had probably a larger and sounder intellect than Peter the Hermit, and all his fanatical compeers; yet the latter were omnipotent and the former were unheard or trampled under foot.

But further; the paramount cultivation of the spiritual powers, the concentration of the mind on religious contemplation, while we can well believe it may and must strengthen that faculty of insight (if indeed the existence if such faculty be not altogether a delusion) from which all our glimpses of the unseen world, all our loftier and deeper spiritual conceptions, are derived—is, as is too sadly known, one of the most frequent and certain causes of insanity.* Not only is it not favourable to health and strength of intellect, but it often upsets the intellect altogether. The topics of reflection are so awful and so grand, the tension of mind required to grasp them is so great, the glimpses gained or fancied are so dazzling, the whole atmosphere of thought is so ethereal, that more than ordinary strength of nerve and brain must be needed to ward off the natural results. Where the ineffable mysteries of the Divine Presence and the Unseen World are truly *realised*—where we try to "live *as seeing Him* who is invisible"— how can that calmness which is essential to wisdom,

---

* Many of us are familiar with Sir James Mackintosh's beautiful letter to his intimate friend Robert Hall, perhaps the finest spiritual intellect of our generation, on his recovery from an attack of insanity.

"It is certain the child may be too manly, not only for his present enjoyments, but for his future prospects. Perhaps, my friend, you have fallen into this error of superior natures. From this error has, I think, arisen that calamity with which it has pleased Providence to visit you, which I regard in you as little more than the indignant struggles of a pure mind with the low realities around it—the fervent aspirations after regions more congenial to it—and a momentary blindness produced by the fixed contemplation of objects too bright for human vision. I may say in this case, in a far grander sense than that in which the words were originally spoken by our great Poet:

    'And yet the light that led astray
      Was light from heaven.'"
      —*Memoir of Sir James Mackintosh* i. 253.

that sense of proportion on which sanity depends, be maintained ? Our most daring spiritual flights, our furthest spiritual glimpses, then, are attained only at an awful risk, and by brains on the verge and in immediate peril of unsoundness. It may even be that it is a certain incipient disorder of mind or tendency to such disorder which predisposes men to these dangerously exciting topics.

We shall be reminded probably that there was One who once walked upon the earth in whom the spiritual and intellectual elements of character were not only in perfect harmony, but reached the fullest development of both. To those, however, who believe that Jesus was more than Man ; to those even, who believe that though not strictly Divine, he was for a special purpose endowed with an exceptional organisation, we may reply that, on *their* supposition, his case confirms rather than impugns our general position. If, for the attainment of this two-fold perfectness, supernatural endowment were required, it follows that ordinary humanity must rest content with a more humble or one-sided development. Those on the other hand who imagine Jesus, though splendidly and rarely gifted, to have been perfect only within the attainable limits of humanity—*i.e.*, not to have been Divine, but only the possible ideal of the human—will not feel offended by the suggestion, that an unprepossessed observer would assign to Christ not a *philosophical* but a purely *spiritual* pre-eminence ; — that we should not look upon him as the greatest *Thinker*, even on religious topics, that Humanity has given forth, but as the one who most truly conceived the Spirit of God, and realised that conformity with His will, which we are told should be the aim of our being here, and which we believe will be the loftiest attainment of our life hereafter. If we are right as to the intrinsic distinction and usual discrepancy between intellectual and spiritual supremacy, we see at once the mistake, and how deep it lies, of those, on the one hand, who conceive that, because Christ is our perfect pattern and our spiritual ideal, he must necessarily be also the depository of all truth and the teacher of perfect wisdom, and of those, on the other, who finding him intellectually limited and in error, conclude thence that he could not be the Divine Example which they yet feel instinctively that he was.*

---

* " Christ, as the incarnate Logos, was the consummation of moral excellence, so far as that is compatible with the unalterable conditions of humanity. Learning and science and artistic skill are not embraced in the attributes of the Logos. In these respects Christ was a man of his own age and nation,—believing and speaking on all speculative topics, on every subject that stood outside the conscience and its eternal relations with God, like the multitude among whom he dwelt. Through this inevitable limitation of his intellectual being, he acted with more power and effect on the spiritual condition of his contemporaries; and from the marked contrast between the grandeur and purity of his religion, and the simplicity of his worldly wisdom, he has acquired a more than earthly influence over the mind of ensuing generations. The unrivalled pre-eminence of his spiritual example we cannot now deprive of its claim to a higher reverence, by imputing it to extraordinary philosophic culture or the perceptions of an intellect raised far above the standard of his time."—(*Rev. J. J. Tayler's Sermons*, p. 75).

Further. We find that the spiritual faculties are constantly most predominant and liable to the most extreme development in those whose physical organization. is the least sound and strong, and under those constitutional conditions which are unquestionably abnormal and disordered, or bordering on such and tending to become such. They are more remarkable in women than in men : and in those men whose nervous system is preternaturally excitable, disproportionably dominant. The close connection between hysteria and what we may term " religiosity" has long been known :—so peculiar is the predisposition of hysterical patients to see spiritual visions, to fall into religious trances, to have or to be convinced they have communications with the unseen world, that some physicians regard these things as only phases and symptoms of that many-faced and many-voiced nervous malady. The trances to which St Paul was subject, and in which he is believed and believed himself to be favoured with spiritual manifestations, appear to have been precisely similar to modern instances of religious trance. Works on Medical Psychology abound in illustrative cases, in which the exaltation and preternatural vividness of some cerebral faculties almost resemble the development of a new sense, and have by some been regarded as such.* Prolonged sleeplessness,—*pervigilium*, as physicians term it—is well known to be a fertile pro-

---

* See Wigan, Abercromby, Conolly—also Bertrand *Varietés de l' Extase*. Also various pamphlets, which may be called the literature of " the unknown tongues."

ducer of this exaltation of the natural powers of vision or imagination. The old Sages who pretended to develop superhuman capacities in human nature, insisted on long abstinence from sleep, as an indispensable condition of initiation. The ascetic religionists who dwell so strongly on the necessity of fasting for the production and cultivation of religious sentiments and emotions, well know what they are about. Prolonged abstinence from food, or a very inadequate amount of it, has a specific effect in stimulating, enhancing, purifying, and *intenerating* the devotional part of our nature; in goading the brain to an unnatural state of susceptibility, as physicians would say,—in emancipating the spirit from the gross shackles of the flesh, as Divines would prefer to express the same fact; in producing that state of mind which it is usual to call specifically "*spiritual.*" The same condition of preternatural vividness and lucidity of mental vision frequently occurs in the crisis of dangerous fevers, and on the approach of dissolution. Schiller and Blanco White, a few hours before they breathed their last, felt that "many things were growing clear to them." *Yet all these states are unquestionably morbid,* or on the point of becoming so.

At what price to the soundness of the understanding and the health of the natural affections, this special and abnormal development of the spiritual faculties is purchased, let the history of creeds, the biography so saintly men, and the life and writings of the religious world of our own day, bear sad and humiliating testimony.   What inconceivably monstrous and self-contradictory tenets have been accepted at the command of spiritual visions!   What delusive information have not the excited ' senses of the Soul ' imposed on the bewildered reason !   What irrational conceptions have not the keenest understandings often been compelled to entertain !   How many deplorable examples have we had of men of the finest intellect compelling that intellect to ' eat dirt,' when the religious element in their composite nature had fairly got the upper hand and established itself in the supremacy of an irresponsible Autocrat !   How fearfully omnipotent is excessive religiosity of temperament in blinding the understanding to the simplest conclusions, in screening from detection the most untenable delusions, in masking the most flagrant inconsistencies, in preventing us from recognising the plainest truths or the most obvious errors, though both were written in sunbeams,—may be learnt from almost every article of our popular theology.   To such an extent has this gone that the antagonism of Faith and Reason has been erected into an axiom, and the subordination of the Understanding to the Imagination—of the Intellectual to the Spiritual faculties—has been preached by the pious as the first of duties.

The sad havoc which the excessive development of the religious temperament makes in the natural affections, where the intellect has not been proportionally cultivated, or has not been enthroned in its due supremacy, is a more lamentable phenomenon still.

Truly it has "separated chief friends," perverted healthy sympathies, "turned wholesome hearts to gall," dried up and trampled out all the sweet humanities of life. Under its influence wives have become cold to their husbands, and mothers cruel to their children; the purest earthly love has been withered by the unnatural competition of the self-called divine; crime it has gilded with the hues of virtue, and the most ferocious barbarism it has fancied was both clemency and duty. It has led those under its despotic sway to look upon all the gentler emotions, the tenderer affections, the more vivid sympathies, with which God has hallowed and beautified our earthly life, as snares, weaknesses, and sins,—and the trampling of them out as the most acceptable service that could be rendered to a jealous and engrossing Deity. It has poisoned the very source of all that is lovely and endearing in our composite being. It is to no purpose to say that these effects are produced only in weak and disordered minds:—they are produced in minds disordered and weakened by the very process of spiritual aspiration; they are produced, even in great minds, whenever the religious element acquires complete predominance over the intellectual. Of course, if the natural affections assert their rights, and the intellect maintains its due supremacy, the effects we have spoken of it do not ensue—but neither, then, does the spiritual faculty reach its culminating point.

If the position we have endeavoured to establish in

the foregoing pages be sound; if, of the three components of which man's complicated nature consists, no
one can reach the highest culture and development of
which any one is susceptible, except by unfairness, injury or peril to the others ; and if those faculties es
pecially, which we denominate 'spiritual' and have been
taught to regard as our noblest, can only attain supremacy
under bodily conditions which imply or threaten disease,
—then it would seem to follow :—

That the ideal of humanity *on earth*—the perfection which we are intended to attain here—is to be
sought, *not in the surpassing development of our highest
faculties,* but *in the harmonious and equal development of all.*   In proportion as a man's physical
organisation is neglected, maltreated, or impoverished
in the exclusive or predominant culture of his
understanding or his imagination—or in proportion as
the religious and devotional element within him is
stimulated and cultivated at the expense of the Intellect—in *that proportion does he depart from his proper
standard and thwart and traverse his allotted destiny.*

That the existence of faculties capable—as we
know by actual proof—of a degree of elevation and
perfection which is only attainable on earth in abnormal
and disordered conditions, points towards a future state
and a different organization—to conditions, in a word,
under which the perfection, possible and therefore designed, of those faculties can be achieved.   They can
scarcely, we may assume, be meant to remain for
ever in an imperfectly developed state : yet that

state is the one clearly assigned to them on earth. With a more finished and ethereal frame, the Intellect will be able to strive and soar without crushing the body, or starving the affections, or discouraging the Soul; and the Soul may reach heights unattainable below, and gaze undazzled on splendours that here only blind and bewilder its unprepared and unfitted vision.

That the design of the Creator, and therefore the duty of man, upon earth, is not the highest development of the *Individual*, but the perfection of the *Race*. The former, as we have seen, must inevitably be reserved for other conditions or another state: the latter is attainable in this. Nature has placed, if not impassable barriers in our upward path, at least warning beacons against the attempt to overleap them. She has not only cautioned us against the *extreme* cultivation of the intellectual and spiritual man, but has condemned that cultivation by assigning disease as its inevitable consequence and condition. In forbidding us to surpass the limits of the *thoroughly* BUT HARMONIOUSLY *developed* specimens of Humanity, she has assigned to us the welcome and feasible task of *bringing up the whole human Race to those limits* :—Not to make strong and healthy frames into Hercules' and Athletes, not to make wise men into Platos, Bacons, or Goëthes, not to make saintly men into Wesleys, Xaviers and St Bernards, but to make all men vigorous and sane, wise, good and holy, in the measure of their just and well-balanced capacity ; not to urge the exceptional few to still more exceptional attainments, but to bring the many to the level of the few. Two glorious futures lie before us: the progress of the RACE here, the progress of the MAN hereafter. History indicates that the individual man needs to be transplanted in order to excel the Past. He appears to have reached his perfection centuries ago. Men lived then whom we have never yet been able to surpass, rarely even to equal. Our *knowledge* has of course gone on increasing, for that is a material capable of indefinite accumulation. But for power, for the highest reach and range of mental and spiritual capacity in every line, the lapse of two or three thousand years has shown no sign of increase or improvement. What Sculptor has surpassed Phidias? What Poet has transcended Eschylus, Homer, or the author of the book of Job? What devout Aspirant has soared higher than David or Isaiah? What Statesman have modern times produced mightier or grander than Pericles? What Patriot Martyr truer or nobler than Socrates? Wherein, save in mere acquirements, was Bacon superior to Plato? or Newton to Thales or Pythagoras? Very early in our history individual men beat their wings against the allotted boundaries of their earthly dominions; early in History God gave to the Human Race types and patterns to imitate and approach, but never to transcend. Here, then, surely we see clearly intimated to us our appointed work :—viz., to raise the masses to the true standard of harmonious human virtue and capacity, not to strive ourselves to overleap that standard; not to put our own souls or brains into a hotbed, but to put all our fellow-men into a fertile and a wholesome soil. If this be so, both our practical course and our speculative difficulties are greatly cleared. The timid fugitives from the duties and temptations of the world, the selfish coddlers and nursers of their own souls, the sedulous cultivators either of a cold intellect or of a fervent Spiritualism, have alike mistaken their mission and turned their back upon their goal. The Philanthropists, in the measure of their wisdom and their purity of zeal, are the real fellow-workmen of the Most High. This principle may give us the clue to many dispensations which at first seem dark and grievous; to the grand scale and the distracting slowness of Nature's operations; to her merciless inconsideration for the individual where the interests of the Race are in question.* Noble souls are sacrificed to ignoble masses; the good champion often falls, the wrong competitor often wins : but the Great Car of Humanity moves forward by those very steps which revolt our sympathies and crush our hopes, and which, if we could, we would have ordered otherwise.

---

* So careful of the type she seems,
So careless of the single life.—*In Memoriam.*

V.

THE SIGNIFICANCE OF LIFE.

Some men seem to be sent into the world for purposes of action only. Their faculties are all strung up to toil and enterprise; their spirit and their frame are alike redolent of energy. They pause and slumber like other men, but it is only to recruit from actual fatigue; they occasionally want quiet, but only as a refreshment to prepare them for renewed exertion, not as a normal condition to be wished for or enjoyed for itself. They need rest, not *repose*. They investigate and reflect, but only to estimate the best means of attaining their ends, or to measure the value of their undertaking against its cost: they think, they never *meditate*. Their mission, their enjoyment, the object and condition of their existence is WORK: they could not exist here without it; they can not conceive another life as desirable without it. Their amount of vitality is beyond that of ordinary men: they are never to be seen doing nothing: when doing nothing else they are always sleeping. Happy Souls! Happy *men*, at least!

There are others who skim over the surface of life, reflecting just as little as these and not reposing much oftener; whose sensibilities are quick, whose temperaments are cheerful, whose frames are naturally active

but not laborious; on whom nature and the external
world play as on a stringed instrument, sometimes
drawing out sweet sounds, sometimes discordant ones;
but whom the inner world seldom troubles with any intimation of its existence; men whom the interests of
the day suffice to occupy; the depth of whose souls are
never irradiated by gleams or stirred by breezes "from
a remoter life." They too are to be envied. The
bees and the butterflies are alike happy.*

There are other spirits whom God has cast in a different mould, or framed of less harmonious substance;
men gifted with that contemplative faculty which is
a blessing or a curse according as it is linked with a
cheerful or a melancholy temperament—according as
it is content to busy itself only with derivative and
secondary matters, or dives down to the hidden foundation of things, according as it assumes and accepts
much, or is driven by its own necessity to question
every thing, according as it can wander happily and
curiously among the flowers and fruit of the Tree of
Life, or as it is dangerously impelled to dig about its
roots and analyse the soil in which it grows. To such
men existence is one long note of interrogation, and
the universe a storehouse of problems all clamorous
for solution. The old fable of the Sphinx is true for

---

* " Happy the many to whom Life displays
    Only the flaunting of its Tulip-flower;
    Whose minds have never bent to scrutinize
    Into the maddening riddle of the Root—
    Shell within shell—dream folded over dream." . .

                                    R. M. MILNES.

them : Life is the riddle they have to read, and death, sadness, or the waste of years, is the penalty if they fail to interpret it aright. A few, perhaps, may find the key, and reach " the peace that passeth understanding." A larger number fancy they have found it, and are serene in their fortunate delusion. Others retire from the effort; conscious that they have been baffled in the search, but, partly in weariness, partly in trust, partly in content, acquiescing in their failure. Others, again, and these too often the nobler and the grander souls, reach the verge of their pilgrimage still battling with the dark enigma, and dying less of age or malady than of the profound depression that must be the lot of all who have wasted life in fruitless efforts to discover how it should be spent and how regarded ; and which even a sincere belief in the flood of life which lies behind the great black curtain of Death, cannot quite avail to dissipate.*

But, whatever may be the form or issue of the search, no man gifted with the sad endowment of a contemplative and questioning turn of mind, can reach mature life without earnest meditation on the great problem

---

* " And though we wear out life, alas !
    Distracted as a homeless wind,
  In beating where we may not pass,
  In seeking what we shall not find ;—

  Yet shall we one day gain, life past,
    Clear vision o'er our Being's whole,—
  Shall see ourselves, and learn at last
  Our true affinities of Soul !"

M. Arnold.

of himself and of the world, the inner and the outer
universe ; without seeking whence he came and whither
he is bound :—

> " The Hills where his life rose
> And the Sea to which it goes."

He yearns to know the meaning of existence ; its aim
and purport ; in what light he is to look upon it, in
what way he is to use it. The necessities of his nature
forbid him to lead a provisional life, either mentally
or morally ; he wants to *sail*, he cannot be content to
drift; he must know his haven and steer his course.
Sentient and conscious existence to him is a problem to
be solved, not a summer day to be enjoyed,—at least
he must ascertain whether it *is* this last, before he
can tranquilly accept even its joys. He is, and must
ever be

> ——" a Being holding large discourse—
> Looking before and after."

What then is Human Life, its significance, its aim,
its mission, its goal ?

To the opening mind—at least when so placed as
to be exempt from the sordid cares and necessities of a
mere material existence—it seems like a delicious feast:
the most magnificent banquet ever spread by a kind
Creator for a favoured creature, the amplest conceivable
provision for a Being of the most capacious and various
desires. The surface of the earth is strewed with

flowers : the path of years is paved and planted with enjoyments. Every sort of beauty has been .lavished on our allotted home, beauties to enrapture every sense, beauties to satisfy every taste. Forms the noblest and the loveliest, colours the most gorgeous and the most delicate, odours the sweetest and the subtlest, harmonies the most soothing and the most stirring; the sunny glories of the day; the pale Elysian grace of moonlight, the lake, the mountain, the primæval forest, and the boundless ocean; "silent pinnacles of aged snow" in one hemisphere, the marvels of tropical luxuriance in another; the serenity of sunsets; the sublimity of storms; *every thing* is bestowed in boundless profusion on the scene of our existence : we can conceive or desire nothing more exquisite or perfect than what is round us every hour. And our perceptions are so framed as to be consciously alive to all. The provision made for our sensuous enjoyment is in overflowing abundance : so is that for the other elements of our complex nature. Who that has revelled in the opening extacies of a young imagination or the rich marvels of the world of Thought, does not confess that the Intelligence has been dowered at least with as profuse a beneficence as the Senses! Who that has truly tasted and *fathomed* human love in its dawning and its crowning joys, has not thanked God for a felicity which indeed "passeth understanding!" If we had set our fancy to picture a Creator occupied solely in devising delight for children whom he loved, we could not conceive one single element of bliss which is not here.   We might retrench casualties ; we might superadd duration and extension ; we might make that which is partial, occasional and transient, universal and enduring ; but we need not, and we could not, introduce one new ingredient of joy.

So varied and so lavish is the provision made for the happiness of man upon this earth, that we feel intuitively and irresistibly, that Earth was designed to be a scene of enjoyment to him—that it was created and arranged expressly for this end ;—nor can either sophistry or sad experience, in any sound and really sincere mind, impair this conviction.   We feel at once that there is something crumbling in the premises and rotten in the logic that can ever attempt to persuade us of the contrary.   It is true that we see around us much suffering ; that the mass of men are happy only partially, fitfully, imperfectly ; that no man is as happy as the provision made for him indicates that he ought to be.   But this neither does shake our conviction, nor should it.   For the more we study Nature, the more do we attain the certainty that nearly all this positive suffering and scanty joy is traceable to our neglect or transgression of her laws—not to the inadequate provision made for human happiness, but to our unskilful use of that provision ; —that the misery now prevalent is not a consequence of Nature's original or ultimate design, but a contravention or postponement of that design.

This is TRUTH, but not the whole truth, nor the only truth.   Life was spread as a banquet for pure, noble, unperverted natures, and may be such to them, ought to be such to them, is often such now, will be such always and to all in future and better ages. But, as at the Egyptian festivals, so at the great festival of existence, a veiled spectre ever sits to remind us that *all* is not said—that the word of the enigma is not yet decyphered. Even when centuries of progress shall have realised the Earth's ideal, Life can never be solely or completely a Drama of holy and serene delights, so long as Death stands for ever by to close it with a Tragedy.

And this will *always* be so. Prudence and temperance may lengthen life ; Science may reduce casualties and mitigate disease ; fewer may be cut off in infancy ; more may reach the possible limit of earthly duration ; a larger and larger number in each successive age may be allowed to play out the whole piece ;—but when all is done, life, longer or shorter, comes to the same end : —if those we love do not go from us early, if the things we are concerned in interest us to the last, still the day comes—and *is always in prospect*—when we are called upon to leave all that has gladdened the eye, enchanted the ear, stirred the intellect, soothed and satisfied the heart,—to abandon the only scene we have ever gazed at, to close the only book we have ever read in, to exchange the known for the unknown—*to go out*—to cease or to appear to cease, to be. Death is even more than this, though we are accustomed to disguise it to ourselves with gentle words and beautiful fancies and glorious anticipations. We may speak of it as an exchange of one sort of an existence for another—of a disappointing reality for a perfected ideal; as "walking into a great darkness;" as "long disquiet merged in rest;" as entering upon untrodden and inviting worlds; as launching forth upon waters of which the darkest feature is that we cannot see, but must be content to believe in, the further shore.

> " Or we can sit
> In serious calm beneath deciduous trees,
> And count the leaves, scarce heavier than the air,
> Which leave the branch and tremble to the ground;
> Or, out at midnight in a gliding boat,
> Enjoy the waning moon and moralize,
> And say that Death is but a Mediator
> Between the lower and the loftier life."

But these are all figures of speech. They may express a truth: we strongly believe they do. But they do not express the simple fact of Death as it strikes our unsophisticated sense; as our natures regard it before religion or philosophy has imposed, or endeavoured to impose, silence on the instincts of the heart. To these native instincts Death is the great "sleep which rounds our little life;" it is a wrench from all that has made up our being for long years of thought, sense and feeling; it is a loss of the only existence we can truly *realise*;—not journeying into a new country, but obviously, ostensibly, so far as all appearances go, an END of the journey we have travelled for so long. We need not deceive ourselves. Death, even to the most fervent believers in the Great Hope, can never be other than a Mystery: to others it must remain God's saddest, deepest, most disturbing mystery.

It must be so to *all.* The gayest and most joyous spirit that ever sported from the cradle to the grave has this tragic element as inextricably interwoven with its life as any of us. The refined, the loving, the tender, and the noble,—whose existence has been one beautiful and harmonious poem,—the music of whose nature has never jarred,—who have extracted from their career on earth every pure delight, every permitted extasy of the senses and the soul, which the Creator fitted it to render,—find the same inexorable Darkness awaiting them at the end of their pilgrimage, if not breaking it off abruptly in its brightest and most perfect hour. The mightiest Intelligences, who have put life to heroic uses, who have waged noble warfare and toiled for noble ends, who have " rowed hard against the stream," who have enrolled themselves in the glorious army of God's warriors and workmen,—these, too, know that they may every hour expect the falling of the curtain ; and that, fall when it may, it is sure to find them with their work unfinished and their goal unreached. Those who most enjoy life, and those who best employ it, must close it amid the same impenetrable shadows.

And this solemn fact is not merely a distant certainty, to which we may shut our eyes till the time comes : it is everywhere before us ; it forces itself on our attention, forbids us to forget it. It does not merely await us at the close of our journey ; it crosses us at every step, its alarum startles us every hour ; it insists on being a *constant* guest, at our homes, or in our thoughts. We *must* reckon with it ; we *can not* put it by ; it gives us no peace till we turn manfully to face it, to wrestle with it, to understand it, to settle with ourselves how we intend to regard it during life and to meet it when it comes. It continues the most *waylaying* thought of the thoughtful man, till he silences its importunity by listening to all it has to say, and reasoning it back into the tomb ;

> " Or place it in some chamber of the soul,
>   Where it may lie unseen as sound, yet *felt*—
> Making life hushed and awful."

Again, Life is a scene of much suffering and sorrow. It is true, as I have argued, that a vast amount, probably far the greatest amount, of this is gratuitous and avoidable. Much of it arises from ignorance of the laws of nature, which the growing wisdom of centuries will dissipate. Much of it arises from a violation of physiological and moral obligations, which in the course of ages the human race will learn almost universally to obey. Much of it arises from social errors which we have already begun to recognise as errors; much from a discrepancy between our theory and our practice which we are even now awakening to the necessity of removing. A vast proportion of the evils which we see around us we know to be curable, and we think we see the mode and the epoch of their cure. The more sanguine among us are already dreaming of the day when the actual of Humanity shall approach within sight of its ideal, and when the original programme of the Creator shall at all events be approximately realised.

But when all this has been done—to say nothing of the long ages of the MEANWHILE—when the perfection of a nature inherently imperfect shall have been reached,—there will still remain a large residuum of grief and pain incapable of avoidance or elimiuation, and which we must therefore accept as one of the permanent elements of the problem presented to us for solution. Life — as constituted by God, not as spoiled by man—is not only a scene of designed enjoyment, terminated by a strange, mysterious and almost contradictory crisis : it is a scene also of inalienable suffering—a scene whose habitual harmonies are jarred upon by discordant sounds, whose bright skies must at times be overcast by clouds of portentous darkness, whose hymns of praise and pœans of rejoicing will often be exchanged for the sharp cry of pain and the wail of inextinguishable grief. Perfect our nature and our social systems as we may, there will still be casualties to stretch us on a bed of anguish to which no skill can bring effective or permanent relief ; there will still be chambers of long and wearing sickness where the assiduities of the tenderest friends cannot hinder the sufferer from longing for the visit of the last, mightiest, kindest friend of all. There will still be bereavements of the affections, not always created by the grave ; severances of Soul, for which there is neither balm nor lethe ; vacant places by the hearthstone which nó form again may fill;—and as long as generation succeeds generation and families are linked together ; as long as the young are coming on the stage while the old are leaving

it; as long as Nature commands us to cling so passionately to what we yet must lose so certainly and may
lose so suddenly and so soon; as long as Love continues
the most imperious passion and Death the surest fact
of our mingled and marvellous humanity, so long
will the sweetest and truest music upon earth be always
in the minor key.*

And in "the long meanwhile"—during which the
goal of human attainment is scarcely perceptibly
approached—the world does seem such a stumbling
botch and muddle; Man himself is such a " pie-bald
miscellany " with his

> " Bursts of great heart, and slips in sensual mire; "

the discrepancy is so vast between our highest actual
and our most moderate ideal; the follies of men are
so utterly astounding, to one who has seen them close;
their weaknesses so profoundly despicable; their vices
so unspeakably revolting; their virtues, even, so casual,
halting, and hollow; Life is such " a comedy to those
that think, such a tragedy to those that feel; " its pages
are so sadly, incomprehensibly grotesque! Generation
after generation of the young rush sanguinely into the
arena, confident that they can solve the puzzle, confident
that they can win the victory. Generation after genera-

---

* " We look before and after,
  And pine for what is not,
  E'en our sincerest laughter
  With some pain is fraught,
Our sweetest songs are those which tell of saddest thought."
                                                SHELLEY.

tion of the old step down into the grave baffled and bewildered, vexed at the dreary retrospect, mortified at the memory of long years eagerly wasted in following " light that led astray;" mourning over brilliant banners torn and soiled, over heights still unscaled, over fields and trenches filled with the martyrs of Humanity. The drama can be only half discerned, or half played out ; or it may be that we have not yet got the clue to the meaning of the Most High.

Yet perhaps, if we consider patiently enough, some conclusions may be reached, some light may be seen to move over the dark and restless waters, imperfect and fragmentary indeed, yet not altogether inadequate, —not enough for a philosophic scheme, nor yet for a dogmatic creed, but enough for a trusting faith, enough to guide and quiet us in life, enough to enable us to bear to die.

———

That life was given us to be enjoyed few men in their sober senses, not distracted by unendurable anguish or rendered morbid by a perverse theology, have ever seriously dreamed of doubting. The analogy of the lower animals confirms the common consciousness. Human infancy holds the same language. The brutes that perish, but never speculate, and the young whose native instincts are not yet marred by thought, alike listen to nature and alike are joyous. The earth is sown with pleasures, as the Heavens are studded with stars—wherever the conditions of existence are unsophisticated. Scarcely a scene that is not redolent of beauty; scarcely a flower that does not breathe sweetness. Not one of our senses that, in its healthy state, is not an avenue to enjoyment. Not one of our faculties that it is not a delight to exercise. Provision is made for the happiness of every disposition and of every taste—the active, the contemplative, the sensuous, the ethereal. Provision is made for the happiness of every age, for dancing infancy, for glowing youth, for toiling manhood, for reposing age. So clear does this seem to our apprehension, that we do not hesitate to pronounce that a man who has not been happy in life has missed one of the aims of his existence ; he has failed of fulfilling the Creator's purpose ; his career has been a *carrière manquée.* Exceptional cases there may be, as there are anomalous organisations: these are among the "insoluble problems" of philosophy. But if a man with the material of enjoyment around him and virtuously within his reach, walks God's earth wilfully and obstinately with a gloomy spirit and an ascetic temper, closing his eye to beauty, shutting up his heart to joy, paying his orisons in groans and making misery his worship, we feel assured that he is contravening his Maker's design in endowing him with life; he is perverting His gifts; he is just as truly running counter to God's will by being intentionally wretched as by intentionally doing wrong.

Of course, as we all know, there are circumstances that peremptorily forbid happiness, circumstances when it can only be purchased by such a dereliction of duty as robs it of all its innocence and nearly all its zest, circumstances under which we are called "to endure hardness, as good soldiers of Jesus Christ." These cases, wherein happiness would be sinful, are just as much, *but no more*, the ordainments of Providence as those more common ones wherein happiness is natural and right: What we mean to assert as a truth which writes itself in sunbeams on the Soul, is, that God has given us the joys of earth to be *relished*, not to be neglected, or depreciated, or forbidden ; to be gratefully accepted as bounties, not to be avoided as snares and perils; that He has scattered them in our path, to gladden and to smoothe, not to tantalize or tempt; that He has graciously called us to the rich banquet of life, not that we may shrink from this wholesome viand lest poison may lurk beneath its surface, nor look coldly and repellently on that delicious fruit as if its beauty were deceptive and unreal, nor refuse that splendid flower, because its colours must fade, and because thorns may be mingled with its leaves, nor comport ourselves either as if we were superior to the weakness of enjoyment, or as if we waited for a nobler feast; but that we should partake of all that He has given with the relish of an unspoiled nature, the moderation of a wise spirit, and the emotion of a thankful heart.

Divines, in that surplice of conventional phraseology which they wear once a week, tell us that Christianity teaches us to look upon the joys of earth as hollow, worthless, transitory, "not to be compared to the glory that shall be revealed," snares to the weak soul, stumbling-blocks to the feeble knees, things to be scorned by those who have in prospect the splendours of a higher world. "We have not so learned Christ." That the joys of earthly life are poor and worthless is an idle lie. That these joys are pale, partial and passing, when compared with the ineffable beatitudes of that world " which the glory of God doth enlighten," in a degree which language cannot measure, we need no words to tell us. *But what of that?* The bliss of Heaven is *yonder*, is future, is unseen; the bliss of earth is *here*, is present, is felt. God has given us the one, *now:* he has not given us the other *yet.* He is not so poor in felicities or so niggard in his bounty that he has not wherewithal to furnish forth two worlds. He does not give us our choice of the two: he gives us, conditionally, both. If Nature is indeed His book, and if we are competent to decipher even the simplest words of His handwriting, He has meant us to be happy here *and* hereafter, perfectly happy hereafter, partially happy here. And *virtue*, not *misery*, is the appointed road to heaven. We are to earn the joys of a Higher existence, not by scorning, but by using, all the gifts of God in this.

It is high time that on this subject we should in some way establish a conformity between our professions and our practice; that we should no longer say one thing and do another; that integrity and self-government should not both be broken down, as they now are, by the established conventionalism of raising a standard that cannot be followed, and pursuing, under protest, a conduct too natural to be rationally abandoned, but on which a formal condemnation is periodically uttered, and for which an act of Indemnity as it were has to be periodically passed. The mischief done to the ingenuous mind in its aspirations after truth and virtue by this flagrant discrepancy between what is affirmed to be right and what it feels to be inevitable, passes calculation.' The moment we clearly recognise that the morality which we hear preached is a code to be listened to, not practised, that moment the *premièr pas qui coûte* has been taken, and the broad way that leadeth to destruction has been thrown open before us. It is absolutely essential, then, that our preaching should be brought into harmony with, not our habitual practice, not the low-pitched level of a virtue which ordinary men find easy, but the fair possibilities of *human* goodness and the wholesome instincts of a nature fresh from the hand of the Creator. It cannot be right to preach anything which is not true; it cannot be right to exhort to anything which is not natural, which is not possible, and which would not be desirable if it were. It is not right therefore to represent this earth as a vale of tears, this life as a weary pilgrimage, the profuse and marvellous beauties that surround us as the concealing flowers scattered over pitfalls, the innocent joys of existence as trials sent to test our virtue in rejecting them, the pure and fond affections of the heart as snares against which we should be on our guard, or as weaknesses to which the Christian ought to rise superior. It is not right to exhort us to "Love not the world, neither the things of the world," in the bald and naked parlance of ordinary preachers. It cannot be right to preach, "Take no thought for the morrow, what ye shall eat, or what ye shall drink, or wherewithal shall ye be clothed," for a man who should practise this would be held guilty of something worse than folly. It is time that those who assume the position of beacon lights and guides should take serious counsel with themselves, and ascertain what they really think, and say nothing but what they actually mean.

Now, of three things we are all in our hearts convinced. We know that many of the best men have been also the happiest. We have all known some men, and possibly more women, on whom the sunshine of God's smile most obviously rested :—

> "Glad hearts, without reproach or blot
> Who do Thy will and know it not,—"

whose hearts were filled with every human affection, fond clinging, passionate, tender ; whose healthy and happy organization tasted with intensest relish every innocent pleasure of a beckoning world; whose fresh pure spirits were a perpetual fountain of delight ; on whose soul all sweet breezes of life and nature played as on a well-tuned harp, and brought forth sounds of richest melody which of themselves were a hymn of praise ; who loved God the more for loving the world which He had made so much; on whom it was impossible not to believe that His eye rested with far other satisfaction and approval than on the sour ascetic or the rigid Pharisee.

Again; the desire of earthly happiness is implanted deep in every human heart. It is instinctive, universal, ineradicable. It is not the highest spring of human effort, but it is the most widely felt and the most intensely active; and will remain such till, in the course of upward progress and purification, the love of duty takes its place. It preserves from apathy; it prohibits despair; it stimulates to ceaseless exertion. It is impossible to believe that God would have endowed us with this eager yearning after what He never designed us to attain; that we should have been thus *ordered* to strive for an object which yet it is sinful to seek thus earnestly or to relish thus intensely. The object for which we are gifted with such an inextinguishable longing cannot be all dust and ashes, nor can it be meant that it should turn to such between our lips. God is not the author of a lie. If earthly happiness be not designed to be sought, attained, and enjoyed by men, then the teaching of Nature is deceptive and we turn over the leaves of her book in vain.

And, thirdly, no one doubts or affects to doubt that we are commanded both by instinct and the moral sense to seek and promote the happiness *of others*. To relieve suffering, to soothe distress, to confer pleasure, to dry the tears of the afflicted, to spread comfort and joy around us, is, we are taught, the noblest function in which man can spend his brightest years and his freshest strength.   Are not those whose lives and powers are devoted to the task of spreading happiness around them, felt to be, in an especial manner, "fellow labourers with God," carrying out His purposes, doing His work?   Are not those who "go about doing good" recognised at once as the peculiar disciples of His exactest image upon earth?   Do we not measure the degree in which men have deserved the gratitude of their species by the degree in which they have con- tributed to assuage trouble and diffuse peace?   And what a hollow and miserable mockery is it then to say that this life was not meant for enjoyment, when to multiply the sum of human enjoyment is felt and pro- claimed to be the most virtuous, sacred, obligatory, god- like work in which Life can be spent !

Nor is there anything in the example of Christ, con- sidered with its context, which in the least militates against this view.   Observe, we know only one year or three years of Christ's life.   Of the thirty years that preceded his public appearance we know absolutely nothing.   Of the brief period of his public career, we know only a few fragmentary facts, selected as illus- trating one phase of his character.   We have no reason whatever for supposing that he did not enjoy life during youth and early manhood.   We have no reason whatever for assuming that, before the stern solemnity of his mission threw all softer and gentler emotions into the shade and gradually en- grossed his whole Being, he had not relished, with all the intensity of a healthy nature and a sensitive organization, every innocent pleasure and every holy and serene delight. We have indications, that, even when his soul was absorbed in the terrible grandeur and the toilsome difficulties of the " work which had been given him to do," he was still keenly alive to the exquisite beauties of that world he was to quit so soon, and to the enjoyment of that domestic peace to which he could dedicate only moments so brief and rare. But even were it not so; even if we had reason to suppose that Jesus of Nazareth, consecrated from his youth to a task that demanded the most unlimited self-sacrifice and the intensest concentration of every faculty and feeling, had no sensibility to spare for the beauty or the bliss of earth; that

> " He looked on all the joys of Time
> With undesiring eyes,"

the fact would have no practical antagonism to our position. From time to time God raises up individuals, cast in a special mould, and set apart for a special destiny, vowed to a special work, men whose entire power, thought, sensibilities seem to lie in the channel of their appointed calling, whose mission is their Joy,* the fiery energy of ·whose purpose burns up every other longing, the magnitude of whose glorious aim

---

* " Yet there are some to whom a strength is given,
  A Will, a self-constraining Energy,
  A Faith that feeds upon no earthly hope,
  Which never thinks of Victory, combating
  Because it ought to combat, ...

dwarfs and smothers every other object. Of such Christ was the first and noblest : but such are no gauges or examples for ordinary men, in ordinary times, with ordinary powers ;—save in this, that moments and circumstances come to most of us some time in our lives, which if we are truly noble we shall seize with gladness, when we, like they, are called upon to forego the lower for the higher office; to remember that though life was given us for enjoyment, it was given us for something nobler also ; and that the very happiness of which it was designed to be the instrument and the stage can only be conclusively promoted by the willing immolation, when needed, of itself. God, through the voice of Nature, calls the mass of men to be happy : He calls a few among them to the grander task of being severely but serenely sad.

The case, however, as thus far stated, is but fragmentary. The happiness of the Human Race is one of the designs of God, but our own individual happiness must not be made our first or our direct aim. To the mass of men, as a rule, enjoyment will come if we fulfil the laws of our Being ; but it was not for this alone, nor for this first, that Life was given. If we set it before us as our chief object; if we pursue it with conscious

---

And, conscious that to find in Martyrdom
The stamp and signet of most perfect Life
Is all the science that Mankind can reach,
Rejoicing fights and still rejoicing falls."

The Combat of Life, by R. M. Milnes.

and relentless purpose ; still more if we seek it by any short cuts or private pathways of our own, or by any road save that by which Providence has prescribed without engaging that it shall lead to any special or certain goal on earth, we may, or we may not, be happy; but assuredly we shall have failed in carrying out a further design of the Creator—at least as indisputable as the first, namely, *The Moral Progress and Perfection of the Individual and the Race.* Let us not " speak unto ourselves smooth things and prophesy deceits." The Cup of Life which God offers to our lips is not always sweet; it is an unworthy weakness to endeavour to persuade ourselves of such a falsehood : but, sweet or bitter, it is ours to drink it without murmur or demur. It is not true that those who obey the laws of God, and listen to his voice, and follow where he calls, are *always* thereby taking the surest and directest way to an enjoyed existence : sometimes His finger points in a precisely opposite direction. Often — usually indeed—" he gives happiness in, gives it as what Aristotle calls an ἐπιγινόμενον τέλος ; but he gives it with a mysterious and uncontrollable Sovereignty; it is no part of the terms on which He admits us to His service, still less is it the end which we may propose to ourselves on entering His service.* Happiness he gives to whom He will, or leaves to the Angel of

---

* Ask we no more—content with these
   Let present comfort, pleasure, ease,
   As Heaven shall with them, come and go—
   The Secret this of Rest below.—KEBLE.

Nature to distribute among those who fulfil the laws on which *it* depends. But to serve God and love him is higher and better than happiness, though it be with wounded feet, and bleeding brow, and hearts loaded with sorrow."

We have already dwelt enough on our conviction that the progress of humanity, the improvement of the world, the mitigation of its anomalies, the extinction of its woes, the eradication of its vices,—in a word, the *realisation of the ideal* of life, is the great design of God and the great work of man. But though the perfectation of the *Race* is the great, it is clear that it is not the sole, purpose or significance of life. The perfectation of the *Individual* is indicated by marks just as obvious. We are sent here and endowed thus not only to do our utmost for the improvement and progress of the world, but to do our utmost also for the development, utilisation, purification, and strengthening of our own individual natures. The riddle of life cannot be even approximately read without this assumption. For, obedience to the laws of God written on the face of Nature, the cultivation of those virtues and affections whose sacredness is written on our hearts, and on which the beauty and the joy of life depend, lead to such progressive excellence. Moreover the advance and elevation of Humanity is most surely promoted by whatever wholesomely, harmoniously, and permanently develops the individual man. It is by the enlightened and disinterested service of his fellow-being that he most surely strengthens and idealises his own nature. He cannot carry forward one of the purposes of Providence without *ipso facto* contributing to the other. And finally, there is one dark page in the philosophy of life which no other creed can irradiate. We mean the fact, so perplexing yet so constant, of men whose youth and maturity are spent in struggle and in failure, and who attain wisdom and virtue only at the close of their career; who begin to see clearly only when clear vision has grown useless; who become thoroughly qualified for the work of life and the service of humanity just as life is ebbing away and the arena of earthly activity is closed to them. Man sometimes seems ordained to spend his allotted span in sharpening his tools and learning how to use them, and to be called out of the workshop the moment his industrial education is complete   If one set of facts point irresistibly to the conclusion that he was sent on earth to do God's work in mending, beautifying, and guiding it, the other more than insinuate the inference that the world is a school where he is to learn his craft, but not the only scene on which he is to practise it, a whetstone on which he is to shape and sharpen his faculties, a sort of *corpus vile* on which he is to experiment, not for its sake only, but for his own. We accept both conclusions : and probably the inconsistency between them is more apparent than real. If the first design had been the only one or the most pressing, the mode in which it is carried out would indeed be perplexingly slow and indirect. Its being interwoven with the second may suggest a clue out of the labyrinth.　God meant man to perfect the world in and by perfecting his own nature : for the latter task MAN has, perhaps, but this brief fragment of Time; for the former God has the whole long life-time of the HUMAN RACE.

Life then is meant for *enjoyment* and for *toil;* but it is meant also that the enjoyment should never be unmingled or supreme, and that the toil should never be wholly remunerative or successful.　This is, then, designed to be an *unsatisfying* world. No hand-writing on the wall was ever more startlingly distinct than this.　The conclusions of Ecclesiastes are echoed by every man to whom experience has given the faculty and the materials of thought.　The intensest joy we have ever felt has been usually so alloyed. The most unalloyed joy we have ever felt has been so passing.

> Medio de fonte leporum
> Surgit amari aliquid quod ipsis in floribus angat.

We can fancy, too, so much purer and brighter than we have known.　Nay, we have caught glimpses of so much that we could neither grasp nor retain.　The actual has been very beautiful; but it is insufficient in the view of a possible far lovelier still.

> " Science for man unlocks her varied store
> And gives enough to wake the wish for more.
> Enough of good to kindle strong desire:
> Enough of ill to damp the rising fire;
> Enough of joy and sorrow, fear and hope,

> To fan desire and give the passions scope;
> Enough of disappointment, sorrow, pain,
> To seal the Wise Man's sentence ' all is vain,'
> And quench the wish to live those years again !"

Then the labours of the ablest and most successful are so disappointing and unfruitful. Of a thousand seeds sown, and watered with blood and tears, only one ripens to the full ear. A thousand soldiers die in the trenches for one who mounts the breach. Half our efforts are in a wrong direction, and the other half are too clumsy or feeble to attain their aim. No! if, at the close of life we can say we have enjoyed much happiness and done some good, we shall have cause for deep gratitude and humble hope; but a sense of complacency, of satisfaction, as of a part fulfilled and a work accomplished, can belong to no man who looks back over his course with a single eye, and in the light of an approaching change. The finer the spirit, the profounder the insight, the more unconquerable is this feeling of disappointment;— an irresistible intimation that this world was not given us to be *rested in*, to be acquiesced in as the only one, or the brightest one; a conviction and a suggestion sent to weaken our passionate attachment to a scene which else it might have been too hard to quit.

Finally, we must conclude that the problem of Man's Wherefore, Whence, and Whither, was meant to be insoluble. When we reflect upon the number of consummate intellects, gifted with every variety of mental endowment and rich in every moral excellence which gives clearness to the vision and depth to the spiritual intuition, who age after age have exhausted thought in fruitless efforts to discern the word of the great Enigma, it seems idle to fancy that we can be more fortunate than they. Centuries have added scarcely one new fact to the materials on which reason has to work nor perfected a single one of the faculties by which that work is to be done. We possess scarcely a single item of knowledge of Divine or of Human Nature which was not as familiar to Plato and to Job as to ourselves: assuredly we have no profounder poetic insight than the one, no finer philosophic instrument than the other. What baffled them may well baffle us also.

Of the dark riddles and incomprehensible anomalies and strange perplexities of which life is full, some very few we *can* unravel; of others we can discern just enough to guess at the solution. The deepest and the saddest must ever remain to try our faith and to grieve our hearts. We see enough to make us believe that there *is* a solution, and that that solution is such as will accord with the serene perfections of the Godhead. We have light enough to walk by, to tread the few steps that lie immediately before us: We need not then murmur or despair or doubt because we cannot see our way through the thick forest and to the end of the long journey. Soldiers must often be content to fight their appointed battle without insisting on understanding the whole plan of the campaign.

That the good are often wretched, and the worthless prosperous and happy ; that sunshine and sorrow follow no rule of effort or desert ; that the beautiful and noble are cut off in youth, and the stained and mean drag their ignominy through a long career; these things we can conceive may be rectified hereafter and elsewhere. That those whose life is devoted to labouring in God's vineyard and carrying out His holy purposes are perpetually called away in the midst of their widest usefulness and on the eve of some signal and fruitful victory; while others whose whole aim seems to be to violate his commands and counterwork his benevolent designs live out their threescore years and ten in mischief and in power,—is a puzzle to which even our philosophy can sometimes suggest the key; since history has shown us that the progress of Humanity is now and then best served by the triumph of the bad man and the discomfiture of the good cause. The infinite slowness with which man advances to his final goal ; the feebleness and vacillation with which he works out his allotted destiny; his frequent apparent retrogressions into barbarism and iniquity ; the ebbs and flows of the tide of civilisation : to all these we may be reconciled by the supposition that perhaps the imperfect conditions of our Being render this progress at once the surest and the fastest possible. But there are stranger and gloomier perplexities than these. There are chastisements that do not chasten ; there are trials that do not purify and sorrows that do not elevate ; there are pains and privations that harden the tender heart without softening the stubborn will; there is "light that leads astray;" there are virtues that dig their own grave. There are pure searchers after truth whose martyr spirit has never reached the martyr's crown, whose struggle for the light which God has commanded them to seek has only led them into "a land of darkness, as darkness itself, and where the light is as darkness." There are souls to be reckoned by the million, low, grovelling, undeveloped, desperately bad, and *which could scarcely, save by miracle, have been other than they are.* What becomes of them? Why are they here? What do they mean?—It is hard to find no answer to such questions. It would be yet worse to simulate content with official answers at once inadequate and consciously untrue,

VI.

DE PROFUNDIS.

"Obstinate questionings
Of sense and outward things;
Fallings from us, vanishings:
Blank misgivings of a creature
Moving about in worlds not realised."
WORDSWORTH.—*Intimations o*

It is not by shirking difficulties that we can remove them or escape them; nor by evading the perplexing problems of life or speculation that we can hope to solve them; nor by saying, "Hush, hush!" to every over-subtle questioner that the question can be answered or the asker silenced. Men cannot go on for ever living upon half-exploded shams; keeping obsolete laws with admittedly false preambles on their Statute book; professing creeds only half credited and quite incredible; standing and sleeping on suspected or on recognised volcanoes; erecting both their dwellings and their temples on ice which the first dreaded rays of sunlight they know must melt away. We cannot always keep clouds and darkness round about us; and it is a miserable condition alike for men and nations to feel dependent upon being able permanently to enforce blindness and maintain silence; to live as it were intellectually on sufferance; to shiver under an uneasy semi-consciousness that all their delicate fabrics of Thought and Peace lie at the mercy of the first pertinacious questioner or rude logician. Yet how rare is the robust faith or the simple courage which boldly interrogates the darkness,

believing that thus only can the light be reached!
The question may not lead us to the truth; but at
least it saves us from sheltering ourselves behind
known or suspected error.

How few of us sincerely and confidently believe
our own creeds either in philosophy or religion!
How seldom do we dare either to *think* them out, or
act them out! Take one example, which opens a
wide field of perplexing speculation.

The received doctrine is that God puts a soul into
every human being at his birth,—*i.e.*, that whenever
man makes a body, God makes a soul, or sends a
pre-existing soul, to inhabit it; or that, in some
mysterious fashion, with the commencement of earthly
life commences also the life of an immortal nature.
On the assumption, then, of man's free agency, (an
essential postulate of all intelligible reasoning on
moral questions) it would seem to lie in man's decision how many souls shall be created or incarnated,
and when, and pretty much to what earthly conditions
and influences. On his determination, or passion,
or it may on his indulgence of a momentary
appetite, depends the question whether an immortal
spirit shall be called into existence, and shall encounter—*having no voice in the matter*—not only the
risks and sufferings of this short human life, but the
incalculable and fearful chances of an unending life to
come. Can this really be so? Are we prepared to
adopt this corollary, or rather this plain statement of
our belief? Yet how can we avoid it? If man has

a soul, when else can it come to him except at birth ? If man's act originate the soul as well as the body, if the soul be an attribute or necessary accompaniment of the body, then this is either materialism, or it makes man the creator of an immortal spirit. He has an unlimited, or at least an indefinite, credit on the Treasury of Spiritual Being.

There is yet another perplexity that meets us here. The moment of birth is a singularly critical and dangerous one. Perhaps our life is never in such jeopardy as at its outset. Whether separate existence shall begin, whether the infant shall breathe and live, or sink back into the limbo of inchoate organisations, often depends upon the skill of the midwife, upon a movement or a stimulus administered in time. Do the awful issues of eternal life really hang upon a thread like this ?

It will be replied that, as an indisputable fact, we know it *does* depend pretty much upon man's will or caprice, or the competence of an accoucheur, whether a human being shall be born to the conditions and casualties of this earthly life; and the difficulties surrounding the other problem are only the difficulties surrounding this one, enormously magnified and extended. Well, then, suppose the assumption of man's power to call immortal beings into existence acquiesced in—no means of escape from it being apparent, save the purely material hypothesis. We proceed.

The Calvinist believes that only a small fraction of the human race can be saved, and that the vast residue will be doomed to endless and unspeakable torments ; that "strait is the gate and narrow the way that leadeth unto life, and few there be that find it ;" that the elect are scanty and the reprobate are legion ; that, of any given number who come into the world, the overwhelming majority will be damned. There is no mistake about it. He does not mince matters. He knows, he believes, he says every day, it is the salient article of his creed, that ninety-nine out of every hundred are predestined to eternal suffering ; that, if he has ten children, it is *probable* that all, it is *certain* that nearly all, will burn in hell for everlasting ages ; that, in fact, except in cases incalculably rare, his married life is spent in furnishing souls for Satan, poor babies for endless misery and damnation, helpless victims for the wrath of God. If he believed all this, would he ever dare to become a father ? If, believing all this, he yet does so dare, where shall we find words strong enough to denounce his hardened and horrible barbarity ? Marriage in itself, the mere condition which renders such consequences possible, must be a sin which no other iniquity can equal. For it cannot be that he believes all his own children will be saved. He cannot lay this flattering unction to his conscience His creed does not permit him to do so. He knows that the Divine wrath is so consuming, and the Divine mercy so scant, and the rescued so incalculably few, that the chances are almost infinite against any child he has. He cannot imagine, as in worldly matters he might, as in spiritual matters other Christians can, that he may by prayer and training secure the salvation of his children. No! his creed tells him that all this is settled beforehand, and cannot be affected by any act or negligence of his. Now, if any earthly father knew that probably all his children—that assuredly nine out of ten—would be seized by ruthless conscription and sent to drag out their whole lives in the severest anguish, who, with a spark of affection or humanity or decent sense of justice, would ever dream of marriage or paternity? Yet the Calvinist knows that they are destined irrevocably to a fate immeasurably more horrible and lasting, yet he multiplies without mercy or remorse? *Does he believe his creed?*

Again. Most Christians now adopt a happier and less dishonouring creed. They are beginning more and more to trust in a good God. They profess to believe that Salvation is for all, and within reach of all, though they differ as to the terms of its attainment. They hold that sedulous prayer, and due care in bringing up their children in the true faith and in sound practices, will, as a rule, secure their eternal existence in indescribable enjoyments. Many, an increasing number, stretch their charity wider still, and indulge in a more universal hope. They believe— and it seems to uninjured lay intellects a necessary corollary from God's goodness that they should believe —that *all* will be ultimately saved, though possibly through much suffering and after various stages of probation; that of all human creatures who once enter upon earthly life, endless and ineffable felicity will be the certain and final lot :—

> "That not one Life shall be destroyed
>   Or cast as rubbish to the void,
>   When God hath made the pile complete."

It follows that on them is conferred the blessed privilege of calling into being nearly as many deferred angels as they please, of creating reversionary heirs of glory and of bliss as surely and as largely as an earthly monarch can create Peers. This being their creed, (and, granting the original premises we see nothing to gainsay in the inferential superstructure,) their logical course of action would seem to be clearly pointed out. They must multiply as fast as they can : not an hour must be wasted, nor an opportunity lost, nor a possible agent unemployed. Celibacy becomes almost a sin, at the least a neglect of duty, a foregoing of privilege, a selfish omission of the means of conferring such ultimate happiness as we can scarcely dream of here. There can be no need for us to pause to consider whether we can support the children we bring into the world, transmit to them healthy organisations, maintain them in comfort or in life, place them in decent or in morally advantageous positions :—all these are matters of very secondary moment, for what is any amount or severity of transient suffering in a probationary state in comparison with that marvellous and enduring felicity which, once in life, is their secure inheritance at last? It may be that the earlier the death the sooner the desired haven can be reached. All that parental care and education can effect is to make their period of suffering and training terminate with this earth. A footing once gained thereon, the rest is a mere question of time, and of the greater or less degree of comfort in which the intervening time is passed before the future angel enters on his inheritance. The greatest benefactor of his species must, therefore, be the man who is parent of most children, and multiplication be the worthiest function of Humanity.

Yet who can admit such conclusions? and who can regard as sound the premises from which they flow?

It would seem clear that, in the eyes or according to the doctrine of the orthodox, those who believe that salvation is to be obtained certainly, and only, through the name of Christ, procreation must be a sin, or at least a calamity and a cruelty among the heathen —innocent or virtuous only among the nations of Christendom; a benevolence in England, a barbarity in China or Thibet.

The pious Theist, who conceives that immortal life is conferred at birth, but that immortal happiness is to be purchased by virtue and desert alone, should regard paternity as *permissible* only where virtue is *possible*, and as *righteous* only where virtue is *probable*. Yet clearly this is not nature's view of the matter, since those classes who are placed in circumstances least favourable to improvement and spiritual development, usually have the procreative habit and faculty the strongest.

———

On any theory it is not to be denied that the difficulties in the way of those who believe in a future life and a spiritual being are extreme. With our limited capacities and scanty knowledge it could scarcely have been otherwise. Perhaps the following train of thought may do something towards suggesting a solution. If birth be in reality the creation of an undying soul with the alternative of future happiness or misery presented to it, *according to its use of this life,* and all that man (by Divine permission or connivance) does is to call into existence a *candidate* for a glorious or a dreadful future, then it is equitably essential that the possibility of the former should be truly *within its choice,*—that it should be placed in circumstances and endowed with sufficient strength and freedom of volition to render its decision *really optional*; that is, that the better fate should be distinctly attainable by its powers and with its inherited or congenital propensities and dispositions. Can we say that this free choice is *bonâ fide* secured to all, or to most ? Yet clearly, if there are human creatures to whom this real option is virtually denied by surrounding conditions, or vicious or defective education, or faulty organization, or innate perverse and ungovernable propensities, or withheld opportunities, then, either they have no soul, or that soul is not immortal, or other lives of fairer probation will be granted them, or—God is indeed the Being he is represented to be in the blasphemies of so many Christian sects. There seems no way out of this inference.

Probably, however, what God bestows at birth is a *germ*, not a finished Entity—not an immortal soul, but a nature capable of being *worked up into a soul* worthy of immortality, an organization rich in the strangest and grandest potentialities—not a possession, but an opportunity—not an inheritance, but the chance of winning one. Perhaps it may be only such natures as develope adequately and in the right direction in this life, that will be heirs of Heaven, and that all others may, as it were, never pass beyond the embryonic or earthly stage of existence. The question of their development must depend upon their inherited organizations combined with the aggregate of influences which surround them. Those who believe in the Darwinian theory of evolution, and measure the distance which man has travelled, according to that grand hypothesis, from the Monad to the Saint and the Philosopher, need have no difficulty in conceiving the scarcely vaster progress which our suggestion postulates. Yet it cannot be disguised that, even on this supposition, we come upon a tremendous moral perplexity, only less startling than those we have already commented upon. For what awful issues then depend upon the parents, often ignorant, often destitute, often

brutal, usually quite insensible or only half awakened
to their gigantic responsibilities! It lies with them
to say—or rather it is determined by casualties and
external circumstances, by organization healthy or
morbid, by location, by opportunities, by a thousand
influences of which they themselves are scarcely more
than the victims· and the shuttlecocks—whether the
children they bring into the world shall be mere
mortal creatures or immortal angels. Is this conjecture
more credible than those we have discarded ? Indeed,
is *any* conception attractive, or reposing, or truly credible
in this "land of darkness, as darkness itself, and where
the Light is as darkness."

"Behold! we know not anything."

Another set of speculations, nearly as perplexing,
must often have been presented to thoughtful minds.
Few travellers trained to appreciate beauty and magnificence in all their manifestations can have surveyed
the gorgeous temples in which the early Indians and
Egyptians enshrined their grotesque idols and their
strange conceptions of Deity, without the half involuntary exclamation:—"Thank God for a false religion! or
at least for the marvellous productions it has inspired."
The same sentiment rises still more irresistibly in the
minds of cultivated Christians, when standing in the
plains of Baalbec or Palmyra, by the waste shores of
Pæstum, or at the foot of the unrivalled Parthenon, and
thinking what sort of gods were they whose worship
suggested those exquisite monuments to the finest

races of the Ancient World, and carried taste almost to inspiration :—" Thank God for a false religion !" A similar impression forces just the same utterance from the zealous Protestant, if he be a man of culture as well as zeal, as he comes forth from the Duomo of Florence or Milan, from St Mark's at Venice or St Peter's at Rome, and marvels at the glorious structures which intense devotion to what he deems little less than anti-Christian faith could rear in the dark days of Catholic supremacy. " Thank God ! " he exclaims, " for a false religion ! " And then as he turns homeward, and stands lost in admiration near the front of Salisbury, or Westminster, or Lincoln, or any other of our own cathedrals, he hears his phrase echoed at his side by the Methodist or Ranter, issuing from a bare, unlovely, whitewashed Bethel in a neighbouring alley, who, half-shocked at the unholy thought, can yet scarcely deny that even the surpassing purity of his own creed does but imperfectly atone for the comparatively wretched house of God in which it has to be repeated. The contrast between the temples inspired by the false faith and the true is painful even to him.

But false religions have inspired grander monuments than temples and cathedrals, and demand our gratitude for achievements of a nobler character. They have been the parents of courage, obedience, endurance, and self-sacrifice. In proportion to the measure of their truth, according to the tenets of their creeds and the fancied attributes of their Deities, they have guided for good or evil the morals of mankind; but they have given to their votaries power to do and to bear, with little direct reference to the characteristics of the faith itself. Often the gods worshipped have been hideous, monstrous, impossible, immoral; often the doctrines held have been revolting and maleficent; often the purest faiths have been disfigured by the most incongruous corruptions: but good or bad, true or false, they have nearly all had one feature in common,—the faculty they inspired of dethroning the present and suppressing self. The *direction* of their influence has been determined by their essence:—the *amount* of that influence, their motive power over humanity, has been in proportion to the absoluteness of the credence they commanded. They have inspired the sublimest virtues and the most frightful crimes; but men have died and slain with about equal confidence for all alike; all alike have had their martyrs and their heroes; life, ease, pleasure, earthly possessions have been readily sacrificed by the devotees of every faith, at the dictate of its authorities and in the certainty of its rewards. In thanking God for false religions, therefore, as for true ones, we are grateful for that which is common to them all,—the power they possess of inspiring human fortitude and human effort.

Recognising, then, that many false religions have exercised in some respects an elevating influence on mankind, and that others, in which truth and error are mingled in various proportions, still largely operate for good, we perceive, too, that in all cases they have this strengthening and ennobling grace, mainly if not entirely, *because they are firmly held,* because no doubt mingles with the faith of the worshipper, or impairs the blind simplicity of his devotion. If he had any misgivings he could not "greatly dare or nobly die." It is only his *certainty* that sends him to the battle-field, or sustains him at the stake, or enables him to bear up through the long and weary martyrdom of life. The very salt of his religion to him lies in his *absolute* conviction of its truth. If he were not positively certain of its divine origin and sanctions, it would lose its magic hold upon his actions and emotions. Now, it is precisely this *certainty* (to which all religions pretend and which is essential to the influence of them all) which, nevertheless, thoughtful and sincere minds know to be the one element of falsehood, the one untrue dogma, common to them all. They may differ on everything else ; the Gods they proclaim may be as discrepant as light and darkness, the articles of their creed may be very approximately true or very manifestly false, their codes of morals may be severally beneficent or noxious, the spirit breathing through them may be the loveliest or the harshest ;—but they all agree in affirming that their faith came to them by more or less direct revelation from on High, admits of no question, and contains no flaw. *In this they all lie :* (all except one, at least, every one admits)—the votaries of each believe that all others lie except their own ; philosophers insist that there is and can be no exception. We Europeans know that the Orientals err in maintaining that Buddha or Vishnu was incarnated in this form or in that, and taught the true faith to man. We Christians know that Jupiter and Minerva never appeared in human shape to give consistence and sanction to the Pagan creeds. We Jews are certain that the law given to Moses on Mount Sinai was never abrogated by a later and sublimer prophet. We Protestants know that the Holy Spirit never dictated to the successors of St Peter the strange dogmas of salvation which those successors are now issuing in its name to votaries who are bound to accept them as absolute and certain truth. We Unitarians and other Dissidents entirely repudiate many of the doctrines which the English Church submissively receives from councils and congresses at which the Spirit of the Most High was asserted to preside; and what the orthodox regard as certain we reject as utterly unsound. And, finally, we Philosophers and men of science know with a conviction, at least as positive as that of any of these Believers, that they are all wrong, that no such dicta have ever been delivered, and that no such knowledge about the Unknowable can be ever reached.

It is, therefore, just this special claim to certainty (to absolute authoritative truth), *which is the inspiring and life-giving power of all religions, which is also the one false element common to them all.* Here then is the startling conclusion alluded to at the outset. It seems to follow that error is necessary to float and vivify truth, that religions hold and exercise their mighty and elevating sway over human imagination and volition, by virtue of the one fundamental assumption or assertion common to them all, and which in all alike is false*.

———

The matter lies in very small compass, and a few words will do as well as many to state it. True

———

* It would lead us too far from our immediate subject to discuss how much the errors mingled with the belief of the ordinary Christian world aided the spread of Christianity at the outset, and serve to give currency and acceptance to it now. Many of these, which we may term *auxiliary* errors, would of course be denied to be errors by the orthodox;—but there is one which has long been recognised and proved to be such, as to which there can be no dispute. Probably of all the secondary causes which contributed to the rapid advance of Christianity in the early times, and gave it its wonderful power over the conduct of believers, none was so effective as the doctrine which it preached, and which appears to have been universally accepted both by Apostles and Disciples,—of the approaching end of the world. No other conviction could have so transformed (as we know that it did transform) the whole nature and views of those who held it. Yet none could be more erroneous. [See *Creed of Christendom*, pp. 181 and 270.] Macaulay has a striking passage in one of his earliest writings, depicting the marvellous aid which the anthropomorphism early imported into Christian conceptions rendered to the progress of the new faith. (*Essays*, i., p. 22). "God, the uncreated, the incomprehensible, the invisible, attracted few worshippers. A Philosopher might admire so noble a conception, but the crowd turned away in disgust from words which presented no image to their minds. It was before the Deity embodied in a human form, walking among men, partaking of their infirmities, leaning on their bosoms, weeping over their graves, slumbering in the manger, bleeding on the cross,—that the prejudices of the Synagogue, and the doubts of the Academy, and the pride of the Portico, and the fasces of the Lictor, and the swords of thirty legions, were humbled in the dust."

religions—that is, religions destitute of this one indispensable false dogma—would not suffice either to guide,
support, inspire, or restrain men, as men now are, nor
to fascinate their imaginations, nor to command their
unhesitating allegiance and submission.   Their imperfect culture, and their low stage of intelligence need
and demand absolute *certainty* and *positive* dogma.
Doctrines which resulted from a mere balance of
probabilities, which were, and avowed themselves to
be, simply the conclusions of mature and enlightened
reason, would have no adequate hold on their belief.
Laws of conduct laid down as imperative, merely as
being conformable to the sound instincts of sound
natures, and as plainly conducive or indispensable to
the good of mankind and of themselves in the long
run, would have no adequate hold on their obedience.
The uncultured mass of mankind—especially in crises
of passion—will neither be moved nor curbed by
being told, or even convinced : " If you act thus or
thus you will contravene the purposes of your Creator,
and injure your fellow creatures and yourself." They
need (what, indeed, in ultimate analysis is merely the
same assertion in a coarser and more concrete form), the
announcement "God spake these words and said,"—and
" Heaven or hell will be your portion according as you
observe them or disobey them." They can realise and
bow down before a revelation which was issued from a
cloud or behind a veil, amid thunder and darkness,
and uttered in their own vernacular by a human
or anthropomorphic voice, — all which accessaries

should in truth be felt as so many reasons for distrusting it; but a revelation whispered by the still small voice of the Most High to the purified consciences and the exercised reason of the selected sages of the race, seems to them announced on mere human authority, and is set at naught at pleasure. The sages, therefore, to whom such religious and legislative wisdom has been vouchsafed—unless their love of truth transcended their love of power and their desire to serve mankind—have habitually clothed the revelations made to them with the *needed* orthodox conventional accompaniments; have falsified their creed in order to float it; have alloyed their pure metal with earthly admixture to' make it workable; and have borrowed for the sacred vision of the Prophet the fallacious but indispensable *imprimatur* of the Priest. Even among communities far removed from that ruder stage when material manifestations of the divinity are in favour, something of the same want is felt, and is supplied in something of the same fashion. The sluggishness and love of pleasure of even comparatively cultivated men need *exaggeration* respectively to stimulate or to control them. A faith, which was avowedly but the outcome of what the highest human intelligences could discover or divine, would never be clung to with credence absolute enough to take men to the stake in its behalf; scarcely even to the battle field, if the battle had not an attraction of its own. A cause, however good and noble, valued only as sober thinkers would value it,—regarded as *probably* and *on the whole* beneficent, as philosophers would express their tepid allegiance—would not inspire sufficient enthusiasm to make men either toil through a laborious life or brave a painful death. How few are the aims which it is not necessary to *over*estimate, if we are to work for them devotedly or to suffer for them gladly! How few are not indebted for their commanding fascinations to the merciful disguises, or the beautifying draperies, or the glorifying haloes, or the magnifying mists which our fancy or our ignorance throws round them!

A corollary would seem to flow from the above reflections which sounds questionable, but the fallacy lurking in which—if it be fallacious—is not easy to perceive. The time, we hope, will come, (and to hasten its arrival should be the aim of all the wise and good), when mankind will have advanced so far beyond their present moral and intellectual stage, that true religion will be as receivable and as influential as false religion is now; when error and exaggeration and mis-statements as to its origin and sanctions will no longer be essential to its dominion over the minds of men. But since, in the meantime, religions *require* for their efficacy the element of untruth of which we have spoken, in exact proportion to the ignorance, torpor, and want of enlightenment which prevail in the world,—how far may it not be permissible, perhaps our duty, tacitly to accept, to acquiesce in, or possibly even to *preach* this fundamental but indispensable misrepresentation? Was the old system of esoteric creeds worthy of the unmeasured condemnation heaped upon it in more ardent days? May it not sometimes be incumbent upon those whose function it is to direct the religious conceptions of a nation, to teach doctrines or histories they do not believe, or at least to assume and to uphold that lying legend which serves as the basis of so much invaluable truth,—of truth, moreover, that would not hold its ground among the mass of men, if the unsoundness of its basis were laid bare? The question is not one of speculative casuistry. It represents a sad and most real perplexity to thousands of conscientious minds. Probably the one safe practical conclusion in the matter will be this; to leave the fallacious foundation, even though a pervading error, alone,—so long as no noxious superstructure is built upon it,—so long as the falsehood is not thrust upon us as the gem and essence of the creed,—so long as it is not called up to warrant dishonouring views of God, doctrines adverse to human happiness and progress, mental fetters and darkness, or priestly insolence or cruelty. It is not that we would give even a momentary countenance to that purely political conception of religion which regards the Ten Commandments as a sort of "cheap defence" of property and life, God Almighty as a ubiquitous and unpaid Policeman, and Hell as a self-supporting gaol, a penal settlement at the Antipodes;—but that in the best creeds as held and promulgated by their wisest votaries, the truth they contain is so noble and beneficent, and the error so nearly confined to the original false assumption at the root, that the balance of good influence is incalculable.

> O Thou that after toil and storm
>   Mayest seem to have reached a purer air,
>   Whose faith has centre everywhere,
> Nor cares to fix itself to form.
>
> Leave thou thy sister when she prays,
>   Her early heaven, her happy views;
>   Nor thou with shadowed hints confuse
> A life that leads melodious days.
>
> Her faith through form is pure as thine,
>   Her hands are quicker unto good,
>   Oh, sacred be the flesh and blood
> To which she links a truth divine.
>
> TENNYSON.—*In Memoriam.*

One more " cry out of the depths," in reference to the oldest and perhaps darkest perplexity of all— *Prayer.*

The instinct of prayer, of appeal for help in difficulty and rescue in peril, is an inevitable consequence and correlative of belief in God, in a Being who can hear and answer, who has made us and who cares for the creatures He has made. It flows from the consciousness of our inferiority and His superiority, of our helplessness and His power. It is an original and nearly irresistible instinct, precisely similar to that which makes the child run to the mother, and the feeble cling to and entreat the strong. We can scarcely imagine its extinction. We cannot picture to ourselves what our nature would be if it were extinguished.

Yet reason and reflection, science and logic, set their face steadily against it, strive to prove the instinct unphilosophical, and are for ever at work paring the doctrine of the efficacy of prayer away. We cannot gainsay them, yet we are unable, cordially and conclusively, to accept their conclusions or to act upon them. Here, as so often in our deeper investigations, we are taught the hard lesson of intellectual humility, by finding corollaries which we cannot admit flowing clearly and strictly from premises which we cannot deny.

The absurdity of Prayer to God, with any belief in its efficacy, comes out most strongly in the practice, which dates from the rudest ages and has survived unbroken to our own,—of two armies on the eve of battle, each appealing to the same God of Hosts to crown their arms with victory. There was sense, or at least consistency, in this in the days when the gods were national deities, rival celestial powers, each of which had his special *protégés* and votaries. No words can do adequate justice to the incoherence of the practice now. Two vast crowds of men, trusting in the same Saviour and worshipping the same God, professing a religion which most solemnly denounces the bad passions raging in their bosoms and the special crime they are about to consummate, draw their swords, load their muskets, range their cannon, and while awaiting the signal to commence their mutual slaughter, kneel down, in all faith and earnestness, to implore the Lord who has condemned slaughter, to render their special slaughter efficacious. Both sets of combatants seek to enlist the Lord on their side, believing, or rather unconsciously assuming, that He is altogether such a one as themselves; believing their cause to be just, they trust that He will favóur it; fancying also, obviously, that even though it be just, He may not favour it unless specially entreated to do so; assuming, too, (unconsciously again) that He is mutable, impressible, persuadable, and can be worked upon by our prayers to do that which He would not have done without them; that is, either to take a different view of the case from that which He would otherwise have taken, or give victory to a cause which, though righteous, He would not otherwise have made to win; to change sides in short.

But the prayer of Armies to the Lord of Hosts is often far more than this, where it is fervent, and really expects to be efficacious or to weigh one iota of a grain in the scale of His eternal purposes. It is a *bonâ fide* petition, almost sublime in its unthinking *naïveté*, that He will interpose to prevent the genius of the opposing generals, the sagacity and topographical knowledge and professional care and foresight of the opposing staff, and the organising skill of the enemy's minister of war, and the dryness of the enemy's powder, and the excellence of the enemy's artillery, and the superiority of the enemy's numbers, from producing their natural, allotted, and legitimate results; and, further, that He will interfere to prevent the stupidity, cowardice, sluggishness of the suppliants, and the ineptitude and knavery of their chiefs, from reaping the fruits which a righteous decree has from all time assigned to turpitude and incapacity. Viewed in this light, the prayer becomes something like an insult. Viewed in any light, it is simply a request that the All-wise and All-mighty Ruler of the Universe will work, not a miracle but a series of miracles, will suspend the whole sequence of cause and effect on which the world depends and on which the actions of men are calculated, to meet a casual crisis in the affairs of one small section of His undeserving creatures. Even in those cases where all human sympathies go with the suppliants, where feeble but indisputable right is on the point of being crushed by overwhelming might, the prayer is still for a miraculous suspension of that pervading law in virtue of which Might, which observes the conditions of success, reigns paramount on earth over Right, which neglects or fails to fulfil them. In specifying these military prayers, we have taken the most startling case, and the one which admits of being most broadly stated; but a thousand others are virtually as illogical, though not quite so revolting to human reason.

Yet in the common affairs of life, prayer—that is, a request for the aid of those wiser or more powerful than ourselves, and confident reliance on that aid,—is our daily practice, and one of the means on the operation of which we most confidently count, and which we distinctly recognise to be perfectly logical and sane.

Why, then, is it permitted by philosophy to pray to man, and not to pray to God? Why is it rational to entreat a tyrant to spare his victim, yet irrational to pray that God will incline that tyrant's heart to spare him? Why is it philosophical, when I am drowning, to beseech a fellow-student on the shore to fling a rope and save me, yet unphilosophical to pray to the deity, equally present and immeasurably abler, to grant me such assistance? Why, when I am sick unto death, may I send for a skilful physician to cure me *secundum artem*, yet may not expect Providence to heal me by a (far easier and simpler) word? Clearly and solely, it would seem, because men are persuadable, and God is not,—because, in the case where human aid is implored, the appeal is a *vera causa;* it can make the tyrant, the friend, or the physician do what otherwise he would not have done. Take the last instance as the simplest one. Thus :—I am ill of a malady which, according to the unchecked operation of those natural and eternal laws which men have studied, and on which they base all their calculations, must prove fatal. I pray that the cup may pass from me, taking nò other step, and God heals me. In this case, not only has a miracle been worked, but an entire derangement of the regular current course of events has been brought about, (for one event cannot be changed without operating on all others) ; not only has all past analogy, by which men guide their actions, been set at naught and the laws of natural sequence suspended, for my behoof ; but, as my recovery, when

I ought to have died, will affect and modify the lot of every one connected with me in the remotest degree, the hearing of my prayer has introduced an entirely new and endless range of consequent events, has negatived the Past and disturbed the Future. But once again :—I am ill of a fatal malady, curable only by one rare drug. I purchase it from a druggist, and I live, I pray a friend, learned in the deeper secrets of chemistry, to confide to me the hidden elixir; he does so, and I am saved. In all this there is no transgression or suspension of natural law, but simple conformity to it. It is in the course of nature that medicines heal; it is in the course of nature that friends listen and assist. The law of nature is that, if the medicine is not administered, I die; that if it is administered, I live; that a friend, if a persuadable being, listens to my entreaties. In this case the prayer is a *causa causans;* it has so acted on the druggist or the friend as to make him do what otherwise he would not have done; he was so made as to be so acted upon; an antecedent which I applied has been followed by its appointed and natural sequence. This reasoning would seem sound. It is certainly in conformity with the instinctive and habitual convictions on which we act, and must act, in our daily life.

If this reasoning is sound, it would seem to follow that the Catholic Church, in sanctioning the invocation of saints, has hit upon the one form of prayer which is logical and philosophic. Assuming the possibility of communication between the living and the spirits who have passed away from earth, and assuming further that those spirits, now endowed with the knowledge and the power belonging to a higher life, still retain something of the affections and pre-ferences of their former state, and favour and protect their votaries, then there is nothing irrational in calling upon them to aid and bless us. They, though translated to supernal spheres, and gifted with larger faculties, are still supposed to be imperfect creatures and not yet partakers of the Divine Nature. They may, therefore, without irrationality be supposed amenable to human entreaties and capable of being moved to exert their super-earthly powers for the benefit of those who adore and trust them. Praying to them is, in fact, just like praying to fellow-beings of a superior order, only still more gloriously endowed than any earthly friends, and still more advantageously placed for answering the claims of the suppliants.

But again: *Is* the above reasoning quite without suspicion of a flaw? If, as philosophers have main-tained, we all and always live under the dominion of settled law; if the present in all points flows regu-larly and inexorably from the past; if all occurrences are linked together in one unfailing chain of cause and effect, and all are foreseen by Him whose foresight is unerring; if indeed they are mere portions of an order of events of which the motive power has been set in action from the beginning,—then is not aid rendered to us by our human friends *in consequence* of our entreaties—as an *effect* of that *cause*—as much a disturbance of the ordained Law of Sequence, as if God Himself had directly aided us in compliance with our prayers to Him? In working out the pre-arranged order of the Universe, men surely are His agents just as much as winds and waves;—to pray to Him to still the latter lest they overwhelm us, is admitted to be unphilosophical, as implying the expectation that a miracle, an interference with the laws of nature, should be worked on our behalf;—to pray to Him to turn the hearts of cruel men lest they should slay us, is admitted to be equally, though less obviously un-philosphic for the same reason. Yet would either result be more a disturbance of established sequences than our being spared or saved by human interposition, if that interposition be, really and truly, caused by our prayers, and would not have taken place without them? Is it not the inescapable conclusion from all this ratiocination, that we are on these subjects dealing with questions which either our imperfect logical instruments are inadequate to handle, or in which our premises are incomplete or uncertain; and in reference to which, therefore, all our reasoning processes land us in contradictions or inadmissibilities? In fine, we are surrounded with mysteries, our own origin and existence being the most obvious of them all; mysteries we cannot clear up or escape from; mysteries as to which, however, we have one plain duty,—namely, since we cannot solve them, firmly to resist the temptation (which is the besetting sin of the undisciplined religious mind) of acquiescing in the pretended solutions offered to us in such abundance by those to whom a state of doubt is a state of torture ; who rebelliously clamour for that certainty which, in moral questions, Providence has vouchsafed only to negations ; and who find it easier to worship a created Idol than an Unknown God.

Probably to every experienced as to every disciplined mind, the one effective silencer and discourager of prayer, is the conviction, which we all accept but can rarely realise, that we constantly pour forth our most fervent supplications for what not only we ought not to obtain, and for what it would not conduce to our well-being to obtain, but for what in a year or a month perhaps we may be most thankful we did not obtain, or most wretched if we did. To grant our prayers would, we well know, be often the greatest unkindness God could do us. We know so little what would make us happy, or what would do us good. If we saw a little truer, a little deeper, or a little further, we should pray to be delivered from the fate we are now passionately praying to attain, as from the worst of earthly evils. To pray for this or that blessing with the proviso, " if it be good for us," is superfluous, for our creed is that God will always give His children what He sees to be good for them. To pray without this proviso, may be, and often is, suicidally intreating for a curse. What blind work then prayer is ! unless confined to the simple monotonous cry, " Thy will be done !" And then as a *Prayer* how needless is that, though as a sentiment of trust and resignation how needful ! * In fine, perhaps the only prayer that the wise can offer, confident that it would be well for us it should be heard, must be reduced to this, " Guide us aright, and deliver us from evil !" Whatsoever is more than this cometh of a faulty judgment and a fainting will.

---

* " Still raise for good the supplicating voice,
But leave to Heaven the measure and the choice ;
Safe in His hands whose eye discerns afar
The secret ambush of a specious prayer.
Implore His aid —in His decisions rest ;
Secure whate'er He gives, He gives the best.
But when a sense of sacred Presence fires,
And strong devotion to the skies aspires,
Pour forth thy fervours for a healthful mind,
Obedient passions and a will resigned ;
For love, which scarce collective Man can fill,
For patience, sovereign o'er transmuted ill,
For faith, that panting for a purer seat,
Counts Death kind nature's signal for retreat—
These gifts for all the laws of heaven ordain,
These gifts He grants who grants the power to gain ;
With these celestial wisdom calms the mind,
And makes the happiness she cannot find."
JOHNSON's Vanity of Human Wishes—Paraphrased
from the tenth Satire of Juvenal.

VII.

ELSEWHERE.

THE belief in a future world, in a prolonged or renewed existence after death, is sincerely held by ninety-nine men out of every hundred among us, even in the educated classes, however unable they may be to give a reason for the faith that is in them, or even to say how they came by it. They may not realise this future, but they do not doubt it, and they would be surprised and shocked to hear it questioned. Yet ninety-nine out of every hundred habitually act and feel as if they had forgotten the doctrine, or had never entertained it. Why is this? Why is it that the other world exercises so slight an influence, and lets in so faint a light, on this? Why do the promises and menaces of the life to come operate so partially and languidly on the feelings and the actions of the life that is? How is it that the attractions of Heaven compete at such a fearful disadvantage with those of Earth? How is it that hopes and fears which come to us magnified through the dread telescope of Eternity are so feebly felt, in comparison with the trivial and transient interests of this " narrow sand and shoal of Time ?" We are

> " Beings holding large discourse,
> Looking before and after ; "—

the histories we read, the scenes we tread, the skies

which nightly remind us of the illimitable wonders of
Creation, all proclaim in language too clear to be mis-
read, too eloquent to be unheard, the infinite littleness
and shortness of what is visible and earthly, and the
infinite grandeur and superiority of what is enduring
and divine ; the earth is strewed with the ruins of things
on which man had accumulated whatever could ensure
stability and permanence ; its surface is written all over
with lessons of the transitoriness of all human interests
and human works.   Of the richest and mightiest cities
of the ancient world the only surviving indications
are the Temples and the Tombs : their dwellings, their
palaces, their theatres, have disappeared,—all the magnificent structures of their genius and their pride, save
those erected to the memory of the Dead, or the worship
of the Undying !   " Passing away " is written on every
thing this world contains ; yet we sit amidst its consentaneous and emphatic teachings, unable to lay to
heart its single moral, engrossed with the shallow
interests of a few brief moments in a passing life, with
the immortal Stars above us, and the Sepulchres of
Nations at our feet ! We are all conscious of this
startling disproportion between the relative magnitude
of the two sets of objects and our relative absorption
in them ; how intent we are upon the one, how neglect-
ful of the other :—divines reproach our insensibility as a
sin ; and we ourselves acknowledge it with an alter-
nate sigh of regret, and stare of half incredulous
wonder.   Where, then, are we to look for the explanation of this strange irrationality ? Why are the joys

of the world to come so feeble to attract, and its terrors so impotent to restrain ?

Can it be attributable to unbelief ? With some, no doubt, this is the principal operative cause. They have no real firm faith in futurity : they *admit* it, but it dwells upon their mind in too nebulous a shape ever to attain to the dignity, or to bear the fruits, of a CONVICTION. What they see and know, therefore, appeals to them with a cogency which can never appertain to what they merely conjecture. On what principles of sense or wisdom should they forego a pleasure that is immediate and certain for a joy, even far greater, that is future, distant, and dim, if not problematical ? Between a certainty and a contingency the conflict is enormously unequal. But it is not of these men that we are speaking. There are thousands who fancy their belief in Heaven and its counterpart is positive, dogmatic, and established, over whose conviction no shade of doubt has ever passed, to whom (theoretically at least) the day of Judgment is as real as the grave, and the immortality of the Soul as certain as the death of the body, whose hopes are never dimmed by the clouds which haunt our hours of weakness and reaction, whom no subtle questionings, no dark misgivings waylay and assail, to shatter and paralyse their energies,—and yet upon whose actual sentiments, estimates, state of mind and course of action, the beckoning effulgence from Heaven or the beacon-fire of Hell have scarce more influence than had upon the ancient world the chill and pallid moonlight of Elysium or the shadowy tortures of the poetic Tartarus. It is not that they are not steadfast believers in these solemn futurities: if you question them, they would class them among the most absolute certainties they know. It is not that for a moment their reason places the pleasures or the pains of earth in comparison with the incalculable retributions of another world; or that their nature is too uncultured to appreciate the immeasurable overbalance of an infinite reversion over a finite actuality. Some other explanation must be sought for.

Can it be found in Man's weak imagination, in the feebleness of his faculty of realisation? Is it that he cannot fully picture to himself, or bring home to his bosom, things so distant and unseen? Is it that, fully admitting them, he cannot feel them? that, though convictions of the understanding, they have not become realities to the heart? No doubt, in a multitude of instances this is the true solution of the enigma. The conceptions of most of us are dull; the power of *presenting* the future to our minds (in the accurate and analysed sense of the expression), of making it present to us, of " seeing Him who is invisible," is a faculty whose strength depends greatly on training, which is vouchsafed to different individuals in very different measure, and to most of us in very scanty measure. It is a faculty, even, which in its complete development is, as previously pointed out, a most perilous endowment, and probably scarcely compatible with sanity. Eventualities too, however certain, of which both the time and the locality are unknown, and of which the nature is not easily *conceivable,* can seldom take a hold proportioned to their magnitude upon minds blunted by living in a world of sense and daily dealing with objective realities alone.

With the vast majority of nominal believers, no doubt, the future is ineffective by reason of its distance: the present overpowering by reason of its nearness. Their will is too feeble, their powers of self-control too little raised above the savage state, to postpone a present indulgence to a future good, to dread a distant agony more than an immediate pang, to forego an actual trifle for a grand reversion. These are the men who sink into luxury and sloth from sheer inability to look forward till the morrow and provide against need, who do evil "because sentence against it is not executed speedily." But there are millions to whom this explanation will not apply; who spend their life in sowing the seed for a remote harvest, who practise daily self-denial for the purchase of some contingent and eventual good, whose whole career is a laborious provision for an earthly morrow quite as distant and far more uncertain than the heavenly one. They sacrifice themselves for a posthumous fame which will not be theirs; they lay by comforts for an old age which in all likelihood they will never reach ; they accumulate, by the surrender of all the enjoyments and amenities of life, a splendid endowment for the family they hope to found,—yet their sons may all die out before them. Here it is not that they cannot sacrifice the actual and visible to the remote and the unseen, but that the locality and the elements of their future are alike misjudged.

None of these solutions of the problem quite explain to us how it is that men who are capable of a strenuous and self-denying postponement of the present to the future, and who are solemn and earnest believers in the Great Hope and the tremendous Fear—yet, practically and habitually, look upon Heaven with so little aspiration and upon Hell with so little dread. We must seek for some other influence which is at work to counteract the natural operation of these mighty conceptions. This influence we believe will be found in the character of the usual representations of the happiness and torments of our future retributive existence. The joys of the world to come have been habitually so pictured by divines that the great majority cannot relish them; and its pains so that they cannot believe them.

In describing these last, it must be admitted that divines have seldom diverged much from the letter of Scripture. The Scriptural delineations of future torments have four characteristics, all singular enough : —they are all physical ; they are eternal ; they are penal, not purgatorial or reformatory ; and they are indiscriminate on all subjected to them. Now, every one of these points is found to be practically almost impossible of credence.

I. It is worthy of notice that throughout the Epistles there is no description of any place or world of punishment; and few references to the existence of such. Paul indeed speaks of the " day of wrath; " " the wrath to come ; " " indignation and wrath, tribulation and anguish, upon every soul of man that doeth evil ; " and both Paul and the writer of the second epistle of Peter mention incidentally the " everlasting destruction," the " perishing " of sinners;—but this is the sum total of their contributions to the subject, which seems scarcely ever to have been present to their minds. In the Gospels, however, the place of punishment is mentioned in several places, generally as from Christ himself; and it is always described in the same or nearly the same language, as " Hell fire;" " flame; " " the place where the worm dieth not, and the fire is not quenched ; " " a furnace of fire "— imagery suggested apparently by the neighbourhood of the valley of Gehenna. In the Revelations the sam conception is (as might be anticipated from the character of the book) still more materialized : there it is " the lake that burneth with fire and brimstone," —the " lake of fire," the " bottomless pit "—&c. In short, wherever Hell is spoken of at all specifically in the Bible, its tortures are described as purely *corporeal;* and Christian writers and preachers in general have faithfully adhered to the representations of their text.*

---

*I am assured that these material conceptions of the place of punishment are not now retained or dwelt upon by any one. Yet I have now lying before me a book entitled " A Sight of Hell," professing to come from the Rev. Father Furniss, C.SS.R., and printed " permissu superiorum," and recommended to be used along with

Now, it is naturally impossible for men of intelligence and cultivation, who are conscious how far the mental surpasses the bodily capacity for suffering, or for Christians,—who have been taught how large a proportion of their worst offences proceed not from the weakness of the flesh but from the wild bad passions of the Spirit,—to acquiesce in this physical delineation of future retribution. Instead of the "majestic pains" adapted to man's complex nature, and capable of such impressive delineation, the torments assigned by ordinary Christianity to the future life are peculiarly and exclusively those appro-

------

the Catechism in Sunday-schools as part of a course of religious instruction. It is one of a series of "Books for children and young persons."

"Little child, if you go to hell there will be a devil at your side to strike you. He will go on striking you every minute for ever and ever without stopping. The first stroke will make your body as bad as the body of Job, covered from head to foot with sores and ulcers. The second stroke will make your body twice as bad as the body of Job. The third stroke will make your body three times as bad as the body of Job. The fourth stroke will make your body four times as bad as the body of Job. How, then, will your body be after the devil has been striking it every moment for a hundred millions of years without stopping?"

Next comes, "A Dress of Fire":

"Job xxxviii.—Are not thy garments hot? Come into this room. You see it is very small. But see in the midst of it there is a girl, perhaps about eighteen years old. What a terrible dress she has on—her dress is made of fire! On her head she wears a bonnet of fire. It is pressed down all over her head; it burns her head; it burns into the skin; it scorches the bone of the skull and makes it smoke. The red-hot fiery heat goes into the brain and melts it. Ezek. xxii.—I will burn you in the fire of my wrath: you shall be melted in the midst thereof as silver is melted in the

priate to this. They are all bodily; yet the body is laid down at death. They are all corporeal; yet we are told that our coming existence is a spiritual one. They are prepared for and addressed to our senseless clay which is mouldering in the tomb, dissolving into its original elements, and perpetually passing into new combinations. The necessary counterpart and correlative of the scriptural doctrine of a material Hell, without which it has no meaning or coherence, is the doctrine of the Resurrection of the body, which Bush, in his *Anastasis*, has shown to be neither tenable nor scriptural. It is impossible for those who believe, as we are taught to do, in the

---

fire. You do not, perhaps, like a headache. Think what a headache that girl must have. But see more. She is wrapped up in flames, for her frock is on fire. If she were on earth she would be burned to a cinder in a moment. But she is in hell, where fire burns everything, but burns nothing away. There she stands burning and scorched ; there she will stand for ever burning and scorched. She counts with her fingers the moments as they pass away slowly, for each moment seems to her like a hundred years. As she counts the moments she remembers that she will have to count them for ever and ever."

The children are then favoured with sight of a boiling boy. " But, listen, there is a sound just like that of a kettle boiling. Is it really a kettle which is boiling ? No. Then what is it ? Hear what it is. The blood is boiling in the scalded veins of that boy. The brain is boiling and bubbling in his head. The marrow is boiling in his bones."

They also have a peep at a baby in a red-hot oven : " Hear how it screams to come out ! See how it turns and twists itself about in the fire ! It beats its head against the roof of the oven. It stamps its little feet on the floor of the oven. You can see on the face of this little child what you see on the faces of all in hell —despair, desperate and horrible."

immateriality of the Soul, in the spiritual and incorporeal nature of our future existence, to accept the doctrine of future torments applicable solely to our fleshly forms, and inflicted by physical elements which can have no power over disembodied spirits. If the place of retribution be in truth a burning lake, and the agents of suffering be the worm and flame, then "flesh and blood" must be the inheritors of Hell, if not of the Kingdom of Heaven; and our earthly frames must be *re-collected*, re-formed, and re-animated at the last day for the special purpose of the penal fire. It may be urged that we do not know what God may do; that we have no right to assume that our next existence will be either an incorporeal one, or one of such "spiritual corporeity" as will be impassible to flame; that God may either re-create our flesh, or endow fire and brimstone with power over our disembodied essence :----possibly; what I affirm is simply this, that those who described Hell as it is described in the Revelations and in the language of Divines, did so with reference to *our mortal frames;* and that the manifest and *felt* incongruity between the σῶμα πνευματικόν and tortures adapted to the σῶμα ψυχικόν,—between an immaterial world, an existence of the Soul, a spiritual essence, and a lake of brimstone, a devouring flame, and a gnawing worm—disarms the latter of all their reality and all their terrors. It may be that in using these expressions, as in so may other instances, the Scriptural Writers spoke metaphorically, and employed such language as would best awaken the dismay of auditors whose merely animal nature could realise animal suffering only, and who were incapable of soaring to the conception of an incorporeal existence. But why then do divines persist in repeating metaphors so singularly inappropriate, and in using the same earthly images when addressing auditors whom at the same time they teach to regard futurity as an *unearthly* state ?

II. The alleged *eternity* of future punishments has contributed in an incalculable degree to prevent the practical belief and realization of those punishments. The common feelings of humanity and the common sentiments of justice which lie deep at the heart of our nature, have, in this instance, proved too strong for the reiterated assertions of orthodoxy, and have steadily refused to accept so terrible a tenet. Yet still, with a *curiosa infelicitas* which is almost stupidity, the Church* still preaches the endless duration of future torments almost as confidently as the existence of those torments. The inevitable consequence is that the general and instinctive rejection of the one tenet entails scepticism with regard to the other with which it is thus persistently bound up. No subtlety of logic, no weight of authority, will induce rightly constituted minds which allow themselves to reason at all, to ad- -

---

* Scarcely, perhaps, The Church; but still the self-styled orthodox, the οἱ πολλοί of the clergy. High authorities among them, however, are beginning to proclaim the doctrine to be as unscriptural as it is revolting. (See, *inter alia*, a Paper by *Anglicanus* in the *Contemporary Review* for May 1872.)

mit that the sins or failings of Time *can* merit the retribution of Eternity—that finite natures *can*, by any guilt of which they are capable, draw upon themselves torments infinite either in essence or duration. Divines tell us—and we all accept the saying—that no virtue on the part of frail and feeble creatures like ourselves can *merit* an eternal Heaven;—but when they demand our assent to the opposite and contradictory assertion that the short-comings and backslidings of the same creatures can and do merit an everlasting Hell, we are revolted by the inconsistency, and shrink back from the corollary involved in the latter proposition.

III. Another point particularly difficult of belief and realisation in the popular doctrine of the sufferings of a future world, is that they are represented as *penal*, not purgatorial, retributive not reformatory. It is not easy to conceive any object to be answered, any part in the great plan of Providence to be fulfilled, by the infliction of torments, whether temporary or perpetual, which are neither to serve for the purification of those who endure them, nor needed for the warning of those who behold them, since the inhabitants of earth do not see them, and the translated denizens of Heaven do not require them. They are simply aimless and retrospective. It is true that in the conception of the philosopher they are *inevitable*, that future suffering is the natural offspring and necessary consequence of present sin : but this is not the view of the doctrine we are considering, nor is the character of the sufferings it depicts such as would logically flow out of the sins for which they are supposed to be a chastisement. The Catholic Church, with its usual profound knowledge of human nature, and ready system of providing for every want and guarding against every objection, has invented purgatory; and by this means, has undoubtedly succeeded in making the belief in and realization of a Hell, possible, to say the least. We may well admit, as Catholics are called upon to do, that inflictions more severe, pangs more searching and more lasting, may be needed and provided in a future world for those whose malignant passions or obstinate carnality the milder chastisements of earth failed to purge away, or who by the unaccountable arrangements of Providence escaped tribulation almost or altogether here. But to believe, as Protestants are required to do, that all these fiercer torments will be inflicted when no conceivable purpose is to be answered by their infliction, when the suffering, so far as human imagination can fathom the case, is simply *gratuitous*,—is assuredly a far harder strain upon our faith; a strain, too, which is hardest on those whose feelings are the most humane, and whose notions of the Deity are worthiest; on those, that is, who have most fully imbibed Christ's sentiments and views.

IV. As if bent upon surrounding their doctrine of future punishments with every thing that could make it thorny and repellant, Protestant Divines usually assume these punishments to be indiscriminate upon all who are condemned to them.　Even the text distinguishing between the many stripes to be awarded to him who sinned knowingly and wilfully, and the few stripes to be inflicted on him who sinned ignorantly, and therefore did not really *sin* at all, is rarely referred to.　Following literally and unintelligently the metaphor of the sheep and the goats—the right hand and the left hand of the coming judge,—Heaven and Hell, in their current language, are two states, with no margin for mediocrity, no debateable or border land between them for those who deserve neither or whose merits are so nearly alike that it is scarcely possible to say which deserve which; but on the contrary, with a great gulph, a broad bold line of demarcation, separating, through all future ages and by boundless distances, those whose measure of sin or virtue while on earth was scarcely distinguishable by the finest and most delicate moral electrometer.＊　On one side is endless happiness,—the sight of God—

> "That perfect presence of His face
> Which we, for want of words, call Heaven,"

for those whom one frailty more, one added weakness, one hair's-breadth further transgression, would have justly condemned to dwell for ever " with the Devil and his Angels," an outcast from Hope, chained to his iniquity for ever, alone with the irreparable !　On the

---

＊ Nay, far worse ;—often those who differed here only in their theological opinions—their reception or rejection of some unintelligible dogma.

other side is Hell, the scene of torture, of weeping and gnashing of teeth; of the ceaseless flame and the undying worm; where he "that is filthy must be filthy still;" torment, not for a period, but FOR EVER, for him for whom one effort more, one *ounce* of guilt the less, might have turned the trembling balance, and opened the gates of an eternal paradise! Human feeling and human reason CANNOT believe this, though they may admit it with lip assent; and the Catholic Church accordingly, here as elsewhere, steps in to present them with the *via media* which is needed. Purgatory, ranging from a single day to a century of ages, offers that border land of discriminating retribution for which justice and humanity cry out. For the best of us have some frailty, some dark stain, which requires to be purged away before we can be fit for admission into a world of perfect purity and love; and the worst of us are conscious of loads of impurity and guilt which, compared with the faults of those sisters or brethren of our race who are "a little lower than the angels," are as a thousand years to a single day.

Yet though Theologians have virtually all but destroyed popular faith in the conventional place of punishment by the language in which they have habitually described it, and the incredibilities with which they have mixed it up, surely, surely, it is not impossible to imagine a future world of retribution in such form and colouring as shall be easy and natural to realize, as shall be not only *possible* to believe, but *impossible* to disbelieve : a world of which we shall feel that if it exist at all, it must be such as we delineate. If the soul is destined for an existence after death, then (unless a miracle is worked to prevent it) that existence MUST be one of retribution to the sinful, and of purgatorial suffering to the frail and feeble, soul. The nature of the retribution will be determined by the nature of the sin ; and the character of the purifying fires will be indicated by the character of the frailty which has to be purged away.

When the portals of this world have been past, when time and sense have been left behind, and this "body of death" has dropped away from the liberated soul, every thing which clouded the perceptions, which dulled the vision, which drugged the conscience, while on earth will be cleared off like a morning mist. *We shall see all things as they really are*—ourselves and our sins among the number. No other punishment whether retributive or purgatorial will be needed. Naked truth, unfilmed eyes, will do all that the most righteous vengeance could desire. Every now and then we have a glimpse of such perceptions while on earth. Times come to all of us when the passions, by some casual influence or some sobering shock, have been wholly lulled to rest, when all disordered emotions have drunk repose

"From the cool cisterns of the midnight air,"

and when for a few brief and ineffectual instants the temptations which have led us astray, the pleasures for which we have bartered away the future, the desires to which we have sacrificed our peace, appear to us in all their wretched folly and miserable meanness. From our feelings *then* we may form a faint imagination of what our feelings will be hereafter, when this occasional and imperfect glimpse shall have become a perpetual flood of light, irradiating all the darkest places of our earthly pathway, piercing through all veils, scattering all delusions, burning up all sophistries; — when the sensual man, *all desires and appetites now utterly extinct,* shall stand amazed and horror-struck at the low promptings to which he once yielded himself up in such ignominious slavery, and shall shrink in loathing and shame from the reflected image of his own animal brutality;—when the hard, grasping, sordid man, *come now into a world where wealth can purchase nothing, where gold has no splendour and luxury no meaning,* shall be almost unable to comprehend how he could ever have so valued such unreal goods ;—when the malignant, the passionate, the cruel man, *everything which called forth his vices now swept away with the former existence,* shall appear to himself as he appeared to others upon earth, shall hate himself as others hated him on earth. We shall see, judge, feel about all things there perfectly and constantly, as we saw, judged, and felt about them partially in our rare better and saner moments here. We shall think that we must have been mad, if we did not too well know that we had been wilful. Every urgent appetite, every boiling passion, every wild ambition, which obscured and confused our reason here below will have been burnt away in the valley of the shadow of death; every subtle sophistry with which we blinded or excused ourselves on earth will have vanished before the clear glance of a disembodied spirit; nothing will intervene between us and the truth. Stripped of all the disguising drapery of honied words and false refractions, we shall see ourselves as we are: we shall judge ourselves as God has always judged us. Our lost or misused opportunities; our forfeited birthright; our glorious possibility—ineffable in its glory; our awful actuality—ineffable in its awfulness; the nature which God gave us—the nature we have made ourselves; the destiny for which He designed us— the destiny to which we have doomed ourselves; all these things will grow and fasten on our thoughts, till the contemplation must terminate in madness, were not madness a mercy belonging to the world of flesh alone. In the mere superior mental capacities, therefore, consequent upon spiritual life, we cannot fail to find all that is needed, or can be pictured, to make that life a penal and a purgatorial one.

But there will be more than this. We shall find in the same suffering and remorseful world, those whose emancipation we would now purchase at any cost, had we anything wherewith to buy it; those whose nurture we neglected, those whose temper we soured, those whose passions we aroused, those whose reason we perverted, those whose conscience we confused and stupified,—those, in a word, for whose ruin we are answerable. We shall have to bear their despairing misery, their upbraiding looks : worse than all, we shall have to bear, here again, *our own present perception of our Past.*

But there is yet another retributive pang in wait for the sinful soul, which belongs to the very nature of that future world, namely the severance from all those we love who on earth have trod the narrower and better path. The affections do not belong to the virtuous alone ; they cling to the sinner through all the storms and labyrinths of sin ; they are the last fragments of what is good in him that he silences or lays aside or tramples out ; they belong not to the flesh but to the spirit ; and a spiritual existence, even if a suffering one, will but give them fresh energy and tenacity, by terminating all that has been antagonistic to them here below. Who shall describe the yearning love of a disencumbered soul! Who can adequately conceive the passionate tenderness with which it will cling round the objects of its affection in a world where every other sentiment or thought is one of pain! Yet what can be more certain, because what more in the essential nature of things, than that the great revelation of the Last Day (or that which must attend and be involved in the mere entrance into the Spiritual State) will effect a severance of souls—an instantaneous gulf of demarcation between the pure and the impure, the just and the unjust, the merciful and the cruel—immeasurably more deep, essential, and impassable than any which time or distance or rank or antipathy could ·effect on earth. *Here* we never see into each other's souls:* characters the most opposite and incompatible dwell together upon earth, and may love each other much, unsuspicious of the utter want of fundamental harmony between them. The aspiring and the worldly may have so much in common and may both instinctively conceal so much, that their inherent and elemental differences may go undiscovered to the grave. The soul that will be saved and the soul that will be lost may cling round each other here with wild affection, all unconscious of the infinite divergence of their future destiny. The mother will love her son with all the devotion of her nature, in spite or in ignorance of his unworthiness: that son may reciprocate his mother's love, and in this only be not unworthy: the blindness which is kindly given us hides so much,† and affection covers such a multitude of sins. The pure and holy wife and the frail and sinful husband

---

* " We live together years and years,
   And leave unsounded still
Each other's springs of hopes and fears,
   Each other's depths of will.
We live together day by day,
   And some *chance* look or tone
Lights up with instantaneous ray
   An inner world unknown."   R. M. MILNES.

† " Or what if Heaven for once its searching light
   Lent to some partial eye, disclosing all
The rude bad thoughts that in our bosom's night
   Wander at large, nor heed Love's gentle thrall?

can live together harmoniously and can love fondly
here below, because the vast moral gulf between them
is mercifully veiled from either eye. But when the
great curtain of ignorance and deception shall be withdrawn—" when the secrets of all hearts shall be made
known "—when the piercing light of the Spiritual
World shall at once and for ever disperse those clouds
which have hidden what we really are from those who
have loved us and almost from ourselves, when the
trusting confidence of friendship shall discover what a
serpent has been nourished in its bosom, when the
yearning mother shall perceive on what a guilty wretch
all her boundless and priceless tenderness has been
lavished, when the wife shall at length see the husband whom she cherished through long years of self-
denying and believing love revealed in his true
colours, a wholly alien creature; what a sudden, convulsive, inevitable, because natural, separation between
the clean and the unclean will then take place! The
gulf *which has always existed* is recognised and felt at
last; corruption can no longer consort with incorruption;
the lion cannot lie down with the lamb, nor the
leopard with the kid. One flash of light has done it

Who would not shun the dreary uncouth place,
    As if, fond leaning where her infant slept,
A mother's arm a serpent should embrace:—
    So might we friendless live, and die unwept

Then keep the softening veil in mercy drawn,
    Thou who canst love us though Thou read us true."
                                Keble's Christian Year.

all. The merciful delusions which held friends together upon earth are dispersed, and the laws of the mind must take their course and divide the evil from the good. But though the link is severed, the affection is not thereby destroyed. The friend, the husband, the lover, the son, thus cut adrift by a just and natural though bitter retribution, *love still ;* nay, they love all the more fervently, all the more yearningly, in that they now discern with unclouded vision all that bright beauty, all that rich nature of the objects of their tenderness, of which their dim eyesight could on earth perceive only a part. Then will begin a RETRIBUTION indeed, the appropriate anguish, the desolate abandonment of which, who can paint, and who will be able to bear ! To see those we love, as we never loved till then, turn from our grasp and our glance of clasping and supplicating fondness with that unconquerable loathing which virtue *must* feel towards guilt and with which purity *must* shrink from stain : to see those eyes, never turned on us before save in gentleness and trust, now giving us one last glance of divine sadness and ineffable farewell ; to watch those forms, whose companionship cheered and illuminated all the dark places of our earthly pilgrimage, and once and again had almost redeemed us from the bondage and the mire of sin, receding, vanishing, melting in the bright distance, to join a circle *where they will need us not,* to tread a path to which ours bears no parallel and can make no approach ; and THEN to turn inward and downward, and realise

our lot, and feel our desolation, and reflect that we
have earned it :—what has Poetry or Theology pictured
that can compete with a Gehenna such as this !

———

Divines have been nearly as unfortunate and as far
from reality in their delineations of the joys of Heaven
as of the pains of Hell.   The conception formed by one
mind, and that one a peculiar, narrow, and abnormal
mind, of a state of bliss has been stereotyped, and
called Heaven.   The picture which excited and engrossed the fancy of the author of the Book of Revelations has been thrust upon all other men, however
diversely constituted, as " the Heaven of the Bible,"
the Paradise of God, the place which Christ " was gone
to prepare for us."   It was to be a scene of gorgeous
splendour and of ceaseless worship.   Those who
did not relish or earnestly desire such a life, those
whose imaginations were not kindled into transport
at the picture, or who ventured to form a different
conception of supernal bliss from that which floated
before the visions of the elect, were held to show a
carnal and unregenerate nature which could have
neither part nor lot in so sublime a world.   It is true
that more human divines spoke of re-union with the
loved, as well as of admission to the throne of the Most
High, of the companionship of kindred and friends, as
well as of " the presence of the power of God," and of
perpetual praise and prayer.   But this was regarded as
a concession : it was scarcely rigid orthodoxy : it was
undeniably not the most prominent feature of " the glory

to be revealed." It lay in the back-ground of all the splendid and sublime imagery of St. John. Those poor human souls who felt almost justified by the language of their Master in loving their brother whom they had seen more than God whom they had not seen, and who felt that, whether justified or not, they did so and could not help doing so, were scowled away from the Gate of the Eternal City. Worship was to be the sole need, occupation, joy, of the beatific state. What wonder that the humble, the unimaginative, the tender, the HUMAN—felt no yearnings towards the cold, strange, pallid unreality!

It is not to be denied that the favourite delineations of Heaven are almost wholly suggested or coloured by the Book of Revelations, in which the descriptions, magnificently splendid and sometimes sublime, are yet, if we except seven verses of the twenty-first chapter, almost wholly material. And not only so, but the material elements are by no means the noblest that might have been chosen. The New Jerusalem is painted as something between a gorgeous Palace, and a dazzling conventicle. The picture is of a CITY—of Thrones of Sapphire, and Crowns of gold—of rainbows of emerald—of walls and pavements of jasper and topaz and amethyst and chalcedony—of streets of glass and gates of pearl :— brilliant ingredients, no doubt, to an Oriental imagination, but

> " Poor fragments all of this low earth,
> Such as in dreams could hardly soothe
> A soul that once had tasted of immortal truth."

The writer's conception of what befitted the Temple of the Lord and the dwelling of the redeemed embraced rather the rare curiosities than the common loveliness of nature : palaces and jewels and precious stones,—not gentle streams, and shady groves, and woodland glades, and sunny vallies, and eternal mountains, and the far-off murmur of a peaceful ocean. *His* Heaven was a scene of magnificent ornamentation rather than of solemn beauty ; of glory, not of love and bliss. It might kindle his fancy : it chills ours. Even our material paradise would be differently pictured. There *may* be all these things in Heaven ; but there will be what will throw all these accessaries into the shade. "There may be crowns of material splendour ; there may be trees of unfading loveliness ; there may be pavements of emerald, and canopies of the brightest radiance ; and gardens of deep and tranquil security ; and palaces of proud and stately decoration ; and a city of lofty pinnacles, through which there unceasingly flows a river of gladness, and where jubilee is ever rung by a concord of seraphic voices. But these are only the accessaries of Heaven. They form not the materials of its substantial loveliness. Of this, the man who toils in humble drudgery, an utter stranger to the delights of sensible pleasure, or the fascinations of sensible glory, has already got a foretaste in his heart. It consists not in the enjoyment of created good, nor in the survey of created magnificence. It is drawn in a direct stream through the channels of love and contemplation from the fulness of the Creator. It emanates from the countenance of God, manifesting the spiritual glories of his holy and perfect character on those whose characters are kindred to his own. And if on earth there is no tendency towards such a character, no process of restoration to the lost image of the Godhead, no delight in prayer, no relish for the sweets of intercourse with the Father now unseen but then to be revealed,—then, let our imaginations kindle as they may at the beatitudes of our fictitious Heaven, the true Heaven is what we shall never reach, because it is a Heaven we are not fitted to enjoy."*

The most repellent mistake of Divines in their delineations of Heaven has perhaps been the *uniformity* they have attributed to its beatitudes. Men in this life exhibit *infinite* varieties of character, craving and capacity—and all this within the limits of virtuous desire and of righteous effort. We see individuals here, differing from each other in almost every taste and sentiment, in the characters they specially admire, in the objects they most strenuously aim at—of whom nevertheless we cannot pronounce that one is a more faithful servant of duty, or likely to be more acceptable to God than another. There are good men of every phase and peculiarity of goodness: there are ardent and unwearied " fellow-labourers with God " in every corner of the vineyard—in all the

---

* Dr Chalmers.

countless departments of His infinitely varied husbandry. There are those whom God sanctifies for the patient endurance of His heaviest will. There are those whom he energises for rough duties of conflict or of toil—of daring strife or plodding drudgery. There are those "who serve, yet only stand and wait." There are those whom he softens and purifies that they may radiate love and serenity around them. There are those, finally, whom He has set apart to glorify and serve him by the discovery of truth and the diffusion of knowledge. The variety which we observe among the candidates for Heaven here below, belongs then to *human* nature, not to *fallen* nature; it inheres not in our imperfections but in our *incompleteness;* it exists in us, not because we are earthly and sinful, but because we are men and not angels—because in a word we are that peculiar modification of sentient and intelligent existences which it has pleased the Creator to make us—and no other.

If this were not so; if God had made us all in one mould, so that we differed from one another only as we were more or less frail and guilty; if there were some one ideal standard, divergence from which by special development in one direction or another were in itself a lapse from good; if unmurmuring submission, if stern resistance to evil, if daring and aggressive energy, if overflowing and all-embracing love, must each abnegate its peculiarity and put on its opposite, before it could do God's work or obtain his smile; if the stern soldier of duty must become the melting child of tenderness and pity; if, in fine, God meant mankind to be a *regiment in uniform*—not a hierarchy of Servants, each with his special mission and his special capacity to perform it, and sentiments and characteristics in conformity therewith ;—then there might be some ground for the idea that Death will be a process of mental and moral assimilation, and that as they enter the immortal state, God will pass a flattening-iron over all who "shall be found worthy to attain to the resurrection of the Just," and smooth out every salient individuality whether of capacity or aspiration. But who that contemplates the varied forms of human excellence, all sanctioned by Divine approval, can find either probability or comfort in so strange a doctrine! "In my Father's House are many mansions."

If, then, we are to preserve our essential identity in that other world—and on what other supposition can we even conceive or desire a future existence ?—individuals must be marked by divergencies analogous to those which have prevailed on earth. With a purged vision and a spiritualised being, those exclusive and disproportionate estimates which so aggravate and perpetuate discrepancies of aim and character below, will of course be corrected ; but that the active and energetic spirit should at once become contemplative, that the earnest enquirer after truth should at once merge into the worshipper, or that she whose whole soul was love should suddenly become the Seraph searching after knowledge,—these are metamorphoses which have no analogy with what we know of the Divine action, and which we can see no reason whatever to anticipate. The *nature* which God bestowed has an individual stamp and character which belongs to it, and cannot be separated from it. Its errors may be corrected, its exuberances pared away, its deficiencies supplied, and its scope enlarged, but it will remain a distinctive and integral existence, through Eternity, as in Time.

If this be so, then, the spiritual world cannot be the state of uniform and monotonous existence which orthodoxy paints it. What divines have done for themselves, let each of us do for ourselves. They have drawn Heaven as they fancy they ought to desire it; let us picture it such as we imagine it may be, as far as faint human words can go. In doing this we shall be putting aside in favour of our own dim taper no superior light or knowledge which has been bequeathed to us; for with the exception of the Apocalypse (which we may put aside with as little scruple as Luther did), one of the most noticeable peculiarities of the Scripture references to heaven is their vagueness and *reserve;* they tie up and chill our aspirations by no definite chart or picture of that future world; the canvas only is given us: we may paint upon it nearly what we please.

For, be it remembered, what is promised to us, or what we are permitted to anticipate, is a state of existence which *will be Heaven to us;* not one which, though it may be a beatific vision to our differently constituted neighbours, would seem a dreary desert to ourselves. For example, to me God has promised not the heaven of the ascetic temper, or the dogmatic theologian, or of the subtle mystic, or of the stern martyr ready alike to inflict and bear; but a heaven of purified and permanent affections—of a book of knowledge with eternal leaves, and unbounded capacities to read it—of those we love ever round us, never misconceiving us, or being harassed by us—of glorious work to do, and adequate faculties to do it—*a world of solved problems,* as well as of realised ideals. The many mansions in my Father's House are many not in number only, but in variety. Our allotted mansion will have been prepared for *us;* not for some one else with whom we have little in common but the original elements of our nature, whose trials, powers, arena, duties have all been different.

And first. It will be a world of Peace and Rest, for the weary and heavy-laden will be there. None but those—and how many there are God only knows —who through life have been bowed to the earth by a weight of care and toil and ceaseless pressure which often seemed too heavy to be borne, have an idea of the perfect paradise which is comprised in that one word—" REST." " He giveth His beloved *sleep.*" *

---

* " Of all the thoughts of God that are
Borne inward unto Souls afar,
  Along the Psalmist's music deep—
Now tell me if that any is,
For gift or grace, surpassing this—
'He giveth His Beloved sleep.'
MISS BARRETT.

To feel the burden roll from their shoulders, as it did from that of Christian, as they pass the threshold of the Shining Gate, to know that the race is ended, that the haven is reached, that the strained nerves may be at length relaxed, that the unsleeping vigilance which so tasked their strength is needed no more, and that a repose that can never be broken may be suffered to steal over the worn and wearied frame! "I thank thee, O God! that the hard struggle of living is over." This is the first instinctive conception of heaven to those

"Whom Time has wearied in its race of Hours,"

as they sink to sleep when the sharp malady of life is over, grateful for the quiet of the grave and the hope of a serener world.

And another class of the weary will be there, resting at last in the beautiful and tranquil world they thirsted for so long, where the spirit shall be always willing and the flesh never weak—those, I mean, worn out less by the fatigues of the world than by the strife of a turbid temperament; to whom urgent appetites, boiling passions, and a critical position have made life an hourly conflict with the world, the flesh, and the devil ; who, though they have endured to the end, have been torn to pieces by the internecine struggle, and have over and over been on the point of resigning the contest in despair. We are most of us like this : and a Heaven which shall put an end to "the fatal war which our desires have too long waged with our destiny" may still be our inheritance and home. We may have sinned frightfully and long; we may have been feeble, faithless, half-hearted, and cowardly; relapse may have succeeded relapse, till mercy would have been wearied out if mercy were a human thing; but the essential point still is, that the Great Day, whenever it come, shall find us *not turned back*, but, however distant, halting, covered with the mire of innumerable falls, "with our face. set *as though we would go* to Jerusalem." If so, we shall have "saved our souls alive;" our flickering lamp may need the tenderest care to keep it still alight and to feed it with the oil which may ultimately nourish it into a steady and enduring flame; our pale souls may, in shrinking and humiliation, have to take the lowest place among the remotest ranks of the countless hosts which circle the Eternal Throne; ages of effort may lie before us; appalling arrears of work which ought to have been done on earth may stretch in endless vistas before us; those at whose side we would fain have walked through the sweet pathways of the Spiritual Kingdom may be for ever beyond our reach, (for, alas! there is no *overtaking* possible in that just world;) but at least we shall have carried with us the germ of an Immortal Being over the threshold of that scene where nothing that enters can ever die.

And the young will be there, with their yet untamed and unblunted energies, not wearied and disheartened, as lifelong labourers are here, with rolling the stone of Sisyphus up an interminable hill. And the aged will be there, with their contemplative and passionless serenity. And for both will be provided an appropriate work and an appropriate enjoyment. For that world can scarcely be pictured as an idle one. The Great Spirit will have behests to be carried out, to be the ministers of which will be the rich reward and the eternal occupation of activity and strength. It may be that all these behests might be far more easily, far more simply, carried out without the intervention of translated human effort; it may be that there, as here, a will, a word, would suffice for the instantaneous result: " He spake and it was done; He commanded, and it stood fast." But here, we know, He works through human agency : why should we not imagine that there the analogy of His dealings will be preserved, and that men, become angels, will be His agents in Heaven. For the Just not yet made Perfect,* there will be missions of mercy, to rescue the despairing; missions of aid, to strengthen those who strive ; missions of consolation, to comfort those who weep; missions of instruction, to guide the blind ; missions of conflict, to combat and to conquer evil. There will be worlds to be guided and redeemed, worlds, it may be, to be created, worlds to be " brought out of darkness into His marvellous light." And the loving soul will be sent to bind up

---

* And doubtless unto thee is given
A life that bears immortal fruit
In such great offices as suit
The full-grown energies of Heaven.

In Memoriam.

the broken hearted · and the serene soul to breathe peace
to the cumbered, the harassed, and the way-worn ; and
the fiery soul to do loyal battle with the powers of
evil. The Hero will have a field of holy conquest
assigned him, in which he need fear no defeat and will
have to weep over no tarnished or dear-bought victory.
The Prophet, who on earth spoke so often to deaf ears,
with imperfect knowledge, and an uncertain mind, will
be sent forth upon a wider mission, with ampler cre-
dentials and sublimer powers. No healthy energy
need fear to lie unused, no virtuous activity will waste
away in idleness, no sword of true temper will rust
within its sheath.*

And the wise and searching of this world will be
there : those who, with pain and toil, with untiring

---

* Peace is God's direct assurance
    To the souls that win release
From this world of hard endurance—
    Peace, He tells us, only Peace.

To this life's inquiring traveller,
    Peace of knowledge of all good ;
To the anxious truth-unraveller,
    Peace of wisdom understood.

To the lover, full fruition
    Of an unexhausted joy ;—
To the warrior, crowned ambition
    With no envy's base alloy.

To the ruler, sense of action,
    Working out his great intent ;—
To the Prophet, satisfaction
    In the mission he was sent.

            PALM LEAVES—*by Lord Houghton.*

zeal yet with small result, used the faculties which God had given them to decypher and comprehend the wonders laid before them; whom piety and science had combined to consecrate—the Priests of Nature; the Martyrs of knowledge. The things which here they saw only "through a glass darkly," they will there discern in the full illumination of the light of God. The whole curtain will be drawn up, of which here they could only for a moment raise a corner, and the field of vision, so bounded here, will be without limit or horizon there. Earth has shown them but the title-page of a Book which it will be given them to *read* in Heaven. Their utmost efforts here have shown them but the smallest portion of the wonderful facts of this little planet. *There*, will be before them, inviting their research and feeding it with fresh results through immortal ages, not only our Earth, but the System to which it belongs—next that firmament composed of countless myriads of stars with their attendant worlds, of which that system forms one of the smallest units—then all those remoter galaxies, the bare existence of which is all that we can discover here, which lie embosomed in abysmal space far beyond the furthest limits of our Milky Way. There will be the secrets of Time as well as those of Space for us to learn, the footsteps of the Eternal in all worlds during those immeasurable epochas and ages of the Past, which Geology and Astronomy dimly agree to indicate: the existencies, the evolutions, the tragedies, and the redemptions which now we can barely and dimly conjecture, but which then will form the feast and pasture of our daily life. There will be forms of Being to investigate, far up through gradations and cycles which distance all human fancy, their nature, history, feelings, motives, and destiny.

> " Here must I stop,
> Or is there ought beyond?   What hand unseen
> Impels me onward through the glowing orbs
> Of habitable nature, far remote,
> To the dread confines of eternal Night.
> To solitudes of vast unpeopled space,
> The deserts of creation, wide and wild,
> Where embryo systems and unkindled suns
> Sleep in the womb of chaos?—Fancy droops,
> And Thought, astonished, stops her bold career."
>
> *Mrs Barbauld.*

And thousands of pious and perplexed inquirers will be there, who, during long years of faith and meditation, sought, and sought in vain, the solution of the dark enigmas of existence, whose prayer was for LIGHT (ἐν δὲ Φάει καὶ ὄλεσσον); whose spirits, aspiring for ever to pierce those sad and solemn mysteries which cast such midnight gloom over all thoughtful souls and drive the less trustful to despair, for ever fell back baffled, and disheartened, but unshaken in fidelity and love.   They have prayed and hoped for Heaven, not as a scene of happiness or recompence, but as a world of Explanation, where their questions would be answered and their difficulties solved.   On earth the grievous and incomprehensible dispensations of Providence beset them before and behind, and laid a heavy hand upon them, but could not drive them from their

anchor of hope sure and steadfast; will not their confidence be justified to them in their "Father's House ?"*

For years, generations, centuries, they saw glorious
efforts baffled, pure high hopes discomfited and
crushed, good seed, sown with care and watered
with the blood of martyrs, choked or carried off, and
never fructifying; they saw fraud and rapine, brutality
and barbarism rampant and omnipotent,—and justice,
truth and innocence trampled in the dust; the good
cause ruined and the bad triumphant; the servants of
God every where defeated and his purposes apparently
thwarted and over-ruled; they saw myriads of His
creatures doomed through life to darkness, to suffering, to hopeless ignorance and inevitable vice; and
they stood aghast, shuddering, and perplexed at the
seeming contravention of the Divine decrees. These
mysteries made their wretchedness here. Will not
the solution of them make their happiness hereafter?
And as with eyes purged from the mists of mortality,
and powers strengthened by the elixir of-spiritual life,
they approach those problems which were too intricate
and too profound for earthly intellects to grapple with,
will they not marvel how simple is the key that
opens and elucidates them all !

The loving and the tender will be there. It would

---

* " They trusted God was Love indeed,
    And love Creation's final law—
  Though Nature, red in tooth and claw
  With ravine, shrieked against the creed."
                    In Memoriam.

seem even as if Heaven was in some especial manner their rightful inheritance : Love is so infinite, and its earthly horizon so bounded, its earthly development so imperfect, its earthly catastrophes so sad ; its undying tenacity, its profound tenderness, and its boundless yearnings seem so incongruous, as contrasted with its frail objects, and its poor performances, and its momentary life. There are those, and the denizens of our anticipated world may consist of them in overwhelming proportion, of whose nature affection has been the mainspring, the strength, the sunbeam, the beauty; whose heart has been their chiefest treasure ; to whom fame, ambition, power, success, have been at best only the casual and outside objects of existence ; who, in a word, lived on love. Generation after generation, age after age, through the countless cycles of the Past, human creatures have linked themselves together, never dreaming that their connection was limited by time, or that their ties would be severed by the Great Destroyer, and have consigned the husk and framework of their cherished companions to the dust, never doubting that these comrades watched over them from the spiritual world, and were waiting to receive them when the years were ripe. Millions in all times have walked courageously into the Great Darkness, satisfied that they were going to rejoin the company of those whose places had been long "left void in their earthly homes;" and, after long yearnings, to satisfy again "the mighty hunger of the heart" in the fulness of eternal joy ;—whatever human affections have been pure, fervent, self-sacrificing, devoted and enduring, look forward to Heaven for their renewal, their resting-place, and their full fruition. If this expectation be delusive, what instinct of the heart can henceforth be trusted?

And the aspiring and spiritual will be at home at last,—those whose thoughts have been all prayer, to whom the blessings promised to the meek, the mourners, and the merciful are as nothing compared to that pronounced upon the "pure in heart;" to whose thought all other beauties of the heavenly city are swallowed up in this: "that there is no need of the Sun, neither of the Moon, to shine in it, for the glory of God doth lighten it, and the Lamb is the light thereof." THEY SHALL SEE GOD. What this may mean; what may be the nature of that vision by which finite and created Beings can be enabled to behold the Infinite and Eternal Spirit of the Universe; in what manner, or through the bestowal of what new powers, His awful Presence will be made manifest to the souls of the Just made perfect,—we cannot even attempt to realise. It may be that the very purity which they have striven after here and attained there, will endow them with a clearness of sight denied to the less unstained of the redeemed, in virtue of which they can penetrate to the inner circle which surrounds the Throne, and reach the immediate Presence of the Most High.

———

Whether in the lapse of ages and in the course

of progressive Being, the more dormant portions of each man's nature will be called out, and his desires, and therefore the elements of his Heaven, change ;⁓-whether the loving will learn to thirst for knowledge, and the fiery and energetic to value peace, and the active and earnest to grow weary of struggle and achievement and to long for tenderness and repose, and the rested to begin a new life of aspiration, and those who had long lain satisfied with the humbler constituents of the beatific state, to yearn after the conditions of a loftier Being, we cannot tell. Probably. It may be, too, that the tendency of every thought and feeling will be to gravitate towards the great Centre, to merge in one mighty and all-absorbing emotion. The thirst for knowledge may find its ultimate expression in the contemplation of the Divine Nature,—in which indeed all may be contained. It may be that all longings will be finally resolved into striving after a closer union with God, and all human affections merged in the desire to be a partaker in His nature. It may be that, in future stages of our progress, we shall become more and more severed from the Human and joined to the Divine ; that, starting on the threshold of the Eternal world with the one beloved Being who has been the partner of our thoughts and feelings on this earth, we may find, as we go forward to the Goal, and soar upwards to the Throne, and dive deeper and deeper into the mysteries and immensities of Creation, that *affection* will gradually merge in *Thought*, and the cravings and yearnings of the Heart be calmed

and superseded by the sublimer interests of the perfected
Intelligence ;—that the hands which have so long been
joined in love may slowly unclasp to be stretched forth
towards the approaching glory ;—that the glance of
tenderness which we cast on the companion at our side
may become faint, languid, and hurried before the earnest
gaze with which we watch " the light that shall be
revealed."   We might even picture to ourselves that
epoch in our progress through successively loftier and
more purified existences, when those who on earth
strengthened each other in every temptation, sustained
each other under every trial, mingled smiles at every
joy and tears at every sorrow ; and who, in succeeding
varieties of Being, hand in hand, heart with heart,
thought for thought, penetrated together each new
secret, gained each added height, glowed with each
new rapture, drank in each successive revelation, shall
have reached that point where all separate individuality
and all lower affections will be merged in one absorb-
ing Presence ; when the awful nearness of the Perfect
Love will dissolve all other ties and swallow up all
other feelings ; and when the finished and completed
Soul, before melting away into that Sea of Light which
will be its element for ever, shall turn to take a last fond
look of the now glorified but thereby lost companion of
so much anguish and so many joys !*   But we cannot

---

* " He seeks at least

" Upon the last and sharpest height,
   Before the spirits fade away,
   Some landing-place, to clasp and say
' Farewell ! we lose ourselves in Light.' "

yet contemplate the prospect without pain : therefore it will not be *yet* ; not till we can contemplate it with joy : for Heaven is a scene of bliss and recompense, not of sorrow and bereavement.——Why therefore picture it at all ?

———

All these speculations may of course be utterly futile and irrelevant, and the discrepancy may be so vast and so essential between the material and the spiritual world that no pictures sketched by human pencil and filled in with earthly colouring will bear the faintest resemblance to the sublime and inconceivable reality. Perhaps no soul still shrouded in the flesh can worthily or even approximately dream of "the glory which shall be revealed" :——the mere step from death into the higher life will so change, convulse, and recreate all the elements of our Being, that what now seems to us supremely to be desired——the felicity of which the prospect has guided, strengthened, and consoled us here, the joys for which we have cheerfully bartered all the beautiful possessions and the rich promises of Earth—— may then appear to our "unscaled vision" poor, pale, worthless and inadequate, and that the ineffable reality may not only transcend but utterly *traverse* all our aspirations. But if so, it is obvious that the mere fact of our seeing it aright would cancel its influence upon us. The action of a future world as a control on our deeds and a stimulus to our desires depends upon its being such, upon our believing it such at least, as we can conceive of and aspire to. If it is to operate upon us it must be picturable by us. Only through our ideas of it can it influence our lives.

Why then quarrel with our conceptions because necessarily imperfect, and probably much more—as all finite ideas of the Infinite, all material description of the Spiritual, must be ? Why seek after a fidelity of delineation or an etherealisation of conception of which the consequences must be so fatal and benumbing ? Heaven will be, if not what we desire now, at least what we shall desire then. If it be not contracted to our human dreams, those dreams will be expanded to its vast reality. If it be not fitted for us, we shall be prepared for it. In the true sense, if not in our sense, it will be a scene of serene felicity, the end of toil, the end of strife, the end of grief, the end of doubt : a Temple, a Haven, and a Home !

APPENDIX.

I⊤ is not only probable, but, I apprehend, quite certain, that no country is really peopled up to its full possible limit of plentiful subsistence. But there are two or three countries in Europe which may be considered to *approach* this limit,—and these, therefore, we will adopt as our standard of comparison ;—the more readily as they differ materially in their physical conditions. One of them, Belgium, has a climate by no means enviable, and a soil originally and in many parts the reverse of fertile. Another, Lombardy, has a soil naturally rich, a warm and genial sky, and great facilities of irrigation. Some of the cantons of Switzerland maintain probably as large a population, and certainly as prosperous and well fed a one, as can anywhere be found, — Zurich, Appenzell, Argovie, Thurgovie, for example. Of these we will select Zurich.* Of course the comparison we are instituting cannot be a very exact or rigidly conclusive one, inasmuch as countries vary indefinitely in their natural advantages and their capacity for supporting inhabitants. Still there are not many in Europe much better off in this respect than Lombardy, nor much less favoured than Belgium ; while Zurich presents an instance of the condition which may be reached by a people who unite good sense and good government to *fair* natural advantages.

---

* Some of the cantons, and some which we believe are more purely agricultural than Zurich, have even a denser population ; thus Basle has 420, Argovie 398, and Thurgovie 368 to the square mile.

Inhabitants to a Square Mile (English).

Belgium	440	Ireland	180
Lombardy	370	German Confederation	180
Zurich	365	Austria	164
England and Wales	350	Switzerland	157
Holland	300	Spain	90
United Kingdom	225	Turkey in Europe	76
Italy	225	Russia in Europe	30
France	180	Sweden	22

It would appear clear from this comparison that of all
the states of Europe, only Great Britain, Belgium, Holland,
Switzerland, and perhaps Italy, can be regarded as amply
populated.   There are three of the largest which assuredly
are very far from being so,—viz., Spain, Russia, and
Turkey.   France, with a soil and climate in the aggregate
superior to those of England, supports only half the numbers, though she supports them no doubt more exclusively
from the produce of her own soil.   A great part of the
north of European Russia is, we know, unfitted for the
production of human food, though yielding largely the
materials for human warmth, clothing, and shelter.   But no
one who is aware how wretched is the state of agriculture even in the provinces most favoured by nature, and
over what a vast part of the empire these provinces extend,
and how sparse is the population which now inhabits them,
can doubt that the country as a whole could support with
ease 250,000,000 instead of 60,000,000 as at present.
The case of Turkey is almost as strong.   The productiveness of many of its provinces is well known ; yet with the
same area as France she counts only 16,000,000 of people,
instead of 36,000,000, and with four times the area of
England, and a far finer climate, she only maintains a
population smaller by one-eighth.   Spain is just as back-
ward, and more blameable, for her soil and climate are, or
might be made, productive in the extreme.   Her extent is

nearly as great as that of France (183,000 square miles to 207,000), yet her population per square mile is only one-half that of France and one-fourth that of England. What increased numbers she might support may be guessed from the fact that some of her provinces do even now show nearly 250 to the square mile. She might easily support 70,000,000, instead of her present 16,000,000, and still not exceed the proportions of Belgium, a far less favoured land. Hungary, too, ought to be specially noted. It contains now about 11,000,000, or not more than 135 to the square mile. Considering the extraordinary fertility of her soil, she might unquestionably find room for 30,000,000, if human ignorance and folly interposed no artificial obstacles. On the whole it is a moderate calculation that the 270,000,000 of which the population of Europe now consists, might become 500,000,000, without any crowding or *necessary* inconvenience.

A much larger number is pointed at by another mode of calculation. It is estimated (for authorities, see Alison on Population, ii. 480), that an acre of wheat can supply three persons with food, and an acre of potatoes ten persons. But people must be clothed, housed, and warmed, as well as fed ; and for these purposes wood must be planted and domestic animals must be kept. We may therefore allot (say) one acre and a half to each individual for all his needs—assuredly a liberal estimate, for in the Canton of Zurich, an acre and a quarter is even now found sufficient. Now Europe contains 2,421,000,000 of acres ; and if we throw aside, being guided by the average of Ireland (one of the worst lands in this respect), one-third as unavailable by reason of its being water, or rock, or high mountain, or unmanageable bog,—it would still maintain, at the above proportion, 1,070,000,000, or four times its present population. If we allow 2 acres per head, it would support above 800,000,000.

I have no idea of examining the actual and possible density of population in Asia and Africa in any detail. Our knowledge of those quarters of the world is too imperfect, and their statistics far too loose to render any such investigation in the least degree satisfactory. A reference to a few specific facts is all that is necessary. Thus, the population of the Asiatic provinces of Turkey shows only 24 to the square mile, yet Syria and Asia Minor and parts of Mesopotamia are among the most favoured countries in the world, and used in former days to sustain far greater numbers than at present. To the traveller of to-day, they present the appearance in many parts almost of a' desert land. There can be no doubt that under a good government, and with a sensible and energetic race, they might contain ten times their actual numbers, and still not approach the density of Belgium or Lombardy. Their 16,000,000 may easily beeóme 160,000,000. Probably nearly the same may be said of Persia.

The African dependencies of the Ottoman Porte are said to contain only about four inhabitants to the square mile. But much of their territory is desert. If, however, we look to South Africa, we find an almost unlimited territory thinly inhabited, yet capable of rich cultivation, and swarming with animal life in its lower phases. The entire of Africa is estimated according to the latest authorities to have an area of 12,000,000 English square miles, and a population of 120,000,000, or about 10 persons to the square mile. But British Africa, of which we know most, has an area of about 120,000 square miles, and a population of 350,000, or not three to the square mile. It is obvious that here we have space for nearly indefinite expansion. A five- or ten-fold increase (i.e., about 1,000,000,000 for the whole continent) would be no extravagant estimate of ultimate possibilities, especially since recent discoveries have proved that even Equatorial Africa can sustain large and populous nations in what to them is plenty.

But it is in America and Australia that we shall find the widest field for the dispersion and multiplication of mankind. America, it may be said, is only just beginning to be peopled. Except in a few localities it is only *sprinkled* with human beings. To say nothing of the older regions of the Hudsons' Bay Territory, there is a vast district lying between Canada and Vancouver's Island, with scarcely any inhabitants, though capable of containing many millions.* A great portion of this district is represented as singularly fertile, far more so than the corresponding longitudes belonging to the United States. Yet the Red River is the only settlement yet inhabited by Europeans, and these are few in number. The day will come, there can be little doubt, when it will be the centre of a nation of 50,000,000. The population of the Canadas was in 1861 only 2,500,000, or less than 8 to the square mile. It might easily become 75,000,000, or 240 to the square mile. As we proceed to the United States, we find that the oldest provinces, though far the poorest by nature, are the most densely peopled. The six New England States averaged, in 1860, 49 inhabitants to the square mile, Massachusetts reaching as high as 130. The six Middle States, including Maryland and Ohio, averaged 70,—Ohio and New York, the one with its vast tracts of rich soil, and the other with its commerce, industry, and great cities into the bargain, only showing densities of about 62 and 80 respectively. We say nothing of the Slave States, which only averaged 18 to the square mile,

---

* Article in "Edinburgh Review," British America, April, 1864.

nor of the desolate territory, near the Rocky Mountains. But if the seven North-western States and Texas were peopled even to the extent that New England and New York have already reached—say 60 to the square mile —they would contain a population of 30,000,000; 200,000,000 is a moderate estimate for the future members of the Great Republic.

Mexico is a splendid country, of vast capabilities, both of soil and climate. Its present population is estimated at 8,000,000, or about 8 to the square mile. In Humboldt's day, a far larger area contained only 5,800,000 souls. The country, there can be no doubt, would be scantily peopled at 160 to the square mile, or twenty fold its present number of inhabitants. Of Central America we know little, except that its population was once far greater than at present. Parts only of its surface are unhealthy, and even these probably not necessarily or incurably so. The best geographers estimate its actual inhabitants at about 2,000,000, or 13 to the square mile. It certainly might maintain five or tenfold that number. As for South America, it is impossible to state with any approach to accuracy, either what numbers it does or might contain. Enormous areas of its surface cannot be said to be inhabited at all, though very copiously endowed by nature. Thus—

Chili has to the square mile about			6
Brazil ,, ,,	nearly		3
Peru ,, ,,	,,		2
Paraguay ,, ,,	,,		4
The Argentine Republic	,,		1
Uruguay and Patagonia ,, not			1

There is certainly ample room yet for 200,000,000 or 300,000,000 on the continent of South America, and as certainly for another 100,000,000—probably twice or thrice that number (for each successive exploration discovers fresh wealth of fertile land)—in the great colonies of Australasia.*

No one who even looks over these statistics can avoid the conclusion that the earth is not yet one quarter—perhaps not one-tenth—peopled. No one who reads books of travels in much detail can avoid having this conclusion deepened into a vivid impression and conviction. The entire population of the globe is calculated by the best geographers to beabout 1,100,000,000, and probably this is rather an extreme estimate. Of this Europe furnishes nearly 300,000,000, and Asia upwards of 600,000,000, leaving only two for the vast continents of North and South America, Africa, and Australia. We cannot form even an approximate conjecture of the length of time which has been needed for the prolific powers of man, acting under the disadvantageous circumstances of comparative ignorance and social barbarism, to people the world up to its present numbers. It may have been 20,000 years; it may have been 200,000; it may have been incomparably more. No one, we fancy, whose opinion is worth considering on a scientific question, would place it below the smallest figure I have named. No doubt the increase of the human race may be expected to proceed

---

* The average density of the two Americas is about 6 to the square mile. "The Gazetteer of the World" states that of Africa at 7, of Asia 32, and of Europe, at 82. These, however, are only rough estimates.

New Zealand contains as nearly as may be the same acreage as the British Isles, but New Zealand has only a population of 100,000, Britain a population of 30,000,000, or 300 times as great, yet New Zealand is probably superior to our islands both in soil and climate. Australasia has a larger area than Europe—upwards of 3,000,000 square miles. There is nothing, so far as we know at present, to forbid the expectation that it may one day maintain an equal population.

at an accelerated pace in future, unless there should be some
retarding influence among yet unrecognised physiological
laws, such as we have hinted at. Agriculture has
made vast improvements; famines are not to be dreaded
as formerly; few now in any country die of want, and
fewer will die from this cause every year, as the world
grows older; communication between distant lands—between those whose population is redundant, and those whose
land is cheap and plentiful—becomes easier day by day, and
mankind may now disperse as fast as they multiply; wars,
too, and pestilence may, it is to be hoped, grow rarer and
less desolating; and assuredly the average duration of individual life is on the increase. Still it is plain that before
the earth can be peopled up to its fair limit of density—the
limit, that is, compatible with an ample supply of the necessaries and comforts of life—a sufficient number of generations or ages must elapse to permit all the influences
developed by civilization to expand and operate. TIME is
all we want, and time, in adequate measure, we may surely
count upon.

Not only is the earth not yet a quarter peopled, but even
the inhabited portion is scarcely yet a quarter cultivated.
In many countries the soil is barely scratched. Even in
England it is not made to yield on an average to more than
one-half of its capacity. Perhaps only in Belgium, Switzerland, and Lombardy, do the *actual* and the potential produce
of the soil in any measure correspond. We can pretend to
no accurate estimate of the number of bushels of wheat, or
tons of hay or of root crops which an acre of ordinary land
under good farming might be made to yield, nor to any
statement, proveable by authentic statistics, of what such
land does yield, as at present handled. All we can do is to
collect a certain number of reliable facts from the best

authorities bearing on such comparison. The conclusion will be as convincing as if we were able to draw it out in formally calculated tables.

The average yield of wheat in England is considered to be about $3\frac{1}{4}$ qrs., or 26 bushels per acre. The author of " Lois Wheedon Husbandry," on not special land, and with no manure beyond the straw, obtained for 19 years an average of 34 bushels. A farmer in Hertfordshire, also not peculiarly favoured, averages 30 from all his land, and has often reached 47, and even 57 bushels per acre. Mr Lawes, another farmer in the same county, has averaged 35 and 36 for 12 years, and in 1863 and 1864, he reached as high as from 40 to 55, according to the manure he used (" Times," Oct. 19, 1864). Even 60 bushels to the acre has been achieved in good years.

Of oats in England, the ordinary yield is 40 bushels to the acre. But 60 are often reached, and 80 by no means unfrequently.

In Ireland the average of wheat is about 24 bushels to the statute acre, and of oats about 40. The variation between the produce of different counties in the same year is enormous—ranging from $7\frac{1}{2}$ cwts. to 12 cwts. of wheat, and from 11 to 19 cwts. of oats—and in the same counties in different years, from 8 to 14 cwts.

Of mangel wurzel, some farmers grow 30 tons, and some 60 or 64 to the acre. Of swedes some 16, and others 40 tons.

It is clear then that the average actual produce of cereals and root crops in England falls short, probably by one-half, of what it might be even with our present lights and practice, and of what actually is obtained by individuals in many instances. Belgium and Lombardy surpass our best farming, with perhaps very few exceptions. It is stated ("Gazetteer of the World,") that the wheat yield of Belgium is 32 bushels for 2 of seed, or 16 fold ; whereas that of Great Britain is only 8 to 10 fold.*　But France, we find, falls as far short of England's average in its agricultural productiveness, as England's average falls short of England's best. France has as good a soil and a far better climate than we have, and, to set against deficient science and inadequate manure, has the advantage of *la petite culture* in a very high degree.　Yet, on the unquestionable authority of M. Leonce de Lavergne, its yield in every article is only half of ours. The following are a few of his statements :†—

The yield of oats in England is 5 quarters to the acre, and sometimes as high as 10 ; in France it is only $2\frac{1}{2}$ quarters.　The yield of wheat in England is $3\frac{1}{2}$ quarters to the acre, or 25 hectolitres to the hectare ; that of France averages only 12 hectolitres to the hectare.　In the case of animal production the disproportion is even greater.　England is estimated to maintain two sheep per hectare—France only two-thirds of one sheep.　Each cow in England is estimated to yield 1,000 litres of milk—in France only 500. The average yield in meats of cattle slain in France for food is 100 kilogs.—in England 250.　"With 8 million head of cattle and 30 million of hectares to feed them on, British agriculture produces 500 millions of kilogs. of meat.　France, with 10 million head and 53 millions of hectares, only 400 millions of kilogs."　M. Leonce de Lavergne sums up by a calculation, showing the entire gross produce of soil (animals and vegetables) in the two countries, the result of which is

---

* McCulloch (Geog. Dict.) states the produce of the Waes county, the most fertile and highly cultivated part of Flanders, to be $20\frac{1}{2}$ bushels of wheat and 41 of oats to the acre.

† Economie Rurale de l'Angleterre, c. ii., iii., iv.

that England yields 200 francs' worth per hectare, and France only 100 francs.

We are accustomed to consider the western provinces of Canada and the United States as offering about the most fertile and unlimited wheat fields in the world. Nearly boundless in extent they certainly are, and for the most of extraordinary natural fertility. But this only enhances our surprise at finding how very moderate the present yield even of their best lands actually is, and our conception of the vast difference between what they do and what they might produce. The best lands in Canada, and Michigan, and Illinois, for example, are far superior both in soil and climate, to the good lands of England; yet neither their average nor their maximum produce in wheat approaches ours. Our average, be it remembered, is about 26 bushels to the acre, and our maximum may be put at 60. In the state of New York the average is 14, and the maximum about 20. In Michigan the average is 11, and the maximum 18. New Brunswick the usual yield is 18, in Canada West 13, in Ohio 15. Yet in most of these districts the soil is represented to be of almost inexhaustible richness—virgin soil in fact. The above figures are collected from Johnstone's Notes on North America—a first-rate authority on these subjects. There can be little doubt that English farming on Michigan or Ohio land would give a result far exceeding anything yet obtained in either country,—and why should this combination not be? Is it not certain that some day or other it will be? In order to give some conception of the vast space yet to be travelled over before even the cultivated portions of the temperate regions yield the amount of human sustenance that they are capable of yielding, we will place some of the above facts in a tabular form,—calling attention merely to the circumstance that the soil and climate (those of Great Britain) which stand at the head of the list, are, of all those mentioned, about the least favoured by nature.

Produce of Wheat per Statute Acre in Bushels.

Michigan	average	11
Canada West	„	13
France	„	13
New York	„	14
Ohio	„	15
New Brunswick	„	18
American	maximum	19
Belgian	„	20
English	average	26
„	maximum	60 *
Possible American	„	80

It is clear from the above comparison that we are not over-stating the case, when we say that the actual produce of some of the most extensive and fertile wheat fields in the world is not above one-third of the potential produce, even on the loose agricultural system which at present prevails almost universally. And the same proportion probably holds good of nearly all other crops. But a few facts, fully ascertained and placed beyond doubt, will suffice to satisfy us that an increase far beyond what has been just mentioned, is within our reach.

Economy of seed is one mode in which the available yield of cereals may be greatly increased. The ordinary consumption of seed wheat in the broadcast sowing commonly practiced is $2\frac{1}{2}$ bushels, or 10 pecks, to the acre, and this as we have seen, yields an average crop of about 26 bushels, or *ten-fold.* In drilling, or "dibbling," 1 bushel, or 4 pecks, is held to suffice, and to yield heavier crops—often 30 bushels, or *thirty-fold.* In one case 4 pecks of seed yielded

---

* This is the maximum yet reported in regular farming. Mr Hallet, however, by his process of wide sowing and selection, had reached a rate of 108 bushels per acre. (*Journ. Agric. Soc.* xxii, p. 377.)

40 bushels, or *forty-fold.* One experiment tried in the
State of New York, where only 2 pecks of seed were used,
showed a yield at the rate of 80 bushels to the acre, or *one
hundred and sixty-fold.* ("Year Book of Agricultural Facts,"
1860, pp. 110, 129, 131.) But all these cases fade into
insignificance before those recorded by Mr Hallett, as the
result of a long series of careful experiments. The extent
to which economy of seed is possible may be guessed from
the statement made in reference to the "tillering," or hori-
zontal spreading out of the seeds of wheat, "that the stems
produced from a single grain having perfect freedom of
growth will, in the spring, while lying flat on the surface,
extend over a circle three feet in diameter, producing at
harvest 50 or 60 ears." Now, an ear contains sometimes
50 grains or more. The above increase, therefore, is 2,500
at least. Of the extent to which economy of seed has
been practically carried experimentally, we can produce no
more signal or instructive instance than the following :—
Two adjacent fields, similar in all respects, were selected and
sown with the same seed wheat. In the one case 6 pecks
per acre were sown, and yielded 54 bushels, or 934,000
ears ; in the other case, 4½ pints per acre were used, plant-
ing them in single grains a foot apart, and the yield was
1,002,000 ears, or a larger quantity than was produced at
the other side of the hedge *from more than twenty-one times
the seed employed.*—("Journal of Agricultural Society," xxii.
p. 372, *et seq.*) But, allowing this to be an extreme case,
it is clear that 2 pecks, if not 1, will suffice where 10 are
now habitually used ; and the saving thus effectable would
be equivalent to a virtual increase of the wheat crop from
8 to 10 per cent.*

---

* Mr Hallett found that a field planted with 6 pecks per acre
yielded only 54 bushels, and one of inferior soil, planted with *one*

Selection of seed is another point to be noticed. Of the gain attainable by this precaution, the celebrated "pedigree wheat" exhibited in 1861 may be cited as probably the best example. In the article just referred to, published in the "Journal of the Agricultural Society," Mr Hallett gives a detailed account of his experiments, and their remarkably successful result. By simply selecting a couple of ears of moderate size, and excellent quality originally, and then in successive years sowing only, and carefully, the best and largest grains from the produce thus inaugurated, he had in five years doubled the length of the ear, increased the number of ears springing from one grain from 10 to 52, and the number of grains in the ear from 47 to 123. I will not go into any further detail, which, for my purpose, is quite unnecessary ; but two points brought out by Mr Hallett are important as showing the *possible* powers of reproduction in the wheat plant when properly treated : "I have now (he says) a field of seven acres planted with the produce *of a single grain* planted two years ago—one acre of it with the produce of a single ear planted one year ago." Again: the ordinary yield in fair farming, that is where two bushels of wheat are used for seed, he states, is considered to be about one ear, or 100 grains, for every two grains sown, or about 50 fold. His best grain produced the first year 688 fold ; after two years' repeated selection, 1,190 fold; and after four years, 2,145 fold.

The use of *appropriate manures* is another mode by which the produce of the soil may be increased to an amount as yet incalculable. Though *careful* husbandry, such as is practised in Belgium and Lombardy, and in some parts of

---

peck, yielded 57 bushels, showing that the extra quantity of seed used was worse than thrown away. He estimates the average *waste* of wheat thus caused in England at a million of quarters annually (Vol. xxii., p. 380).

France, where *la petite culture* prevails, is by no means in its infancy, yet *scientific* husbandry is. By scientific husbandry, I mean the adaptation of the crop to the soil, and the use of appropriate manures which will return to the earth what the present crop needs, or what previous crops have exhausted. Attention to, and comprehension of, the latter point, date from Professor Liebig's works, *i.e.*, from our own time, and indeed are not yet diffused. Thousands of facts bearing on the subject might be accumulated, but they are not needed. We will cull a few, mainly from Liebig's " Modern Agriculture." Where an unmanured plot yielded 15 lbs. of grain, and a similar plot supplied with inappropriate manure gave 16 lbs., the plot treated with the fitting nutriment gave 36 lbs. (p. 57). Mr Lawes records an experiment where the proportionate result was as follows (p. 77) :—

Yield without manure	1000lbs.
With one sort of manure	1690lbs.
With the right manure	2000lbs.

Liebig considers (p. 267) that by the use and improvement of phosphate of lime, " the amount of provender for cattle has been increased as much as if the area of every field for green crops had been doubled." What the introduction of guano has done for agriculture—especially for the turnip* and the sugar cane—we have all a general idea. A couple of hundred weight per acre, according to Lawes and Caird, will, even for wheat, give an increase of eight bushels of grain, or 30 per cent., besides 25 per cent. in straw ; and one ton of guano is equal in value to 33 tons of ordinary farm-yard manure.—(" Nesbit's History of Guano," p. 21, 25.)

Again, another indication of the vast increase of food

---

* In one case the unmanured field yielded 17 tons, and that treated with guano 31 tons.—(*Journ. Agric. Soc.*, xxii. p. 86.)

obtainable from land already settled and cultivated may be found in a comparison of the number of cattle and sheep which may be kept on a given acreage, by merely grazing, and by arable cultivation and stall feeding, either exclusively or in combination with grazing. Thus a cow requires from three to four acres of pasture land ; whereas *one* acre of well managed land under tillage would suffice ; some say even less. (Consult Morton's " Cyclopædia of Agriculture.") If this be correct, the production of animal food might be doubled in Great Britain, and trebled nearly everywhere else, by a simple change of system, and the application of more labour to the soil, without the addition of a single acre. M. Leonce de Lavergne states that on an average England keeps two sheep on a hectare, and France only two-thirds of a sheep. In the case of cattle the comparison is still more unfavourable to France, both as regards the size and number of animals. The milk yielded by each cow is double in England, and " with 8,000,000 head on 30,000,000 hectares, England produces 500,000,000 of kilos. of meat, while France with 10,000,000 head on 53,000,000 hectares only produces 400,000,000 kilos." Thus France has not only a vast distance to travel before she reaches England, but England has at least as far to travel before she reaches an easily attainable ideal. Other countries, *à fortiori*, are still further behind the possible.

There is yet another mode in which the amount of human life sustainable on a given area, and therefore throughout the chief portion of the habitable globe, may be almost indefinitely increased, viz., by a substitution *pro tanto* of vegetable for animal food. Practically of course we should never wish to encounter the risk of again feeding a whole people mainly on potatoes, though Irishmen have thriven on that diet, and though an acre in potatoes will sustain three times the amount of human life of an acre in wheat. But a given acreage of wheat will feed *at least* TEN times as many men as the same acreage employed in growing mutton. It is usually calculated that the consumption of wheat by an adult is about one quarter per annum, and we know that good land produces four quarters. But let us assume that a man confined to bread would need two quarters a year; still one acre would support two men. But a man confined to meat would require 3 lbs. a day, and it is considered a liberal calculation if an acre spent in grazing sheep and cattle, will yield in beef or mutton more than 50 lbs. on an average;—the best farmer in Norfolk having averaged 90 lbs., but a great majority of farms in Great Britain only reaching 20 lbs. On these data, it would require 22 acres of pasture land to sustain one adult if fed only meat. It is obvious that here, again, is the indication of a vast possible increase in the population sustainable on a given area.

But there is much more yet, all tending in the same direction, and confirming our former inferences, if it were needful, or if we had time to go into it. There is an enormous area employed in the production of mere superfluities, such as tobacco, and in *dispensable* luxuries like tea and wine. There are the boundless riches of the sea, as yet not half explored, or utilized, or *economized*. We all know how salmon has been rendered scarce, and how easily it might again be made plentiful, as shown by Alexander Russel, in his entertaining book. If sea fisheries were protected by a law making it illegal to destroy fish while breeding—giving them, that is, a couple of month's immunity, it is calculated that this article of food might be at once increased ten-fold in quantity, and probably reduced twentyfold in price. For every female mackerel or herring destroyed in full roe, about 500,000 ova perish.

Finally, there is every reason to believe that *cooking*—

scientific cooking, that is—by which we mean the intelligent treatment of food so as to extract from it the utmost amount of healthful nutriment,—is in its infancy, or rather has scarcely entered into life. Probably it is not too much to say that at present, owing to our ignorance, carelessness, and clumsiness on this head,—added to the extravagance and excess of some,—one-half the food consumed is *wasted;* and that twice the numbers now living on the globe— certainly in many of the most civilized countries of it— might be maintained on the *existing* produce of the soil.

TURNBULL AND SPEARS, PRINTERS EDINBURGH.

POSTSCRIPT

SEVENTH EDITION.

THE passage in the last chapter of these Enigmas (p. 263-267), describing "the severance of souls" assumed to be the inevitable consequence of the purging of our vision at the Last Great Day, has, I find, given much pain, and drawn forth sharp dissent, in quarters where I would fain have caused neither. I am bound to say that I recognise the justice of the animadversions, and I grieve for the distress I may have caused.

Mr Thom says :—

"Mr Greg's own picture of future retribution contains elements more cruel, more painful to a Christian heart, more purely gratuitous, than any theory of physical sufferings. Those who on earth were, blessed with a wealth of love of which their unknown sins made them unworthy—and which of us is worthy of the love we all receive?—are represented under the light of the eternal day as '*loving still*,—nay, loving all the more fervently, all the more yearningly, in that they now discern with unclouded vision all that bright beauty, all that rich nature of the objects of their tenderness, of which their dim eyesight could on earth perceive only a part,' yet as doomed 'to see those they love, as they never loved till then, turn from their grasp, their glance of clasping and supplicating fondness, with that unconquerable loathing which virtue *must* feel towards guilt, and with which purity *must* shrink from stain,—to see those eyes, never turned on them before, save in gentleness and trust, now giving them one last glance of divine sadness and ineffable farewell,—to watch those forms, whose companionship cheered and illuminated all the dark places of their earthly pilgrimage,—receding, vanishing, melting in the bright distance, to join a circle *where they will not need them*, to tread a path to which theirs bears no parallel and can make no approach.' Is there anything in the physical separation of Dives and father Abraham, with the great gulf between, across which, however, they held communication,—the poor soul in torment shewing a tender care and love for his brethren in the flesh,—so hard, so arbitrary, so needless, so unreal as this? What analogy of Providence on earth, what spiritual law of God, requires this local separation, this ineffable farewell, this unconquerable loathing, these receding paths which never approach again, as the doom of one whose stains of time had yet left his heart so fond, eager, and imploring?"—*Theological Review*, July 1873, p. 404.

Miss Cobbe writes thus, in the same periodical :—

"In speculating on the awful probabilities of 'Elsewhere,' Mr Greg lays it down, as if it were an obvious truth, that love must retreat from the discovery of the sinfulness of the person hitherto beloved, and that both saint and sinner will accept as inevitable an eternal separation. Further, Mr Greg thinks it possible that at the highest summit of finite existence, the souls which have ascended together through all the shining ranks for half an eternity of angelic friendship, will part company at last, Thought for ever superseding Love. 'Farewell, we lose ourselves in light.' It would, perhaps, be wrong to say that the two views hang logically together, and that the mind which (with all its capacity to understand and express the tenderest feelings) yet holds that there may even possibly be something more divine than Love, may well also imagine that Love cannot conquer Sin. But is it not only by a strange transposition in the true table of precedence of human faculties that either doctrine can be accepted? Let us suppose two persons loving each other genuinely and tenderly in this life (so much is granted in the hypothesis). The very power of the worse to love the better truly and unselfishly, is, *ipso facto*, evidence of his being love-worthy, of his having in him, in the depth of his nature, the kernel of all goodness, the seed out of which all moral beauty springs, and which whosoever sees and recognises in his brother's soul cannot choose but love. . . . . . The poor, self-condemned soul whom Mr Greg images as turning away in an agony of shame and hopelessness from the virtuous friend he loved on earth, and loves still at an immeasurable distance,—such a soul is not outside the pale of love, divine or human. Nay, is he not, even assuming his guilt to be black as night, only in a similar relation to the purest of created souls, which that purest soul holds to the All-holy One above? If God can love *us*, is it not the acme of moral presumption to think of a human soul being too pure to love *any* sinner, so long as in him there remains any vestige of affection? The whole problem is unreal and impossible. In the first place, there is a potential moral equality between all souls capable of equal love, and the one can never reach a height whence it may justly despise the other. And in the second place, the higher the virtuous soul may have risen in the spiritual world, the more it must have acquired the Godlike Insight which beholds the good under the evil, and not less the Godlike Love which embraces the repentant Prodigal." —*Theological Review*, July 1873, p. 454.

The force of these objections to my delineation cannot be gainsaid. and ought not to have been overlooked. No doubt, a soul that can so love and so feel its separation from the objects of its love, cannot be wholly lost. It must still retain elements of recovery and redemption, and qualities to win and to merit answering affection. The lovingness of a nature—its capacity for strong and deep attachment —must constitute, there as here, the most hopeful characteristic out of which to elicit and foster all other good. No doubt, again, if the sinful continue to love in spite of their sinfulness, the blessed will not cease to love in consequence of their blessedness. If so, it is natural, and indeed inevitable, to infer that a chief portion of their occupation in the spiritual world will consist in comforting the misery, and assisting in the restoration of the lost whom they have loved. We shall pursue this work with all the aid which our augmented powers on the one side, and their purged perceptions on the other, will combine to gather round the task,—and in the success and completion of that task, and in that alone, must lie the consummation of the bliss of Heaven.

But this is not the only, nor perhaps the most irresistible inference forced upon us by the above considerations. If so vast an ingredient in the misery of the condemned consist in the severance from those they love, this same severance must form a terrible drawback from the felicity of the redeemed. How, indeed, *can* they enjoy anything to be called happiness hereafter, if the bad—*their* bad, not strangers, but their dearest intimates, those who have shared their inmost confidences, and made up the intensest interests of their earthly life—are groaning and writhing in hopeless anguish close at hand? (for everything will be close to us in that scene where darkness and distance are no more). Obviously only in one way,—*by ceasing to love:* that is, by renouncing, or losing, or crushing the best and purest part of their nature, by abjuring the most specific teaching of Christ, by turning away from the worship and imitation of that God who IS Love. Or, to put it in still terser and bolder language, How, *given a Hell of torment and despair for millions of our friends and fellow-men,* can the good enjoy Heaven except by becoming bad? without becoming transformed, miraculously changed, and *changed deplorably for the worse?* without, in a word, putting on, along with the white garments of the Redeemed, a coldness and hardness of heart, a stony, supercilious egotism, which on earth would have justly forfeited all claim to regard, endurance, or esteem? Our affections are probably the best things about us—the attributes through which we most approach and resemble the divine nature; yet, assuming the Hell of Theologians, those affections must be foregone or trampled down in Heaven, or else Heaven will itself become a Hell. As a condition, or a consequence, of being admitted to the presence of God, we should have to forswear the little that is Godlike in our composition. Do not these simple reflections suffice to disperse into thin air the current notions of a world of everlasting pain?

One further corollary may be briefly indicated. Hell, if there be such a place or state, though a scene of merited and awful suffering, must be full of the mighty mitigations which Hope always brings, and can scarcely be devoid of an element of sweetness which might almost seem like joy, if the consciousness

be permitted and ever present to its denizens, that
"elsewhere" Guardian Angels—parents who have
'entered into glory,' wives who cluster round the
Throne, sisters and friends who have 'emerged from
the ruins of the tomb, and the deeper ruins of the
Fall'—are for ever at work, with untiring faithful-
ness and the sure instincts of a perfected intelligence,
for the purification of the stained, the strengthening
of the weak, the softening of the fierce and hard, and
the final rescue of them all.

February 1874.

WORKS BY W. R. GREG.

POLITICAL PROBLEMS FOR OUR AGE AND COUNTRY.

In one Volume, demy 8vo, pp. 342. Cloth, 10s. 6d.

CONTENTS.

I. Constitutional and Autocratic Statesmanship.
II. England's Future Attitude and Mission.
III. Disposal of the Criminal Classes.
IV. Recent Change in the Character of English Crime.
V. The Intrinsic Vice of Trade Unions.
VI. Industrial and Co-operative Partnerships.
VII. The Economic Problem.
VIII. Political Consistency.
IX. The Parliamentary Career.
X. The Price we pay for Self-government.
XI. Vestryism.
XII. Direct *v.* Indirect Taxation.
XIII. The New Régime, and how to meet it.

"A large section of the educated classes may welcome in Mr. Greg a confident guide to lead them towards doctrines which they are inclined and yet afraid to accept."—*Saturday Review.*

"It is always a pleasure to read Mr. Greg's political or literary writings......But if you like the companionship of a robust intellect that braces all whom it comes in contact with, and can be chivalrous enough to admire feats of strength and moral courage, whatever their object be, and if you like to commune with a political writer who is no mere political attorney, you will bear with Mr. Greg's rough points, and will frankly own him to be one of the ablest of living political writers. His intellectual gifts are numerous."—*Scotsman.*

"We are always compelled to admire, but very seldom allowed to agree with Mr. Greg's political writings. He is an idealogue, with the style of a consummate journalist and the knowledge of a practised statistician."—*Spectator.*

It can hardly be necessary to say to any one who knows anything of him, that Mr. Greg is always a thoughtful and able writer, and that we do not enjoy him the less when we happen not to agree with him "—*Echo.*

"It is perfectly unnecessary to say that his 'Political Problems' is a very able work. Everything produced by Mr. Greg is characterised by great ability, and marks of deep and earnest thought."—*Civil Service Gazette.*

"Favourably known to the more thoughtful section of the public by his 'Literary and Social Judgments,' Mr. Greg now strengthens his position by a volume of essays more uniformly serious in aim, and worthy of attentive perusal."—*Weekly Dispatch.*

"W. R. G. is thoroughly individual, and what he thinks for himself he does not hesitate to say."—*Edinburgh Evening Courant.*

"It is very refreshing to meet with a writer like Mr. Greg, who handles the most pressing social and political questions at once acutely and profoundly, and yet with a rare amount of independence of all the sections of current opinion."—*Westminster Review, April,* 1870.

"Mr. Greg thinks clearly, and expresses his thoughts in vigorous language. He rarely writes on a subject without having taken considerable trouble to master its details. And the questions which, in his 'Political Problems,' he offers for solution, or attempts to solve, are of great and immediate importance. For all these reasons his book will repay study."—*North British Review, April,* 1870.

THE CREED OF CHRISTENDOM; its Foundation and Superstructure.

Second Edition, in one Volume, crown 8vo, pp. xx. and 280, price 6s.

"We do not hesitate to say, that for a man of sound mind to read this book through slowly, and to retain his belief in the verbal inspiration of the Mosaic Record, is a moral impossibility."—*Spectator.*